Lisa Dickenson was born in the wrong body. She was definitely meant to be Beyoncé. Despite this hardship, she grew up in Devon attempting to write her own, completely copyright-infringing versions of *Sweet Valley High*, before giving Wales a go for university, and then London a go for the celeb-spotting potential. She's now back in Devon, living beside the seaside with her husband and forcing cream teas down the mouths of anyone who'll visit. She is sadly still not Beyoncé.

Follow her on Twitter for all her book news and Beyoncé-related chatter: @LisaWritesStuff.

Also by Lisa Dickenson

You Had Me at Merlot
Catch Me If You Cannes

the TWELVE DATES OF Christmas

Lisa Dickenson

sphere

SPHERE

First published in Great Britain in 2015 by Sphere

1 3 5 7 9 10 8 6 4 2

Copyright © Lisa Dickenson 2013

A CIP catalogue record for this book
is available from the British Library.

ISBN 978-0-7515-5729-9

Typeset in Caslon by M Rules
Printed and bound in Great Britain by Clays Ltd, St Ives plc

Papers used by Sphere are from well-managed forests
and other responsible sources.

To Phil, Manpreet, Mum & Dad and to all
of you, you big Christmas sparkles

And to myself, because I wrote
the damn thing

Date One

The Royal Opera House, Covent Garden

Claudia's underwear was evil and it was going to ruin everything. She fanned herself, one eye on the clock. She would not cry over a stupid cheap corset she'd got off the internet, even if it was completely locked to her body, upside down, and she had to leave in three minutes' time for her first really posh date in years.

'Get – off – me.' She gripped the material and pulled down with all her might, but it wouldn't budge.

Online, the corset had looked far more Agent Provocateur than Moulin Rouge fancy dress, but it would still be a treat for Seth at the end of their enchanting evening. Only when she'd done it all the way up the front to find her bosoms still page-three-free did she realise her error. Then it wouldn't undo. The damned hook-and-eyes had become ensnared in the fabric and the more she pulled and tugged the more it gripped hold of her.

Tonight had to go well. If everything was perfect and romantic they could do this more often and things wouldn't seem so … flat. Their relationship was *fine*, but watching other people's lives on TV together every night and cooking the same old dinners in their PJs was making Claudia worry life was passing them by. She was not going to be stuck in a rut at thirty, so it was time to do something about it.

She heard his footsteps coming towards their bedroom.

'Wait!'

'What?' Seth called through the door. 'We've got to go.'

This corset would not derail their big night. With a shot of strength to rival the Incredible Hulk, Claudia struggled, tore and ripped the corset off her body, releasing her pink skin. Panting, she allowed herself a five-second victory dance before grabbing the first undies that came to hand.

'Just wait there a minute.' She sat down in front of her dresser and twisted a handful of diamantés into her dark hair, then ripped the cellophane wrapper off a second packet and went to town with them, too. You can't have too many sparkles at Christmas. She pouted flirtatiously at her reflection. This was the first time she'd ever worn red lipstick and she *thought* it worked – hopefully it was more Taylor Swift than Joan Collins. Leaning into the mirror, she bared her teeth. The whitening toothpaste was definitely making a difference. 'You're a FOX – oops,' she whispered, dabbing the spit from over-pronouncing the word 'fox' off the mirror.

She pulled on her brand new dress. *Scarlet*, no less. Tonight she would be dazzling and witty, and Seth would see her as his beautiful girlfriend – and not his glorified room-mate – once more.

'I'm ready. No – wait,' she smiled to herself. 'This is our first date: you have to pick me up.' Why she was mimicking Katharine Hepburn's accent she had no idea, it just seemed to fit with 'dazzling and witty'.

There was silence behind the door. 'What are you on about, "first date"?'

'Well, our first date in a really long time. It's special. Knock on the door.'

Claudia heard him sigh, but he banged on the door-frame. 'Hellooooo, I'm here for our date.'

She flung open the door and grinned. After a moment he looked up from his phone. 'You look nice. You ready?'

Claudia shimmied like she'd learned in Zumba. It probably didn't look as hot as she hoped, since she nearly toppled out of her heels. 'Do you like my dress?' she prompted. *Please like my dress. It's for you.*

'Yep, it's nice,' he said, hitting send on his phone and stuffing it into his suit jacket. 'Come on then.'

'It's red. Like LOVE.'

'Yep.'

For crying out loud, Seth, meet me halfway. He couldn't have sounded more lacklustre if he'd tried. But this evening was about more than a red dress, so she brushed it aside and thought with excitement of their evening to come.

Claudia slipped her arm into his as she tottered out of the flat. It was a cold but clear night, and the strings of Christmas lights across the street blended into the starry sky.

This was the best Christmas present she could ask for, the perfect start to the season. This date, hopefully the first of many, was a new beginning for her and Seth, a rekindling of their romance. She was just brimming with anticipation.

'I *love* our first date so far.' She beamed up at Seth, treating him to her megawatt combo of scarlet lips and Hollywood-white gnashers, Marilyn-style. He looked down at her, amused.

'What's with all this "first date" stuff? We go on dates—'

'Not proper dates; the pub with friends doesn't count. This is a *proper* date.' She blew him a kiss. 'It's romantic.'

Seth flung an arm around Claudia's neck and sighed. 'All right, fusspot, let's romance you up. There's nowhere I feel more romantic than at a bloody ballet!' He winked and pulled her in close.

Urgh, Claudia didn't want to see his willy. Not here, in a toilet cubicle of the Royal Opera House, in the middle of *The Nutcracker*. But there it was, gazing up at her. She scowled back.

'I really do need a wee. I wasn't expecting you to follow me in here.' Her eyes shifted to the smug face of the willy's owner.

'Bet you're glad I did though, eh?' Seth twitched his penis so it gave a jaunty bow like the head of a nodding dog. He flexed his fingers thoughtfully in front of her chest then put his hands on his hips. 'Why are you in a huff?'

'This was supposed to be a romantic date—'

'Well what do you call this?' He shook his willy back and forth. 'Mr Romance is ready for you!'

Claudia put her face in her hands, blocking herself from the unblinking one-eyed stare and hoping it would go away. It was very off-putting. It also made her want to laugh, but from experience she knew that wouldn't go down well. 'We're at the ballet, at the *Royal Opera House*, on our first date in ages, and you're in the toilets showing me your own *penis* ballet. Please can we just go back to our seats?'

'And, once again, you don't want to have sex.' Ouch. He'd noticed? Of course he had – she knew he would have – but the less frequent things got, the more often she was able to push it to the back of her mind and act like nothing had changed. Busted.

Claudia emerged from her hands. Seth looked down at her coldly and she felt herself turning as red as her dress; her new 'reignite the passion' dress.

'It's not that I don't want to, I love … that … I just…' She hated confrontation and now was so not the place. 'I just think we need a bit of romance back in our relationship.'

Seth zipped himself back up, furiously. 'I try to romance you every bloody day! And most of the time you're having none of it. When we first got together you'd do it with me anywhere—'

Nice. It wasn't *anywhere*.

'You were sexy and exciting. But I guess you're not that person any more. You're the problem here. YOU ARE THE PROBLEM.'

Claudia wanted to say so much, to voice every frustration and all the pain she'd felt. She knew she needed to put more effort into the relationship, but so did he. They were in a rut because of *both* of them. But it seemed like every time she tried to make things a bit more special, to make their lives more fun, he interpreted that as 'have more sex'. She wanted to tell him, preferably in a profound, witty and indisputable way, how she wanted to feel loved and desired and wooed. She wanted to feel like *The Nutcracker*'s leading lady, Clara, pirouetting out there on the stage, the lucky cow, and to be taken on out-of-this-world adventures. But her brain refused to engage in such thoughts, being completely preoccupied by his words instead. *You WERE sexy and exciting …*

'Sometimes it just doesn't feel like you love me that much any more.' Her voice broke and at that moment she loathed herself. Stop crying. *No.* 'Like it's *only* about the sex.'

He didn't move towards her or wipe her tears. *Touch my face!* she screamed silently.

'Well it's definitely not about the sex now, is it?' His words hung in the air.

She heard her heart thudding, her quiet breathing. She studied the collar of his shirt.

'Five years, Claudia. It's a long time to hold the interest, especially when you're turning me down left, right and centre.'

What was happening? Oh God . . .

She stared at him, dumbfounded, as he flung open the door of the cubicle. He turned back, his face impassive. 'Let's not force this. Sounds like we're both a bit bored. I guess we're done here.'

We're done here? *We're done here?* Had she been dismissed?

As he stormed from the bathroom she stood frozen, staring at her face in the mirror. She looked at her green eyes, her dark hair, her stupid red dress. It was a flared, fifties-style one – not sexy *or* exciting.

Five years. *We're done here.*

A tornado had just blown through her life and ripped it in half in the space of five minutes. Why didn't she just have sex with him more often? Silly dates didn't matter. Dressing up, going out, adventures didn't matter. What had she done?

No! Adventures do matter! It was her life too, her relationship too, and what she wanted out of it damn well mattered. He was such a *dick*. She grabbed a pretty carved soap and mashed it in her fist. Mashed it really hard. Like it was his stupid, pig-headed face.

Claudia washed the mess off her hands and tried to calm down. She walked out of the toilets, half expecting, a tiny bit hoping, to see Seth waiting outside.

No one.

She ascended the plush red-carpeted stairs like a zombie. At the top she bought a packet of wine gums – an attempt to realign her universe – and slipped back into the auditorium.

Let's not force this . . . we're done here.

On stage, the Sugar Plum Fairy twinkled like starlit snow as she danced in front of the ice castle. Her tutu trembled like a bauble on a Christmas tree. The Opera House was a winter wonderland that night, with beautiful sets in glittering creams and ice whites, dancers in pale, delicately embroidered costumes, and a mesmerised audience draped in their best velvets, cashmeres and silks.

And up there, a part of this magical world, were her two best friends in the world: Penny, dancing as part of the ensemble, and Nick, creating this Christmas dreamland backstage. *I should have been part of this.*

Penny's pretty, spotlit face was turned to the audience and Claudia knew she was looking straight at her. Penny twitched her head just a fraction, asking 'What's up?' That's when the tears came. Luckily the ballet was so beautiful she wasn't the only one crying. She'd never see Seth's niece again.

He wouldn't be coming to Ellie and Emma's wedding in three weeks' time. His absence would mess up their seating plan.

How would they divide the saucepan set? She'd take the two smaller ones, she supposed, being a girl. But the smallest didn't even have a lid; it was just a milk pan. *I don't need a milk pan, I need a lid!* She stuffed four wine gums into her mouth in indignation.

On stage, Clara was sighing in the arms of her soldier in front of the magnificent Christmas tree. The music swelled and Claudia's heart sank. She wished it didn't have to end; she wasn't ready to leave this cocoon of music and darkness.

But the lights came up and Claudia stood with the two thousand other patrons to applaud. She clapped and clapped until her hands stung and until everyone else from her row had filtered out. Claudia picked up her bag, wiped the mascara off her face and headed backstage.

Claudia stood for a moment, her hand resting on the heavy, black-painted door leading backstage. She let out a stray choking sob that desperately didn't want to be taken in there with her. And then she pulled herself together. It was a big fat fake pulling-herself-together, but it was a start. She pushed open the door and entered the lion's den.

Noise and chaos enveloped her into the centre of post-performance buzz. Margie, the hard-nut security guard, waved her through, recognising her as the frequent groupie who was always hanging around the dancer and the stagehand.

Racks of tiny-waisted costumes, enormous bunches of flowers, towering sets shifting back to their Act One positions ... Claudia made her way through the corridors, wishing she were invisible and avoiding the eyebrows being raised in her direction. Once she'd been part of this world, back in amateur hour. Now she was painfully aware of how out of place and awkward she was in the big leagues.

It wasn't that anyone was ever outwardly mean, it was just that feeling of being way out of your depth. Penny and she had grown up dancing; mostly ballet, but they would try any class they could get their hands on: jazz, hip hop, salsa.

Then Claudia had stupidly, *stupidly* fallen in the middle of a breakdancing class, tearing ligaments in her ankle and putting her out of action for close to four months. She missed the audition that elevated Penny into a prestigious London ballet academy.

Penny was euphoric. Along with their other good friend, Nick, who'd been accepted into his dream theatre production course, they celebrated hard. She couldn't be happier for them, but Claudia was left behind.

She eventually recovered from her injury, but she'd lost the drive. Whether it was fear, or bitterness, Claudia wasn't even sure she knew. So here she found herself, twelve years out of the game, the outsider.

But Penny and Nick were her family, and that meant battling her way through the maze of tutus, wigs and lighting, squashing down her crap, falling-apart life and congratulating them on being awesome.

Rounding the corner, mumbling 'Oops, sorry, I'm sorry,' to a stretching ballerina whose legs she tripped over, she saw her lifelines.

Nick and Penny were deep in conversation, their brows furrowed. Nick's brown hair was a tousled mess of sweat and dust, his eyes full of concern for what Penny was saying, and he stood in his thinking stance – legs wide apart and his arms folded across his chest. They saw her at the same time and lunged forward, wrapping her in hugs of sawdust and feathers.

'What's happened?' Penny muffled into her ear.

Claudia pulled back, but Nick kept a big hand on her back, holding her close. 'Nothing much – Seth and I had a bit of a fall-out – but you guys were great. Penny, you were the best one on stage, and Nick, I mean …

wow . . . you created masterpieces out there.' This was their night; the Seth drama had to wait.

'Claudia . . .' Nick cupped her face gently, wiping a stray tear with his thumb. 'Talk to us.'

Claudia's resolve wobbled. She couldn't look Nick in the eye without wanting to crumble to the ground and tear at the floorboards with her fingernails. She stared hard at his grubby grey T-shirt, focusing on the rise and fall of his chest.

'It was nothing; we're just . . . sort of . . . maybe . . . not together any more.' She gulped back an enormous sob. 'I loved your Christmas tree,' she told Nick quickly, prodding his pec.

Penny squeezed her even tighter, her white-blonde wig stuffing its way up Claudia's nose. 'How did this happen? Was he so disgusted by my fat thighs on stage he said he didn't want anything to do with you?'

'That was partly it. Then he got his willy out and I said, "No! Get it away!"'

Nick kissed her on the top of the head and took her hand. 'Do you want to see mine instead? It's much better. You'll feel much better. Come on, I'll show you.' He started leading her to the door.

'No, really, I'm fine. I'm fine.' She laughed gently, dropping Nick's hand. 'You guys did ridiculously good tonight. Sorry I'm a rubbish old party-pooper. I'm going to go home now, and I'll catch up with you tomorrow.'

'Wait, we'll come with you.' Penny started yanking clips out of her wig and freeing tendrils of her real hair.

'No, don't be silly, you'd look ridiculous on the Tube.'

'I can leave now. I'll take you,' Nick volunteered.

'No thanks, please stay.'

'Don't be such a pain in the arse. Let me take you home.' Nick tilted his head and gave her the warmest grin in the world. But she just couldn't bear to be around anyone right now.

'NO,' Claudia insisted. 'I really just want to go on my own, please; I'll call you both in the morning when my head's a bit clearer. *Please* go and celebrate your amazing show.' She gave them both a quick kiss on the cheek and felt Nick's hand rest tenderly on her bare arm for a moment. She pulled away and retreated down the corridor.

Claudia exited the Opera House alone. The crowds had left and she was by herself on the dark, chilly street. She stood for a moment, closing her eyes and letting the cold breeze dry her face. How could she go home? But what else could she do? When this date started she had no idea it would end in the kind of awkward 'broken-up couple living in the same house' scene she'd only seen on TV.

This was a ridiculous situation. It had to sort itself out. It had to.

She opened her eyes and turned to walk up the road.

She stopped.

Seth.

He was coming around the corner at the very top of the street. He had come back to her.

Claudia was boiling all the way to her toes with anger and hurt, but relief still swept over her. She realised how much she'd needed to see him; safe, familiar, half-of-her-life him. Her pace quickened.

Then Seth stopped outside the pub on the corner. He broke into a series of cheers and laughs as he greeted a large group of friends.

She watched but he didn't come any further; he hadn't seen her.

He looked cheerful.

She was a mess and he didn't even look a bit sad, or wistful about the life he'd just lost.

He threw his arms around a girl who emerged from the centre of the group.

Who's that?

They laughed together. She looked like one of those fun, sexy, confident girls you both hate and desperately wish you were. Like The Pussycat Dolls.

His hands groped her perfect butt cheeks.

What?

They kissed.

Things. Just. Got. Worse.

Claudia's legs made an executive decision, taking charge before her brain and heart could crumble into each other, inconsolable. They swept her across the road and in through the door of a quiet Italian restaurant. The eatery was mellow at this time of night, with just a few couples sharing desserts and a birthday party taking their time over the dregs of several bottles of wine.

The darkness of red upholstery and mahogany tables shrouded her, and she took a seat on a stool at the far end of the bar, next to the windows that looked out onto the street. Claudia never took her eyes off Seth.

Her whole body was trembling, and the sensation that her heart had been scraped out of her chest made her curl inwards. She laid her small, shaking hands on the window. No, no, no, he can't have cheated on her. Their life together can't have all been a lie. That would mean they could never be together again.

The barman materialised in the corner of her vision. 'Can I get you a drink?' he asked in an Australian accent.

'Can I have a bottle of house red please? One glass?' Claudia whispered, as if Seth would hear her voice in the wind and turn to look at her.

Claudia dragged her eyes from the window for a second to look at the bartender. His name badge read BILLY. He looked like Billy Kennedy from *Neighbours*.

'You look like Billy Kennedy from *Neighbours*.'

'So they say.' He grinned. 'What's your name?'

'Claudia,' she mumbled.

'So, Claudia, this whole bottle's just for you?'

'Yep.' She went back to watching her partner of five years stroking someone else's bottom. She wanted to break every bone in that hand. 'Just for me. Big fat lonely me.'

Pop. Glug, glug, glug. 'Good for you, darl'. You crack on.'

She took some hearty gulps of wine and went back to squinting at Seth, misting up the window with her breath. Was that a look of pain? Was that beardy guy patting him on his back out of consolation? Was he wiping a tear? Ha! Thank God . . .

No.

No, he was crying with laughter at something *she* had said.

'You're not funny,' Claudia hissed, her fingers curling into claws.

'I reckon he's laughing at her fat ugly face.' Billy was standing behind her, tea towel flung over his shoulder, staring out across the street. She half-smiled through the pain.

'What?'

'Yeah, he's thinking, "Bloody hell, what am I doing listening to your drivel, you dumbo. With your boring clothes and your minging hair."'

Her hair *was* a little drab, if you call 'no need to style

because it looks amazing anyway' boring. She scrutinised Billy's face. 'Minging?'

He nodded. 'Minging.'

'I feel sorry for her,' Claudia said. 'She probably doesn't even know how grating that laugh can get.'

'I like your dress, by the way.'

Claudia had been best friends with her dress at the start of the evening. Now she looked at it bitterly, like you would a faux-pleasant co-worker who's thrown you under the bus in front of your boss.

'Date night gone wrong?'

'Dunno.' Claudia sighed and had another gulp of wine. 'It's the only date I've been on in yonks, so maybe it's normal now for the boy to bugger off halfway through.'

'I've never been on a date with a boy, so I'm not sure. But it doesn't sound quite right.'

Claudia shook her head and gazed outside.

'If you stop staring you never have to see the bastard again.'

'Ah, but I do,' she choked, finishing off the glass and pouring herself another. 'I live with the bastard.'

Billy roared with laughter. Claudia swigged and tried to look affronted, but her features were beginning to slacken as the alcohol numbed them.

'Life's got a way of kicking you right in the balls sometimes, hey? My girlfriend back in Oz cheated on me; we shared a house but she was my landlord and I had to give her two months' notice. You've gotta laugh ...'

Something that could have been a sob and could have been a chuckle burst from Claudia. 'You've gotta laugh ...' She watched the pitiful end to her date, the weight of her own breathing hunching her back until she was resting her cheek on the rim of her wine glass. More than anything she wanted to curl up where she was and sleep. She felt defeated.

'I hate him,' she whispered to no one in particular.

'I think you should confront him,' Billy answered. Claudia swivelled her eyes to look up at him without moving. 'I really think you should. He's got no right to treat you like that; you should do it now, while he can't deny it or try to get out of it.'

'I can't—'

'Yes you bloody can!' Billy whipped the empty glass from under her cheek. She sat up, startled, and wiped the red-wine circle from her face. She couldn't confront him, not in front of all those people. She *hated* confrontation.

But she was a bit pissed.

'Go on, you drunk, bugger off,' Billy said with an encouraging grin. 'Go and tell him which bridge to jump off, do it for all us cheatees who never had the courage.'

Claudia stood, wobbled, and took a deep breath.

She sat down again. She really didn't want to face him. What was she going to say?

Nothing, because she wasn't going to do it. She

would cut through the side streets to the Tube station and avoid him. He never had to know she was there, or that she'd seen him.

'HE SHOULD KNOW I'VE SEEN HIM!' she declared, standing and knocking her stool over onto the polished floor. The sedate diners looked up from their gelati and vino.

Claudia swayed and fixed Billy with a hard stare. 'I AM A WRONGED WOMAN.'

Billy smiled and passed her a shot of limoncello. 'Yeah you are. Drink this and go kick his arse.'

She knocked back the limoncello, gave Billy a salute and stumbled out of the restaurant. Wow, that wine had hit fast. That's what you get for gulping it.

In the cold night air Claudia contemplated throwing up and then settling down for a nap, but instead she slicked on a fresh coat of red lipstick.

Yeah, *powerful red lipstick*.

She stood next to the bronze statue of a ballerina, sitting serenely opposite the Opera House. *Young Dancer* she was called. *Younger Claudia*, she thought miserably, allowing herself a full thirty seconds of melancholy before the limoncello burned the inside of her chest and she felt her temper bubbling again.

She glared at the Young Dancer. 'You cheated on me?' she accused the statue, picturing Seth's laughing face. 'You cheated on *me*?' There were millions of things she wanted to say to him.

She jabbed the statue. 'I hope you have the worst life, absolute crap, because you don't have me any more.' Claudia put her face close to the statue and sneered into her ear. 'Good luck telling your family what an idiot you've been. They love me. But you messed it up.'

The ballerina gazed impassively at her foot.

Claudia's whole body shook and despite the cold her skin prickled with heat. 'You're a nasty, crap cheat!' she seethed.

And he'd blamed *her* for this breakup?

'You're no man, you're a boy, a coward. With a very small willy.' She glared at the ballerina, who sat, indifferent to the verbal abuse.

'I'm going to punch you in the balls.'

But she didn't, because a couple exited the restaurant and gave her a look.

Even in her haze of wine and limoncello she was at least partially aware of how crazy she must seem, going off on one at a defenceless statue. She gave it one last glare, hissed 'You're making me look drunk' into the Young Dancer's ear and straightened up.

'Right then.'

Claudia's head was held high as she approached the pub, and she marched with the determination of a soldier. But the closer she got, the more the hundreds of emotions she was feeling tried to pull her backwards. *Don't do it*, they warned, *you're not ready*.

Her pace slowed and she stepped quietly. Truth be told, she didn't want to do this. Correction, she *wanted* to do this, but she didn't think she *could*.

She stopped a few metres away from Seth, her voice caught in her throat. How had it got to this, where she was scared to speak to her own boyfriend? They were a happy couple three hours ago; they had a whole past of experiences, memories, in-jokes and intimacies. She'd assumed they had a future.

She looked at his face. The face she knew as well as her own. She knew the feel of his eyebrows and his ears, the colour of his eyelashes, the smell of his skin.

Would this really be no more, just like that? Would she never know those things again?

A silent sob escaped as a puff of air. Did *she* know those things? Had *she* felt his browline and smelt his skin?

The group fell silent and Seth turned to face her. She met his eyes and his hand dropped from the back of the other girl's jeans.

They were locked together in that moment. Claudia searched his eyes and searched for the words she wanted to say, but nothing came.

Seth cleared his throat. 'Claud—' He reached for her and she came to life, jumping back from his touch. She looked from his hand to his face.

'That's been on her bum!'

Seth glanced around at his group, his eyes falling on the girl. He looked back at Claudia. 'Look, Claud, like we talked about earlier, we just need some time apart. You go and enjoy the Christmas festivities, it'll do you good.' He smiled at her.

Those damned tears were back, rolling like melting icicles down her cheeks. She scraped them away. *Come on, Claudia, be strong. Don't you dare be a walkover. Tell him what you told that statue.* Anger prowled inside her that she couldn't put into words. Nothing made sense now that she stood in front of him. She begged him with her eyes and her tears to make it better, to fix this horrible misunderstanding.

He shuffled his feet. He looked so uncomfortable.

The girl sniggered: 'This is awkward.'

Claudia tore her eyes from Seth and whipped around to face her. 'What? What? I don't care if this is awkward for *you*, you ... complete ... cow!'

The girl laughed, like any good woman-hating female would. 'You don't get to be involved,' Claudia spat, and turned back to Seth, frantic to salvage something from this confrontation, and too demeaned to risk looking at her again.

Seth was chewing his lip.

Claudia felt desperation seeping from her and hated herself for it. 'Why don't you care?' she implored, searching for some kind of reassurance that he did, and at the same time acutely aware of how embarrassingly needy she sounded.

He said nothing. He just looked at her, a sad expression on his oh-so-familiar face.

'You don't care ...' she whispered. 'It's all just ... okay ... SCREW YOU.'

'Claudia,' Seth purred half-heartedly, 'of course I care.'

She turned her back on them all. She was humiliated. She walked away from the person who knew her the best and cared about her the least.

Turning the corner, Claudia's legs carried her just far enough down the road that she could no longer hear the noise and revelry from the pub. Then she crumbled against a wall, her face in her hands. She felt like an idiot. She'd wanted to come across as strong, to give him a piece of her mind. Instead, she gave them all a good laugh.

She vowed that she would not let her fear of confrontation humiliate her like that again. She was going to change, never again be a scared little woman, and next time she saw him she'd let him know.

The alcohol, pain and confusion made her head swim. Her body needed to buckle with tears but her eyes were dried out, and all she could do was take deep, unsteady breaths, inhaling the sickly-sweet smell of wine gums and limoncello.

There was too much in her brain. She hated Seth for everything he'd done and for everything he hadn't lived up to. So how could she love him as well, and desperately want this all to go away and for him to come back, to choose her and for them carry on with their life?

Her phone tinkled with the sound of reindeer bells; her festive text message alert. Seth?

She dragged her phone from her clutch bag.

It was Nick.

You're ace, you know that, right?

She smiled. Maybe – not now, but in the future – she'd be okay. She had Nick. And Penny.

Every inch of her still felt beaten, but Nick's message was like some strong arms lifting her upright. It was time to go.

Claudia sprawled her way through Covent Garden Tube station, her pink-rimmed eyes looking blankly ahead but hiding a runaway train of thoughts. She made it to the platform with just enough time to shove all her anger against one of the train's closing doors until it huffed, conceded and sulkily let her in. The carriage was nearly empty; Claudia plonked herself down in the middle of a line of blue seats and let out a massive sigh.

The train was *nearly* empty.

Diagonally across from Claudia a late-teenage couple canoodled shamelessly, coming up for air only to glance smugly around the carriage to see who was jealous of their steamy relationship. Urgh. Claudia glared at them.

Their pointy, pale faces and matching floppy haircuts made them look like brother and sister. The girl giggled coquettishly as her double-denimed hipster dribbled on her neck.

Claudia wanted to vomit on their heads. She *really* wanted to. She sighed again, loudly.

With the smug look of Angelina Jolie bagging Brad Pitt, the girl fluttered her hair in the boy's face and he stroked it.

It sent shivers down Claudia's spine and she curled her upper lip. Why were they so annoying?

'Urgh,' she grunted.

The boy looked over and flicked his Bieber-hair out of his eyes. The girl whispered something and licked his ear.

Claudia held his gaze and tutted.

He went back to staring at the girl's jawline from two centimetres away, and she spanked his be-jeaned bottom with her Oyster card.

Claudia, the wine, and her emotions couldn't take it any more. The three of them clubbed together and gave her a voice.

'Get out of her neck, man!' she slurred. The couple looked up, deer in headlights, before he struggled to regain his cool and narrowed his eyes. 'Personal space,' Claudia hissed.

'What's your problem?' he squeaked.

'Your face,' Claudia replied. And then hiccupped.

'At least it's not old. Like your face,' the girl piped up, before sinking back behind her curtain of hair.

Claudia snorted. Her eyelids were becoming heavy and she was beginning to wonder why she'd picked a fight with a couple of teenagers. 'At least my face isn't being sucked on in the middle of the Tube. Sooooo romaaaaaantic.'

'Well your face probably isn't going to be sucked on at all this Christmas. Because it's crap.'

Claudia had no answer to that. The little shit was probably right. She stuck out her lower lip and thought about it, then flicked her eyes towards the girl.

'You'll find out, girly,' she lectured, 'that relationships and snogging is all well and good until your brother here' – she motioned at the boy, who looked aghast – 'puts his hands on your other sister's bum and cocks it all up.'

'*We are now arriving at Baron's Court.*'

Claudia used the pole to heave herself up and tottered clumsily to the train doors. She looked back at the couple, who were having a heated discussion about whether to stand up to the crazy drunk lady or let it go because she might be stronger than them. *Damn right she was stronger than them*. The doors opened and the cold night air rushed into the train.

'I am a wronged woman,' she declared, and fell face down onto the platform.

Ouch. Fresh tears trickled down Claudia's cheeks. It wasn't fair, she didn't want to be hurt right now, she was hurting enough. She pushed herself up from the cold, gritty tarmac and hobbled down the long platform, feeling very alone. London is a noisy, crowded, energising city, but at night certain pockets can be as silent as the countryside.

Claudia exited the station aware that the only sound was the clacking of her high heels. She didn't like this feeling. She was injured and alone, it was dark and really cold, and the damned wine was heightening her emotions even more. She could see her breath misting in front of her face, and a quiet, lazy breeze pushed crackly leaves and cigarette packets across the street.

Claudia stopped and stood still in the middle of the road.

A new fear made her heart thud. She couldn't go home. She couldn't bear it. What if he came back? What if he didn't?

She was all alone, at night, on the streets of London, and she had nowhere to go.

Date Two

Starbucks, Holborn

Claudia unpeeled her face from the sofa cushion one eyelash at a time. Beneath her she left a zebra-print of tear-streaked mascara on the cream fabric. Penny would kill her, if Penny were one to care about such things and didn't regularly lob red wine, pasta and hair dye all over her flat.

She padded to the bathroom and had a good stare at herself. She was still wearing last night's make-up, but not one bit of it was in the place it started out. A false eyelash had nested above her top lip, giving her a Hitler moustache. She tilted her head. *If only I could be a boy* . . .

Her hair glittered faintly with hidden crystals, the few survivors cowering fearfully in her sunken up-do. She wore thick penguin-print pyjamas that belonged to Penny and were, if she was being brutally honest (which right now she felt like being), too short, too tight, less cute and more adult-baby on her than they were on her friend the petite ballerina.

Claudia opened the shirt and looked at her breasts. She lifted one and let drop; it bounced in the manner of a yo-yo. The same result with the other. She stretched a handful of flesh away from her stomach as if it were bread dough.

'You *are* sexy and exciting,' she whispered to her reflection. 'Just look at you.' The bare-breasted, diamantéd Hitler in the mirror struck a pose.

Penny woke mid-morning to the sound of a thousand dying cats in her living room. Following her late-night performance she had found her best friend in a shivering, tearful frenzy on the doorstep of her building, and it took four hot chocolates and three episodes of *The Big Bang Theory* before she fell asleep on the sofa.

Flying out of her room she saw Claudia in the plank position, guttural, inhuman groans bursting out of her. On the TV was Penny's *Insanity Workout* DVD.

'3 ... 2 ... 1!' yelled the presenter, and Claudia collapsed with a last dying wail.

Penny flicked off the TV. 'Why is this happening?' she demanded.

Claudia wiped her sweaty brow on the carpet. 'This morning – well, last night, I suppose – I had the realisation that I am not considered a Sexy Lady. I am therefore becoming said Lady. Starting with a little exercise.' If she just fixed herself everything might still work out.

Penny rolled Claudia over and glared at her. 'You're a very Sexy Lady. Seth is a total moron with no brain cells and shrivelly, cowardly balls. Don't you dare change for him!'

'I'm not – this is for me. I want to be a Sexy Lady for me.' She peeped at Penny to see if she was buying it. 'I'm sorry I got your pyjamas sweaty. And your sofa grimy.'

'Don't care and don't care, but if you're going to start an insane fitness plan then we're going to do it together, because I want to be a Sexy Lady too.'

'You already are a Sexy Lady.'

'As are you! But we do need to get you a change of clothes. Will you let me take you home?'

'No thank you.' Claudia shrank back against the sofa.

She'd stood on the frosty street for a good half an hour the previous night, overwhelmed by the responsibility of deciding what to do with herself. Eventually she'd turned her back on her block of flats and tottered the mile to Penny's house. By the time she'd arrived her emotions were roller-coastering, with certain sharp peaks that she just kept swinging back around to.

She wasn't sexy any more.

He didn't love her.

A Jack the Ripper wannabe could kill her at any moment.

She wasn't exciting.

She'd fallen out of the Tube and cut her knee, and it wasn't *fair*.

Penny crouched down and began untangling Claudia's hair with her fingers. 'We'll be really quick, I'll go in first, check the coast is clear, then you can run in, grab some stuff, pour bleach in his shampoo and we'll be back here within an hour.'

Claudia nodded. She could do this, if Penny held her hand. Seth should be at work anyway. 'I called in sick,' she confessed. Claudia worked at Edurné's, a popular dancewear shop on Neal Street. She liked her job. Really. Her schedule was flexible, she kept herself up to date with the dance industry's news, trends and fashions, and she could match a dancer with their perfect shoe just by looking at them. But she'd been doing the same thing for years, and the truth was she was bored.

'*Quelle surprise*. What's this, the fifth time in the last six weeks?' Penny pulled Claudia to her feet. 'Come on, we'll go in all black, like ninjas. You'll have a great time.'

Fifteen minutes later Claudia was walking through Kensington wearing black leggings and a big black duffel coat. Penny chasséd along next to her, humming a mash-up of the *Batman*, *Spiderman* and *Avengers* theme tunes. Claudia kept quiet, her heart thudding in her chest.

She hated that she was nervous about going to her own home, but what if he was there? She stopped in her tracks. 'What if *she's* there?'

'She won't be there – Seth would have expected you to be home last night, so he wouldn't have brought her around unless he's even more of a knobbertron than I thought.' Penny gently pushed Claudia into a walk again.

Arriving at her block of flats in West Kensington, Claudia stood for a long time staring up at her window. *I won't be able to look out at my view any more*, she mused. She couldn't afford to live here on her own. She'd have to downsize to a studio.

She took a deep breath and plunged into the building. She climbed the stairs listening for sounds of wild sex coming from her floor.

Nothing.

She crept towards her front door. Even Penny had stopped dancing and was moving silently; she was really fulfilling her role of ninja.

Claudia pressed her ear to the door and listened. She listened for sounds of him and the girl, she listened for sounds of silence, and she listened, with hope in her heart, for sounds of crying, of heartbreak, of him sitting in there caring about their split.

Still nothing.

Taylor Swift wouldn't be fannying about like this. She'd have already written a stonking great chart-topper about the whole mess. *Let's do this.*

The second she walked into their flat she saw everything – their photos, their memories, their life. Their open bedroom door, their bed, and that he hadn't been home last night either. Her heart crumpled like a discarded ball of paper.

'Come on.' Penny charged in. Claudia knew she'd noticed the same thing, but was grateful to her for not saying a word. Penny yanked open a cupboard and pulled out Claudia's huge pink suitcase.

Claudia shrank back from the case like it was the enemy. She didn't want anything to change. She wanted to live here, and she didn't want never to see Seth again. She fanned her hot skin and she stuck as close to Penny as if the apartment was booby-trapped.

Penny marched Claudia from room to room filling the suitcase with clothes, underwear and toiletries, not giving Claudia more than three seconds per item to decide if it was coming. Every time Claudia's face wrinkled and she started to say 'I wore that when . . .' Penny would pinch her and move on to the next item.

It'll be over soon, Claudia repeated like a mantra as she averted her eyes from the box of Seth's favourite cereal. *It'll be over soon*.

Claudia and Penny were silent as they walked back to Penny's flat, taking it in turns to drag the heavy suitcase over the uneven paving slabs.

Claudia heaved the case over a particularly angled stone and it crashed with a thud on the other side. She stopped and sighed. *I think I'll have a break to wallow in self-pity.*

Penny took the case from her hand and coaxed Claudia to keep moving. 'Dare I ask what you're thinking, or will that open the floodgates?'

'I'm thinking ...' Claudia considered her words. 'That we had a nice relationship. He wasn't a horrible old knob all the time. I couldn't have seen this coming. Did you see it coming?'

'No.' Penny was thoughtful. 'Generally he's a nice guy, I liked him. Though ... he did think his own crap jokes were funny.'

'Yeah, he thought he was hilarious. I just presumed he was destined to grow up to become king of the Dad-Jokes.' They walked on in silence for a little more. 'We were close, though. I know we didn't ever go on dates any more, but it's not like we didn't have fun together. And it's not like we hadn't had sex for years, it just wasn't ... that often.'

Claudia tried to take the suitcase back from Penny, who shifted it into her other hand and gave Claudia a harsh *bugger off, keep talking* look. So she did.

'We had brilliant holidays, like when we went to Orlando, or Rome. I love his family, and he loves my dad. And Dad thinks he's okay ... We're only halfway through season four of *Game of Thrones* together, Penny!'

'I know, it's really hard,' Penny soothed.

'What I'm saying is, it all feels very out of the blue. I couldn't have predicted this, could I?'

'Absolutely not, and when you're ready maybe you can get some answers from him. But for now, you need to promise me you're not about to blame yourself.'

'Oh no, he's the idiot who messed it all up.' But inside she did feel a bit to blame. She was supposed to bring 'fun, sexy girlfriend' to the table yet over the years she'd begun only to bring her doughy tummy and some cracking TV box sets.

Claudia's phone tinkled. She met Penny's eye and warily pulled it from her handbag. She smiled. Nick.

Fancy a shag now you're single?

Claudia laughed out loud. Nick was the only one who could say something like that to her and not induce further hysterical crying or livid indignation.

No thanks, now a lesbian, no boys allowed.

Fine. Frigid. Let me know when I can come over to Penny's and stare at your lovely face.

Claudia walked a little lighter the rest of the way.

'Can you plump it up a bit?' Penny asked, her arms in the air.

Claudia boxed the sides of Penny's stomach until it stuck out at more of a curve, then went back to circling her with duct tape.

Claudia finished her friend's faux-pregnancy pillow tummy with a flourish, and Penny added the finishing touch by pulling on a billowy blouse. Penny stroked the pillow and admired herself in the mirror.

'You look so beautiful.' Claudia smiled, a tear in her eye.

'Thanks, you too.'

'Thanks.' Claudia squadged her own pillow-baby, which she'd really only fashioned in support of Penny. It felt warm, but other than that she definitely wasn't ready to be pregnant yet. 'So, how does that feel? Still want a baby?'

'I love it, Claud, I love it so much I want to name the pillow. I want to name her Katie Rose and go shopping for tiny furry onesies with ears on.'

Penny was head-over-heels broody for a baby, and at thirty she was over waiting for Mr Right to ride in and play house with her, so she'd chosen to look into the options of having a baby solo. She was bursting at the seams with love, more than enough to equal that of two parents, but she wouldn't be alone – Claudia would be there.

'If I do go ahead with this, will you come with me to appointments or whatever?'

'Of course I will; I'm going to be your husband for the whole thing. Especially if we get to go to a sperm bank, because I'm gagging to know if they really do have porn mags lying about.'

'I'm not sure if they'd let you look. That might be a different, um, wing than where we'd be going.'

'Okay, I'll bring my own.'

'Cool. Don't bring them if we end up going to an adoption agency, though, that might be a bit off.'

'You're always telling me not to look at porn, you're such a nagging wife.'

Penny walked in a circle, holding the small of her back as if the pillow-baby was making it ache. 'Do you think people will judge me? For not actually being a wife?'

'If they do they're living in the past, and I'll give them a good telling-off.'

'Well, maybe not for being unmarried, but what about for not doing this with a man?'

Claudia saw the nervous face of her friend and waddled over to give her a hug, squashing their pillow tummies together. 'You've wanted this for a long time, and if you had a partner I'm sure it would be a great journey together, but you *can* do this yourself. It's allowed.'

Penny nodded. 'You sure you don't want to get one too? We could be single mums together. Sorry, not to be flippant.'

'It's fine, but no thanks. With or without Seth, I am soooo not ready.'

'But you'll hold my hand?'

'Hell, I'll hold your legs apart in the delivery room if you want.' She looked down at their pillows. 'We should totally sumo with these.'

'Let's do it, but we can't when I'm actually preggers. Can we?'

'No, probably not. For now, nothing will stop me defeating my non-up-the-duff nemesis.' She gave Penny a bump with her pillow and sent her flying across the room.

That night, while Penny danced under the icicles at the Opera House, Claudia sat on the living-room floor surrounded by her underwear.

'I'll show you sexy,' she muttered, snipping a peep-hole into the left cup of one of her bras.

Among the scattered, fraying garments were needles and thread, sequins, ribbons and a big plastic bucket filled with warm water, her red dress and two pairs of knickers that were slowly turning pink.

Claudia had spent the evening miserably trying on her lingerie collection in front of Penny's full-length mirror. She didn't feel very hot in it. This wasn't the underwear a sexy and exciting girl would wear. *I bet That Girl's buttocks were encased in some skimpy, lacy number* called a 'cheeky hipster' or 'man-stealer thong'. But Claudia was no city banker. She couldn't skip down to Victoria's Secret on Bond Street and blow a few hundred on teeny colourful triangles with all the trimmings. She had to make do and mend.

Which is what she found herself doing now: sewing sequins onto bra straps, stitching ribbons to the sides of granny-pants and upgrading grey undies to murky pink ones. She was pleased with her progress, and was holding a bedazzled balconette up to the light to inspect her glitter-gluing skills when Penny got home.

'What in God's name are you doing and have you made me some?!' Penny took the bra from Claudia's hand and held it against her boobs. 'Hmm, you're bigger than me. Are these your Christmas presents?'

'No.' Claudia took back the bra and set it down tenderly, the glitter-glue already cracking and falling off. 'This is my sexy new underwear.'

'Oh.'

Penny and Claudia sat in silence, looking at the mess.

'Hang on,' Penny said eventually, and darted off. She came back moments later holding a pair of frilly red tutu knickers. 'You can have these if you like.'

'Um, I don't mean to be rude, but I don't want to wear your old knickers.'

'They're better than your old knickers!' Penny waved the red pants at the chaos in the living room. 'I haven't even worn these.'

Claudia gingerly reached out and took the knickers. They felt soft and silky, and she was longing to put them on instead of the scratchy sequin-riddled ones that were currently burning her bits. She went into the bathroom and tried them, topping them off with her newly peep-holed bra. Okay, the bra looked awful, and Claudia hid her rude boobs with her arm. But the knickers were nice. The frills cascaded over her bottom and when she shook it they rippled like a can-can dancer's petticoats.

She popped her oversized T-shirt back over the top and went back into the living room. Penny was chucking the gloomy pink water down the sink. She turned around. 'Full disclosure: I've worn them once. But I washed them. I think.'

Claudia was washed and scrubbed and had already called in sick when there was a knock on Penny's door the following morning. Penny leapt from her room like a springbok and crouched in front of the door. 'Don't be angry,' she whispered, then stood and flung the door open.

'Dad!' Claudia's father, Joe, was a teddy bear, but fiercely protective when it came to his daughter's happiness. He felt he owed it to her. Claudia knew he worried, and dragging him into London like this was not going to do either of them any good. But even as she thought this, and mentally Chinese-burned the hell out of Penny, a warm sense of comfort washed over her.

'Dad . . . ' she murmured, and raced into his arms.

Joe held his daughter in the doorway for as long as she needed, in which time Penny had made them both cups of tea, cleared the remaining scraps of deceased-underwear fabric off the sofa and retreated to the shower.

Claudia let go, but stuck close to her dad as she led him to the sofa. 'You didn't have to come into town. Did you take the train?' Joe still lived in their family home back in Frostwood, a small village in Surrey. He couldn't bear to part with it, even after her mum, Diana, had moved away.

'Yep, I used my Oyster card and everything,' he said proudly. 'It's fine, love, it only took half an hour or so door to door.'

Claudia squeezed his hand and willed the tears not to overflow. He was such a lovely, sweet liar. It would have taken him at least two hours. She picked up her tea but her shaking hands gave her away. Joe took the mug and put it back on the table. 'I know Penny's a mucky pup, but let's not pour tea all over the place for the sake of it.' He pulled his daughter in close. She let the tears flow.

Eventually, through bubbles of snot and high-pitched snorts, Claudia explained what had happened. Not the part about the evil willy making an appearance in the toilets, though – she left him zipped away.

Joe listened, smoothing Claudia's hair. When she'd finished and his polo shirt was soaked, he nodded thoughtfully. 'This is a good thing,' he said eventually.

Claudia raised her eyebrows and wiped her nose on her hand. 'Seth was tolerable: always pally towards me and seemed to treat you well enough. Liked the sound of his own voice a bit too much. But he's only half the man you deserve. He isn't even that.' He lapsed into another silence. Claudia looked at his crinkled, handsome face. He comforted her. She hadn't known it, but he was the best medication she could have taken in the past two days. Good old Dad.

Her phone jingled and she struggled to slip under the weight of her dad's arm as he was lost in thought. She smiled as she read the text message.

'That better not be him ...' Joe spoke up, unconsciously twitching his hands in and out of fists.

'No, it's Nick. He wants to meet up this afternoon. I've been kind of avoiding him.'

Joe sat up and grinned, the sparkle back in his eye. 'Now Nick I like. I like Nick very much, he's a good chap. Why are you avoiding him?'

'Avoiding all men, I should say. No offence.' She quickly typed back,

> Not ready to face the world yet, can we give it
> another day? Sorry I'm crap, miss your face x.

Joe stood up. 'Well stop being a wet wipe and go and meet him.'

Her phone jingled again.

I have to see you. Today.

Why??? You're such a stalker!

'What's he saying?' Joe asked, craning his neck to see her phone.

'Dad!' she laughed. 'I'm just getting rid of him.'

I have something very important to ask you and it can't wait.

Joe stood and pulled on his coat. 'Come on, daughter, I'm taking you for lunch at that Hard Rock place you like, then you're going to see your boyfriend— I mean, your best friend ...' He threw Claudia a cheeky sideways glance.

By mid-afternoon the temperature had plummeted. The sun was low in the blue sky and frost was forming wherever shadow had settled. Claudia walked briskly between the white-stoned law courts on the Strand, clapping her gloved hands together and burrowing her lips inside her scarf.

What a nice lunch with her dad. She felt calmed but also a pang of homesickness. The wedding of one of her loveliest school friends, Ellie, to her equally scrummy partner Emma, would take place in their hometown on

Christmas Eve, and the gap between seeing her dad today and seeing him then seemed like a lifetime.

She rounded the corner onto High Holborn and spied Starbucks, with Nick sitting on a stool by the window.

She stopped on the other side of the street and smiled at the sight – her Nick, in his Christmas-patterned jumper and three-day stubble, engrossed in the battered copy of *A Christmas Carol* he read every year. He lit up at Christmas; everything was about tradition and magic.

She stamped across the road and pushed open the café door, releasing a happy tinkle of bells and a plume of toasty air. Nick looked up and beamed, jumping from his seat and folding her into a bear hug. He steered her to a stool, gave her a big kiss on the forehead deliberately overloaded with spit, and jogged off to the counter.

Claudia wiped her head and picked up his book. The cover illustration showed a pointy-nosed Scrooge by his fireplace, alone and miserable on Christmas Eve. 'It doesn't look too bad, Ebenezer,' she whispered. 'At least no one's bothering you.'

Nick returned with two mugs overflowing with a volcano of whipped cream, caramel drizzles and sprinkly bits of chocolate. Claudia laughed. 'You remembered.'

She took a sip of her gingerbread latte, the spices and sweet smell igniting the memories of a thousand Christmas moments: cooking with her mum, watching *The Snowman* with her dad, present shopping, tree decorating, light switch-ons, singing Band Aid at full volume while trying to recreate these very drinks at home with Nick and Penny . . .

'Of course I remembered. Yours is gingerbread, Penny's is toffee nut, and mine's—'

'Salted caramel.'

They drank in cosy silence for a few minutes. She could feel his eyes on her behind the syrupy steam that rose from her giant mug. Nick broke the spell. 'Are you going to tell me what happened?'

Claudia picked up Nick's ancient old Nokia phone and fiddled with it between her fingers. 'You need a new phone for Christmas,' she stated.

'You need to try beating my high score on Snake, *then* tell me I'm wasting my time with this thing. And you need to stop trying to change the subject.'

He prised his phone from her hand and gently pushed her latte closer with encouragement.

She didn't want to give him the Dad version; she'd cried enough that day. And she also found that she didn't want to give him the Penny version, which was basically a list of why Seth was rubbish and why she was unlovable. 'We were in very different places, it turned out, and I should have—'

'I don't want the agony-aunt answer; I want to know how you *feel*. Tell me through the art of nineties ballads if that would help.'

'Okay, I *feel* like Seth is a big horrible knobface who

ruined not only our first date in for ever but also a night I was really looking forward to – seeing the work you and Penny had put in to this year's production.'

'Knobface. Got it. Tell me more, let it out.'

'First his willy came out, and I swear it was *glaring* at me, you know?'

'I do know; they can do that. Mine's not much of a glarer, but it gets a real attitude if I hang out on a snowboard too long.' He paused. 'Stop thinking about my junk.'

Too late … 'Anyway, then he accused me of being boring, not who I used to be …' *Hello again, tears, thanks for joining us in the middle of Starbucks*. 'And ended with a rousing chorus of how unsexy I am.'

'Shut your stupid face!' Nick raged. 'I know you better than him, and you're the same fun, exciting, sexy girl you've always been.' Claudia caught his eye for a millisecond and he pulled her in to him. He tugged up the hem of his jumper and flashed a very un-winterly display of naked flesh as he mopped the mascara from her face. At a nearby table, two younger girls spilled their coffees at the sight of his taught, construction-worker stomach.

She felt just a teeny, tiny, barely-there sense of smugness. *He's here with me, ladies*. Just a tiny bit. It didn't mean anything.

He studied her face. 'Seeing you like this sucks. Seth's an idiot.'

'I'm really tired of crying.'

'I know you are.'

She pointed at his book. 'I think I want to be Scrooge.'

'You can't be Scrooge. If we're going to live in *A Christmas Carol*, I want to be Scrooge.'

'Why do you get to be Scrooge?'

'Why do *you* get to be Scrooge?'

'Because I'm miserable and alone and I don't want anyone to be happy.'

Nick thought this through. 'No. No, you have to be Fred, Scrooge's nephew.'

Claudia threw a blob of cream at Nick's face. 'That's the worst character! He's so annoying!'

Nick threw cream back at her. '*You're* the worst character.'

Claudia looked around at the other customers bundled up in their winter woollies, tottering between the counter and the armchairs, laden with hot chocolates and oversized mince pies. The low sunshine streamed through the sticker-covered window, sprinkling the floor and walls with shadows of snowflakes. 'Thanks for bringing me here, Nick, I love it, it's so *easy*. No pressures. It would be a nice date place, don't you think?'

'What do you call this?' Nick asked with mock indignation.

'This isn't a date. If it's a date it's my second one this month, and I got dumped on the first one.'

'This could be a date; I bought your drink, I'm being charming, and I left just enough stubble for you to think I'm sexy but not trying too hard.' He raised an eyebrow.

She thought about it. A date … with Nick …

He whooped. 'You're thinking about it! You're thinking about dating me!'

'No I'm not!'

'Seriously, why don't we call this a date?'

'Nick …'

'Answer me, woman. You're very secretive for a date. Are you trying to be mysterious?'

He was such a pain. 'Because I haven't been on any dates for about three years, so two in one week is just … silly.' *And I feel guilty being on a date, but not with Seth. Even though a date* with *Seth wouldn't be happening.*

'Well it shouldn't be silly for a lovely girl like you, it should be normal. You should be taken on so many dates you're like, "Men, leave me be, I need to have a night at home catching up on *New Girl*."'

She laughed at the image. She did love *New Girl*, though.

'Consider this your official second date of December.'

Why the heck should she feel guilty? She gave in and nodded, holding Nick's gaze. He was a tricksy one.

'Anyway, shut up,' said Nick. 'I have to ask you something, if you can manage not to be so self-involved for two minutes.'

'I can try,' she offered.

Nick was staring at her with twinkling eyes. 'I can only reveal half of why I needed to see you today, and half tomorrow.'

'Go on.'

He put his hands flat on her thighs and bent in towards her. He smelled of caramel and coffee. 'How do you fancy making it three dates in one week?'

She was instantly suspicious. 'Why?'

'Will you go on a very important date with me tomorrow?'

'Three dates? I don't think my heart can handle it.'

'You'll be the most popular girl in school. Or everyone will think you're the biggest slut-bag.'

'I wish. What is it, and why do you need me there?'

'I need . . .'

'Yes?'

'To ask you . . .'

Claudia tapped her foot against her stool. 'Get on with it.'

'If you'll—'

'Hang on.' Claudia leapt up. 'Just going to the Ladies.'

She skipped off towards to the toilets, smirking. She was dying to know what the big secret was, but it was fun playing a little cat and mouse with Nick.

Also, did she imagine it or did she go into flight mode, just a little, sensing this was moving into dangerous territory? Just occasionally, flirting with Nick felt like very thin ice.

She slunk back to their table deliberately slowly. He laughed when he saw her. 'Well played, my dear.'

'Seriously now, spit it out, what's the big deal about tomorrow?'

He gazed at her for a moment. 'I need to ask you if you'll come with me to the work Christmas party tomorrow night.'

Claudia looked away. 'With the Royal Ballet? No, I don't really want to ...'

Nick caught her eye again. 'Come on, for me? I really need you there.'

'You don't need me; those guys are your family.'

'What do you think *you* are? Please?'

'No.'

'*Please?*'

'No, Nick. Thank you for the offer, but ...' She hated sounding petty, but she felt inadequate when she was around the whole company of the Royal Ballet. It was a big fat reminder of the life she had missed out on. 'I don't want to, I feel weird at those things, you know that.'

'Claudia, I think it would be good for you.'

'Why? How could it possibly be good for me?'

'I think you need a little reminding of what life pre-Seth was like.'

She squirmed.

'There's a really good reason that I want you there.'

'What is this reason?'

'I can't tell you yet.'

'Nick!'

55

'Nope,' he said, looking away and glugging the last of his coffee. 'My lips are sealed.'

'Well I'm not coming then.'

'You mean you'd decided you would come?'

'Not if you don't tell me what's going on.'

He sighed. 'You are such a Nosy Nora. I'm not going to ruin the surprise now, because it's something that I want to reveal while you're in the middle of the magic tomorrow. When you're all happy and hopped up on mulled wine.'

'Why would that make any difference?'

He shrugged. 'You might want to thank me, and it might be a much better thank you if you're a bit sloshed.'

She stirred the last dregs of cream in her mug, replaying their conversation. She wanted adventure, didn't she? She wanted to be out of this rut, didn't she? *Then grow a pair*, she told herself. Who knows what could happen?

'Come on, Claudia, DO IT LIKE YOU WANT TO DO ME!'

'Fine, fine, I'll come to the stupid party,' she laughed, shushing him. '*You* should definitely be Scrooge's nephew.'

Nick grinned his huge, contagious grin. 'Brilliant, I can't wait! Now, like I said, I need you there for a very specific, very special reason but I'm not going to tell you what it is so don't hound me for the next twenty-four hours with questions. That's very off-putting for a date. As is non-stop crying. Can you pull yourself together by tomorrow?'

Claudia lapsed into thought and Nick leaned closer.

'I'll make sure it's the night of your year ...'

Her heartbeat quickened. 'That wouldn't be hard.'

'Best night of your life?'

She looked into his eyes. He wouldn't do anything to hurt her. She trusted Nick. 'Sold.'

He leapt up happily and went to buy them another round of drinks. 'Just don't wear those customised undies Penny told me about,' he called back across the café.

Claudia watched him at the counter; at ease, confident, making the baristas go weak at the knees. She'd seen it happen a thousand times: women (and men) entranced by his good looks, and then beside themselves when he showed his true colours of a genuinely lovely goofball. Everyone wanted to be Nick's best friend. She was very lucky to have him as hers.

He glanced back and threw Claudia a whopping, dazzling grin. She felt half the café swoon.

What was she getting herself into?

A Christmas party with the people who made her feel like the world's biggest failure.

A date with Nick. *Nick*. Was it a date? It kind of sounded like one, and these butterflies that had awoken in her stomach were flapping about like they were prepping for one. Hmm. Where had they come from?

And why the secrecy?

Anticipation glittered through her veins.

Date Three

The Royal Ballet's Christmas party, Covent Garden

I'm going to be a ballerina. I'm going to be a bloody ballerina again, for the Royal Ballet.

Be quiet, brain. Claudia moved with the tide of commuters onto the Piccadilly line. Shimmying into a spare gap between an armpit and a suitcase, she raised her hand to the pole, extending her arm gracefully and watching her fingers glide around the metal. Wow. She wondered if anyone else had noticed how lovely and graceful she was. *That's right, I am a ballerina*, she told them silently.

Nick's big secret had churned in her mind all night, which gave welcome relief to the broken heart that had been keeping her awake with its wails.

What's the secret?

Why does it have to be revealed there, among the ballet company?

Why would it be the best night of my life?

Would it change my life?

The idea hit her just before dawn, and over a bowl of

Penny's cornflakes she'd tried to convince herself not to be so silly.

There was *no way* the big surprise was that they wanted her to join the Royal Ballet as a dancer. That was ridiculous.

But she *had* been a really good ballerina, and Nick and Penny had been with the company for a long time. They would have rooted for her to get the job ...

Maybe they needed someone else for the tour – an understudy. Maybe someone was injured and she was to step in and be part of the ensemble.

But they wouldn't pick her; she hadn't done ballet properly for yeeeears.

But it *was* something life-changing, ballet-related and that Nick would think deserved a whopping thank you. Maybe they did want to give her a chance. Bloody hell, they really might be asking her to join the Royal Ballet.

Shush this nonsense.

Silly or not, potentially cracking the secret put a spring in her step, and since this might be her last day before handing in her notice she thought she should face work.

Claudia had just finished fitting a happy hip-hop dancer with split-soled shoes when her phone jingled.

'Is that him again?' grinned her manager, Laura. Nick had been texting her all morning, making arrangements for that night and teasing her with hints of what was to come.

'Well it's not Seth, *again*.'

It had been two days, eleven hours and sixteen minutes since she'd last spoken to Seth. Since he'd told her to 'enjoy the Christmas festivities'. It was the longest they'd gone without communicating since they first got together. At least Nick, work and nervous excitement about tonight were filling the little lost spaces in her thoughts that searched for interaction with her boyfriend.

Claudia had told Laura and Beth, the other sales assistant, about the break-up as soon as she'd arrived at work, getting it over with. Laura and Beth had made the usual sympathetic noises and had brought her a lot of tea, and after the third text from Nick resulting in the third worried glance between the two of them, she came clean and also confessed about her non-date date this evening.

But not the part about the secret. That was hers.

'I *love* Nick,' Beth swooned like some kind of Jane Austen character. 'You two should get married and have beautiful brunette babies and then give me some pictures of Nick with his top off.'

'That's never going to happen. The marriage and babies thing. The photos I could probably arrange, for the price of a few Wispas.'

'It could happen,' Laura smiled.

'It's really not a date, it's … a comfort blanket.' A really comforting comfort blanket, which made her feel wanted and warm and a little less like a discarded old T-shirt.

'Come on,' begged Beth, 'feed my fantasy. Nick is yummy – surely you've thought about him in a not-very-wholesome way.'

'Beth, I've just come out of a long relationship.'

'That does not answer my question.'

'I didn't think about anyone else while I was with Seth; no one else mattered.' What a waste of feelings. 'Nick's always just been there as my best friend in the world. We're really close, but since being with Seth it's never been anything more than that.' Not including the tiny sparks between them yesterday. Maybe she imagined that. Yes, she probably imagined it.

'Wait,' said Laura. '*Since* being with Seth?'

'That's not what I meant.'

'Are you saying nothing has *ever* happened between the two of you?' Beth probed, her eyes sparkling with victory.

'Well …' Claudia hesitated and blushed, to Beth's squeals. 'Okay, okay. We first became friends back in school – with Penny as well – and Nick and I were a little flirty but nothing happened. Then, at the sixth form leavers' ball, I was feeling a bit of a loser: they were going off to their fancy dance and theatre production colleges and I was scared they'd forget me.

'They were playing that Whitney song, "My Love is Your Love", and I'd had a Malibu and Coke too many,

64

and decided to make my move on Nick. I did the whole making eye contact, softening my lips, saying his name quietly – all the things *Sugar* magazine had told me to do – and at the last second he realised what was going on and jumped back.'

'Oh . . . ' Beth whimpered.

'He made a run for it, and we never spoke about it again, bar me talking very loudly the next day about being "sooooo drunk" and "not remembering a thing".'

'So, in a way, you've *always* had a thing for Nick?' Beth asked.

'No, I really haven't,' Claudia answered honestly. That was so long ago, a completely different time. And it had only been a silly teenage thing anyway. It had been nothing like what she'd shared with Seth, which was real, grown-up and out of her hands now. 'It's way, way, *way* past all of that now. Seriously. Laura – you're married, you don't still harbour feelings for your teenage crush, do you?'

'Totally!' she exclaimed. 'The one that got away. You know what I would do on a Friday night with my teenage crush? Sip Hooch in the park as the sun went down, suck love bites out of each other that would put Robert Pattinson to shame, and he'd play the profound songs he'd written about me on his guitar. You know what I did last Friday night? Plucked my husband's nose hair while our three-year-old kicked me in the shins for being too fat.'

65

'Well, it's not like that with us. We're absolutely, one hundred per cent just friends now.'

Beth surrendered. 'Well I hope you have an absolute ball with him tonight, you deserve it.'

Tonight! Her eyes danced around the shop, taking in the pointe shoes, the leg-warmers, the leotards. *Tomorrow I might be handing in my notice. Tomorrow I might be needing these things for* me *again*. Her heart pirouetted, a feeling she could only have imagined two days ago. Everything could change tonight: her job, her dreams, her life. Everything could be better.

'All right, ladies?' yelled the DHL man, sauntering into the shop later that morning. 'I need a "Claudia" to sign for this one, please.' He dumped a large rectangular sparkly silver box on the counter, the kind you buy flat-packed in Clinton Cards.

Claudia signed the electronic doodah and eyed the box. What could possibly be in there? An early Christmas gift? Some elaborately wrapped samples from one of their ranges? A 'sorry' present from Seth? Laura and Beth were bubbling over with anticipation.

Claudia lifted the lid.

What the . . . ?

Inside lay a brown-paper Primark bag, a silver card balanced on top.

'What is it? What does the card say?' Beth asked, her

neck stretching like a giraffe's around the lid of the box.

Claudia was grinning. 'It's from Nick. It says, *I'm not made of money, you gold digger.*'

She drew out a black sequined micro-minidress with spaghetti straps. It was so not her, and Nick knew that very well. He probably didn't expect her to wear it, but he was reminding her to come out of her comfort zone. And that this *was* a date.

'Erm, that's . . . nice?' said Laura.

'No it's not, and he knows it's not. It's just a joke.'

'What *are* you going to wear tonight?' Beth asked.

Claudia hadn't bought a fancy new dress in a long time, and what could she wear that didn't make her think of 'that time when she and Seth', or even 'that time I bought that dress hoping'? She couldn't wear some bobbly old out-of-fashion dress in front of all the popular girls. 'I hadn't thought about that,' she panicked. 'I don't want to wear one of my old dresses. I don't have time to go shopping.' The three of them turned to the sequined dress. No, she couldn't . . .

'You could try it on?' Beth suggested.

So Claudia found herself in the shop's fitting room, standing in front of the mirror looking like a Vegas cocktail waitress. The dress was loose around the top, condom-tight at the bottom and barely skimmed her bum cheeks. It was very inappropriate for this cold weather.

And on that old-woman thought it was time to face her audience. She slunk out into the shop, thankful there were no customers.

'Hope you've got time for a bikini wax!' Beth yelped, and then threw her hand over her mouth. 'Wait, I didn't mean – I can't see – it's just quite short.'

Claudia laughed. 'It's true. Can you imagine me walking into the party in this?' She jutted out her pelvis and strutted across the floor hips first. '*Hello darlings, I am Nick's date, and this is my frouhaha.*' She took an imaginary cocktail from a tray. '*Thank you. And I'll just take one for her downstairs as well!* I can't wear this; the top of my inner thighs won't let me.'

The three girls stood with hands on hips.

'You really don't like it?' Laura asked.

'It really doesn't like me,' Claudia answered.

Taking a pair of scissors, Laura pushed Claudia back into the changing room and, with Claudia still in the dress, started chopping, snipping a good five inches off the bottom. It now fell to just below her stomach. Claudia nodded. 'Well this is much better. Thank you, Laura.'

'Wait there.' Laura left the changing room for a moment. She returned with a gorgeous black wrap-around skirt in floaty chiffon with a cascade hemline, which she tied around Claudia's waist, tucking the half-dress inside then tugging it out just enough that it fell softly over her chest. Then, using a thick silver ribbon, she cinched in Claudia's waist.

Claudia gazed at her reflection. She looked lovely; elegant and womanly. She dared a smile at herself.

'The finishing touch,' Laura said, plucking some ballroom sandals from the window and passing them to Claudia.

'I can't afford those; I have some shoes I could wear at home.'

'No, they won't be the same, you have to wear these. Consider them your Christmas bonus.'

Claudia took the shoes, along with the lovely gesture. She felt herself well up.

'Stop that. Try them on.'

Claudia slipped her feet into the champagne-coloured heels. Ohhh, they were the most comfortable things since furry slippers. The sheen of the satin complemented her skin while the criss-cross straps were an eye-catching detail. The gem on the buckle of the ankle strap sparkled and winked when she flexed her foot, like a big star in a night sky.

I feel ready for a date. The realisation hit her. She knew it was all just fancy packaging, but it made her feel good. Confident. And not because it might make a boy like her, but because it was new, different, fresh. Out with the old.

Claudia stepped from the changing room to give Beth a twirl, just as the shop door opened and Penny stuck her head in, bundled up in earmuffs and woollen accessories.

'Ready?' she asked. She gave Claudia's outfit the once-over. 'Whoa – way overdressed for lunch at Pizza Express.'

Claudia quickly changed and carefully folded her outfit into the silver box. That Nick, he was a handful, but he was very good at taking her mind off things.

Okay, Claudia thought. *Time to get into the Christmas spirit of things. Let's call it a date.*

Date three of December. The butterflies awoke.

'Before I forget, Laura brought in the leaflets I asked for.' Claudia plonked a stack of pastel-coloured NHS leaflets on the table, which detailed the different options when it came to having a baby.

'Yay, thanks, Claud!' Penny grabbed them and started leafing through.

'I know you can find all this stuff on the internet, but doesn't it seem more fun and real to actually *have* these?' Claudia picked one of them up and studied the front. 'Look at this one, with its eighties-style drawing of a lady and a test tube.'

'I like that this one has huge red letters on the front – WE DO NOT PAY SPERM DONORS. I'm excited though, big decisions to come . . .'

'The biggest. Let me know if you want me to crack out the Magic 8 ball.'

'That would be perfect. So how have you been

today?' Penny asked, reaching for another slice of their shared Sloppy Giuseppe pizza.

Claudia chewed and thought. 'I've been okay. I thought going to work would ruin me, but keeping busy might actually be helping.'

'That's brilliant! No crying?'

'No crying, just a minor wobble. But I've had other things to cheer me up.'

'Ah yes, you're Nick's big date tonight. He's very excited. He thinks he's in some golden-era movie and is obsessed with giving you a jaw-dropping evening.'

'He is being such a sweetie pie. He sent a dress to the shop this morning.'

'Awww.' Penny melted like mozzarella. 'He is such a good guy. I'm seeing our little Nick in a whole new light.'

'He is. And he's totally focusing on right now rather than on what's happened over the past couple of days. It's a refreshing break from my own thoughts.' Claudia peered at Penny. 'Do you know what the secret is tonight? Has he told you?'

'Not a peep. All I know is he keeps having hushed conversations with the director.'

The director of the Royal Ballet knows about me!

'I have something to ask you,' Penny said. 'I know you've just finished with Seth, but I was wondering ... how would you feel about going on a blind date?'

'No way.'

'At least think about it. He's a nice guy – the brother of one of the other dancers. He's *très* rich—'

'I don't care how rich he is, I am so not ready to go on a blind date. To be honest, I don't think I ever want to go on a blind date.'

'I think it'll be good for you,' Penny said with authority, despite the cheese dangling down her chin.

'Everyone thinks they know what will be good for me. I absolutely do not want to rush into a new relationship.'

'Who said anything about a relationship?' Penny chuckled.

'I don't need a new man to make me happy. I don't need a man to make me happy *full stop*. I am Rihanna.'

'Of course you don't need to be with someone to be happy. But what I'm suggesting is that you go on a date or two and let yourself feel better about *you*. You've been with Seth for so long. Even if nothing happens with these guys it'll do you good to know that not everyone is like him. And maybe it'll boost your confidence a bit.'

'I don't want to.' Claudia was a grown woman and wasn't going to be pushed into something she didn't want to do. Did Penny assume that because she was damaged right now she couldn't think for herself?

'You're going on a date *tonight*. Why are you so against another one?'

'Because tonight is just a bit of fun with someone I know well. It doesn't have … implications.'

'But it's still going to be date-y. Come on, Claud, it might shave a few days off wallowing in misery.'

Claudia sighed. She didn't have to agree to this. *I can do whatever I want.*

'And if nothing else, it'll help keep you busy, like you just said.'

Her flash of annoyance was subsiding. Maybe she should stop telling herself she didn't want to do things just because she felt she shouldn't. She doubted Seth was in mourning, wherever he was.

She and Seth had broken up because they hadn't said 'yes' to each other enough. If she hadn't said 'yes' to Nick she wouldn't be going to the party tonight, and (maybe) becoming a ballerina once more.

Saying yes was a good thing. Sometimes. *Let's just see if this is one of those times.*

'Yes.'

'Yes?'

'Yes.'

'YES!' Penny wiped her mouth with her napkin. 'That's brill, because I said you'd meet him at Winter Wonderland in Hyde Park at eleven tomorrow morning.'

'What if I'd said no?' Claudia demanded.

'Then I would have called it off.' Penny shrugged. 'You can do whatever you want.'

Nick knocked on Penny's door at bang on six o'clock. Claudia adjusted her silver-ribbon belt and plumped up her high ponytail one last time. *Enjoy date three*, she told herself.

She opened the door to find Nick smiling, handsome in his charcoal suit. 'I can't believe you wore it!' he whooped, taking in her outfit. 'You look stunning.'

Claudia felt herself blush. 'Stunning' was a little overboard. 'I wore *some* of it. Thanks for sending this over, you're very sweet.'

'No problem.' Nick held out his arm and she stepped through the door, locking Penny's flat after her. 'Hope you didn't think it was too much.'

'Not at all, but Laura and Beth are ready to kidnap you and keep you for ever.' She peeked at Nick. 'I had a lot of explaining to do about this not being a date, you know.'

Nick caught her eye and chuckled. Claudia grinned and looked away.

They sat together on the train, with Claudia feeling strangely shy. Her tummy was fluttering as she stared at the Tube map, counting down the stops. She could sense Nick peeping at her from time to time.

Her heart thudded along with the chug-chug-chug of the underground, and she felt her palms sweating. What was she doing? She didn't belong there tonight, with those people. She shouldn't be here with Nick.

What was it about tonight that made her feel like she was walking a tightrope?

Nick took her hand in his. It felt warm and big, and it gripped hers securely. He pulled it over so both their hands rested on his thigh. Claudia stared at it, steadying her breathing.

'I'm going to keep holding this until it stops shaking,' he told her, his eyes fixed on the Tube map.

You're not helping.

They emerged from the crammed Tube station into the bustle of Covent Garden. Christmas music blasted from the shops, all with their doors flung wide open and heaters blowing warmth into the faces of late-night shoppers.

People were everywhere. Some were happily weighed down with a pick and mix of the stores' festive shopping bags, in gold, red and silver. Some were dressed to the nines ready for a night out in London town. Many were standing around the entrance to the station, their faces glowing, as they watched and waited for their friends, families and first dates.

Nick held her hand as they weaved through the crowd. She found herself humming along to the Christmas classics.

'Relaxing a little?' Nick asked.

'A little,' she admitted. You can't stay too jittery when you're washed with songs that remind you of dozing on the sofa with a Chocolate Orange and watching *Home Alone*.

'We don't have to go to the party until you're ready. Shall we just walk around for a while?'

'Will you tell me the secret before we go in?'

'Nope.' Nick shook his head. 'It has to be there. But it can wait. Can I buy you a mulled wine?'

He led her to a wooden hut with fairy lights on the roof and spiced steam rising from enormous steel urns within. Nick leant over a fat garland of green ferns and silver pine cones that was strung across the counter. He ordered two mulled wines. As the woman poured out the thick ruby drink Claudia found herself studying Nick's profile.

What a familiar face. She knew it like the back of her hand, and yet he looked somehow different tonight.

Nervous? Maybe.

Handsome? Maybe.

He was trying so hard to make sure she was happy. Why was her stomach butterflying more than it ever had around him?

He turned back to her with the drinks. 'Enjoy!' He raised his Styrofoam cup to her.

They both took a sip and their eyes met. Claudia quickly shut hers and focused on the heady sensation of the hot wine hitting her tongue. The tang of orange and the mellowness of cinnamon and nutmeg smashed together, and Claudia let loose a blissful 'Mmmm.'

Nick took her hand again and they walked, unhurried, across the cobblestones and into the market. They passed through an archway and found themselves standing under a hundred glossy red baubles the size of smart cars. They hung from the glass roof at different lengths, while two enormous silver glitter balls twinkled in the centre.

Claudia took out her phone, and Nick seized it and motioned for her to step ahead of him, happiness bouncing around his face. 'Stand there, I need a picture of these.'

She grinned at his excitement and dutifully posed for his picture. He angled the camera to capture her and the baubles and then, lowering the phone, asked quietly, 'Can I take one of just you?'

'Sure,' she said, trying to sound natural. This was only Nick. They had a thousand photos of one another. Claudia unbuttoned the front of her coat to show off her outfit in the photo.

'Thanks. It's just that you look really lovely.' He blushed a little and concentrated on the phone. 'And, you know, I'm pretty chuffed with my amazing fashion sense.'

Claudia laughed and tugged on the neckline of the sequined dress. 'You did well,' she concurred. She moved back beside him and instinctively their hands slotted together. She struggled for neutral conversation. 'I had a brilliant time with Jennifer last week.'

'So I heard. Thanks so much for taking her, she's wanted to go for so long.'

'My pleasure, I love hanging out with her.'

Nick glowed with pride. Jennifer was his little sister, who suffered from cerebral palsy. Claudia had taken her to the Making of Harry Potter studio tour. Any excuse for Claudia and Jennifer to hang out and they both jumped at the chance.

Claudia and Nick passed boutique windows dressed in tinsel and spray-on snow, and a Salvation Army brass band wrapped in thick wool coats and knitted hats, gently playing 'God Rest Ye Merry Gentlemen'.

Oh, tidings of comfort and joy . . .

She was ready.

Stepping into the penthouse bar the Royal Ballet had hired for the night, Claudia and Nick were hit with a wall of merriment. A live Rat Pack band belted out the best Christmas songs, from a jazzed-up version of 'White Christmas' to 'Fairytale of New York' with a swing twist. All around them was dancing, cheering, laughing, singing and drinking.

Potted mini Christmas trees lined the walls and reams of multicoloured fairy lights glittered across the low ceiling, creating the atmosphere of a grown-up Santa's grotto.

A girl Claudia vaguely recognised was tottering past with two glasses when she saw Claudia and stopped. 'HI!' she shouted over the band. 'Have a snowball, they're sooo good!' She thrust a goblet into Claudia's hand. Giving Nick a friendly wave, she slunk off into the crowd.

The atmosphere was intoxicating. A grin spread across Claudia's face and she turned to beam at Nick. He grinned back, baring all his teeth, delighted at her reaction.

Claudia took a sip of her snowball, the thick vanilla flavour with the brandy hit oozing down her throat. She watched the joyful crowd for a moment. *Somewhere in there is my big secret.*

Nick led her into the throng.

People she'd vaguely met before greeted her like they were old friends, and those she hadn't welcomed her with hugs and clinks of glasses. She felt at ease. Instantly comfortable. *Happy*.

Relief, surprise – and the snowball – swam through Claudia's veins. Why had she been scared of these people? Why had she never given them a chance? They weren't scorning her, patronising her, looking down on her. They were lovely! And they treated her like one of their own.

Like one of their own. She liked that feeling, a lot. If this was her future she could get away from everything. It wouldn't matter that she'd have to move house and find new love, because she'd be starting afresh. She'd finally be living the life she'd always wanted.

And maybe, just maybe, it would mean that the break-up with Seth was what she'd needed.

That was a scary thought. A thought that needed another snowball.

Nick leant close to her ear. 'Can I get you another drink, Claud?'

She turned her face to him and smiled. His mouth wasn't far from hers. In her ecstatic state she felt playful, and looked at his lips with an urge to press her own against them.

'Can you get me the answer to the secret?'

He laughed, making sure not to move his head too far from hers. 'Not yet.'

'Then another snowball please.'

He gave her a thoughtful look, and edged off to the bar.

Penny appeared, shoving her way through two very sloshed dancers having a spinning contest on the dance floor. She had rosy cheeks and gold tinsel wrapped around her neck. 'I'm tipsy!' she hiccupped.

'I'll be there with you soon: wait for me,' Claudia laughed.

Penny slung a drunk-heavy arm over Claudia's shoulder and turned her to face the bar, her hips boogying to 'Rockin' Around the Christmas Tree' all the while. 'How handsome does Nick look?' she shouted at Claudia, waving her cocktail in his direction.

'Very.'

'Has he told you the biiiiiiiig secret yet?'

'No – he says I have to wait.'

'That man is a tease.'

By the time Nick returned with their drinks Penny had danced off into the distance. Passing her another frothy snowball, he took her free hand and pulled her on to the dance floor.

She looked at his neck. What a delicious neck. She wanted to kiss it a lot. Like, *a lot*. A teenage-vampire lot.

The alcohol and the atmosphere were spinning her hormones out of control. She had to calm down before she did something stupid.

Composing herself, she asked, 'Can you tell me the secret now?'

He straightened up, his laugh tinkling like reindeer bells along with the band. 'No, first I need to show you a merry Christmas.'

He lifted her arm and had her spin underneath. And even though she remembered that her heart was broken, even though she was surrounded by all these professional dancers, at this moment she felt more happy and alive than she had in a long time.

An hour later, Nick and Claudia left the dance floor, sweaty, happy and more than a little splashed with drinks. Claudia flopped down on a wide leather chair; Nick stayed standing.

'I'm ready.'

'You are?' she asked, her heart doing a backflip. *Ready for me?*

'Yep. Wait right there, I'm going to get your surprise.' He raced off around the edge of the room. The surprise. Of course. What else did she think he meant? Her mind was being very silly this evening.

The secret. This was it. Part of her wanted to run. Another part of her wanted to get it over with. She looked around, searching for any hint that would confirm her theory about what the secret was. Make or break time. *I'm going to be a ballerina again.*

Nick was returning, along with a man in a nice three-piece suit. He had grey hair and a friendly face, with lots of crinkles around the eyes – a man who every day saw pleasure in what he was surrounded by.

They drew closer. Excitement bubbled in Claudia like champagne fizz, and she felt the cork was about to pop. She couldn't cope.

BUGGER OFF!

No, don't, come and tell me my fate.

BUGGER OFF!

LET'S GET THIS OVER WITH.

Nick held his arms out, motioning at Claudia. 'This is she. Greg, meet Claudia. She's a star. Claudia, this is Greg, the director of the Royal Ballet.'

Why the hell wasn't she saying anything? *SAY SOME-THING.*

Oh no, what was her body doing . . .

She curtsied. What a loser. Greg let out a light laugh. 'Brilliant to meet you.' He shook her hand warmly.

'Nick's told me *all* about you,' Greg said, giving Nick a pointed look, who studied his beer bottle intently. 'I hear you used to do ballet.'

Claudia nodded. This was it. She really should say something. 'Yes, a *long* time ago . . . ' *SELL YOURSELF*. 'But it feels like yesterday, and sometimes I still do, and I work at Edurné's, just around the corner, and I still feel so involved in the world of ballet and dance.' Stop it, this wasn't an interview. Or was it?

'So you're pretty familiar with the people, you get on with them?'

I do now. 'Yes, absolutely, loads of them shop at Edurné's. They're like my family,' she exaggerated.

'Do you think they'd tell you things, open up to you?'

Claudia touched her hand on her heart. They were *such* a close-knit bunch. 'I think they would.'

'You're okay with late nights, early mornings?'

'Love them both! Who wouldn't want to dance the night away every night?'

'And I'm sure you've learnt a lot about the behind-the-scenes work from Nick.'

'Oh yes, I think it's really important to know exactly what goes into a production, even if you're spending most of your time on the stage.'

'And you like writing, taking photos?'

'Erm, yes, they're occasional hobbies of mine. Do you?' she asked politely.

Greg shook his head. 'Not really, but you seem lovely.

Nick, you're bouncing around like a kangaroo. Do you want to ask her?'

'Claud.' Nick stepped in front of her. 'I've been talking with Greg because there's a lot coming up for the ballet in the next year. The tour, the local performances, the new show.' Claudia's heart raced like a runaway train. 'And Greg mentioned that he needed an extra someone.'

GET ON WITH IT! Claudia's mind screamed at Nick, a blasé, interested smile fixed on her face. She could kill him and his big intros sometimes. *Make me a ballerina,* she willed with all her heart.

'Greg wants someone to put together a book – a year behind the scenes at the Royal Ballet. Like a coffee-table book with some history, lots of photos, how a production is put together, that kind of thing. To be published by a real publisher.'

What?

Nick continued, 'And I told him how much you're still involved in the business and you still love ballet.'

WHAT?

'So we wondered if you'd do this book? Tell the story from backstage?'

Claudia froze, her face mirroring the look of glee on Nick's, masking the huge operation going on beneath the surface of composing her features so they didn't fall into a look of utter disappointment.

They didn't want her to be a ballerina.

Of course they didn't want her to be a ballerina.

They wanted her to be a groupie. To write about them, photograph them, from backstage. To be the outsider she knew she was, but she'd fooled herself into thinking she wasn't.

'Surprise!' beamed Nick.

'Thank you very much,' she said, her voice stilted like a Stepford Wife's.

'What do you think?' Nick asked, like a child giving a Christmas present. He was so excited about this, his big secret. He'd worked hard to open up this opportunity for her.

She was the fool with the idiotic dreams and stupid, unrealistic fantasies.

A tidal wave of disappointment nearly lifted her off her feet. She took a big gulp of her snowball, using the glass to hide her wobbling chin. *Don't be such a massive cry-baby*, she desperately willed herself. *They didn't know what you'd been hoping for*.

None of this was Nick's fault. None of it was anyone's fault but her own.

'Well, if you're sure you don't want me to play the Sugar Plum Fairy ... ' She erupted into shrill laughter. She wanted them to think she was joking, but also say 'My, we hadn't thought of that, what a fantastic idea!' But of course they didn't; they just smiled and waited for her answer.

'Claudia, what do you think?' asked Nick again.

'I think it sounds like a lovely opportunity ... Greg, may I think about it?'

Greg smiled, nodded and patted her warmly on the shoulder before heading off into the crowd.

Nick turned to her like an excited puppy. 'Do you want to do it?'

'That's a bit forward!' Claudia forced another laugh, trying to turn an awkward moment into some *Carry On* humour.

Though she was ruined inside, she couldn't spoil his night. So she did the sensible thing and grabbed another two cocktails from a passing tray. She handed one to Nick and glued on a big grin.

'I'm going to have a really good think about it. It sounds really good; thanks for thinking of me, Nick.' She clunked her glass against his.

'But do you think you might? You could put together a whole book, just you, and you get to work with me and Penny.'

'Yes, lovely, it's a brilliant opportunity. Lovely, yes ...'

'Do you mind that I waited until now to ask you? I just really wanted you and Greg to meet first, and for you to spend a bit of time around the company, who are fun and they really like you – I know you've found it a bit weird before.'

'Yep, you planned it all very well.'

'Did you guess what it was? Did you have any idea?'

'I had absolutely no idea. This is definitely a big surprise.'

'A good surprise?'

She pressed her lips together and nodded, willing him to stop talking for two minutes.

Penny materialised, tumbling into the two of them. 'HAS HE TOLD YOU THE SECRET?' she bellowed. 'IS HE REALLY A WOMAN?'

'It's better than that,' Nick said. 'Tell her, Claud.'

'Nick and Greg have asked me to put together a book. About the Royal Ballet. From backstage.' Did she sound excited? Grateful? Or like a petulant misery guts?

'A book? Pleeeeease put me on every page.'

'She's going to dedicate it to me, though,' Nick laughed. '*To Nick – my hot date turned hot recruitment consultant.*'

Claudia chuckled along with them, swigged down the rest of the cocktail and swayed. How many had she had? Who cares? She had to get out of this chaotic head of hers.

Nick wrapped an arm around her and squashed her into him. 'Right, now that's out the way, let's celebrate properly. MERRY CHRISTMAS!' he boomed across the room.

'MERRY CHRISTMAS!' she boomed back, determined not to let another thing bring her down, and a delighted Nick kissed her on the top of the head and led her back to the dance floor.

Claudia toppled off the low table, landing in a giggling heap in Nick's arms. Her dance-off rival, Penny, raised her arms above her head and whooped.

The party was in full swing, and Claudia had eagerly suppressed the anticlimax of the big reveal. So things would stay as they were. She'd carry on working in the shop. Same old. She'd experienced twenty-four hours of a reignited dream, but now it was back to reality. And right now, her reality was Christmas party, cocktails and new people.

She loved these people. She would friend them all on Facebook.

Nick was tipsy himself, a dopey smile plastered on his face. 'I like that you're happy,' he shouted in her ear.

'What?' Claudia leaned closer.

'I LIKE THAT YOU'RE HAPPY.'

'How could I not be happy? I'm a freeeeeeeee woman!' Claudia shimmied to the festive music, loose in Nick's arms.

She felt blissfully comfortable with Nick. Had she ever felt this comfortable with Seth? Had he *ever* encouraged her to dance with him? No. Seth Shmeth.

'Seth Shmeth,' she said to Nick.

'What?' he ducked his head down to her level. Laughing, Claudia dragged him by the hand to the balcony.

Claudia sighed a sigh and tucked herself into Nick's

arms against the cold breeze, her cheek resting on his chest. 'You smell nice,' she slurred.

Nick laughed softly. Claudia looked up. 'Mistletoe!' she cried, spying a plump bunch hanging over the doorway. Nick followed her gaze. A little voice interrupted her drunken haze. *Don't say it.*

'Let's snog – it is Christmas,' she burbled.

What did I just tell you?

Nick chuckled. 'We can't do that, I'd be taking advantage, you drunken old hag.'

Claudia moved closer, matching his breathing. It was deeper than hers. She watched his mouth.

They were so close she could smell the mulled wine on his lips. His breath fluttered against her eyelashes.

She wanted to do this. She knew it was a silly, friendship-rocking thing to do, but she wanted it. She wanted him. And she could feel it; he wanted her too. Something had shifted between them and there was no going back.

She dragged her gaze away from his lips, up his face and into his eyes. He was looking at her; scared, happy, confused.

Claudia tilted her chin and brought her lips to within an inch of his.

A thought flitted by: *I don't know who you are to me any more.*

Claudia moved forward. *I want this.*

Nick moved back.

He dropped his arms. She rocked on her heels. *No ...*

'Claudia,' Nick whispered.

She stepped back, widening the space between them. What had she done? What had *he* done?

'Claudia,' he said, stepping forward.

She moved further along the balcony. Nick looked injured. Well so he should.

'You did it again?' she accused, watching pain slice through his features. They were both transported back to that teenage night as they stood at opposite ends of the balcony.

'You're drunk, it shouldn't be like this.' Nick looked so sad.

Claudia couldn't comfort him. She was humiliated. She really *wasn't* sexy and exciting. She was an idiot. All night, she'd been an idiot. 'I'm going to leave. I'm going home,' she choked, pushing past him and heading for the door. He tried to hold her hand but she ripped it away as if it burned.

'Please don't go,' he begged. She turned away from him. 'I'll take you home.'

She shook her head, hiding her shamed face. 'Please, just leave me on my own.'

She could sense him hesitating behind her. His voice cracked. 'I'll get Penny to take you home.'

Claudia met his eye. 'If you have any shred of care, don't tell her what happened.'

He looked stung. What could they say to each other? Claudia turned from him again, her face in her hands.

A minute later she heard him walk through the door, away from her.

Date Four

Winter Wonderland, Hyde Park

Claudia miserably crunched her way through the burnt bacon Penny had served up for breakfast.

Rejection, rejection, rejection. Kirstie and Phil should make a new show. It could star Claudia putting herself in a series of situations with men, each more outstandingly embarrassing than the last, and at the end she'd have to decide who she wanted to be dumped by first.

She felt like a prize idiot.

'I feel like a prize idiot,' she told Penny.

Penny snapped a piece of bacon in half. 'Why? So you got a bit pissed at a Christmas party. Join the club.'

Penny and Claudia had been nursing their immense hangovers with salty food for half an hour now, but it was barely helping either of them.

Claudia carefully made her way over to the sink, filling two glasses with water and plopping Berocca tablets into each. She handed a fizzing glass of the neon-orange liquid to Penny and slumped back to her seat.

Penny turned her grey face away from the drink. 'I'm

so glad we left when we did; good call. I don't think our bodies could have taken any more snowballs.'

Claudia grunted and rested her cheek on the breakfast bar. She hadn't mentioned a word about Nick.

'Nick looked like he was having a great time,' Penny said, dipping her bacon in the drink to moisten it up.

Claudia grunted again.

'He was pretty worried about you at the end, though – face like death when he came to find me. Well, face like ours right now, to be honest. I laughed my head off for a full three minutes when I first saw him, I was like, "Maaaaan, you look so rough!" Maybe Nick was just wasted too, and the hangover kicked in early.'

Hearing his name made Claudia's insides shrink in shame. She was so humiliated. She had to change the subject.

Penny got in there first. 'Oh!' she cried, and immediately cringed at the noise of her own voice. 'So what are you going to do about the job? Are you going to come and work with me? Please say yes, please say yes.' She sounded as excited as she could muster when feeling this ill.

Dammit! Another confusing thing to block up Claudia's head. She lifted her face from the counter-top.

'I don't know; it sounds a bit shit.' She spat out the last word with more venom than she intended. It didn't sound *shit* – a little part of her acknowledged that it sounded quite good – she just *felt* shit about the whole thing. Why the hell had she talked herself into thinking she'd be asked to be a ballerina again?

'You don't want to do it? But you're so bored at the shop—'

'It's not like this would be any better. Both aren't actually doing what I want to do.'

'What *do* you want to do?'

The question hovered about in the kitchen. Claudia felt too embarrassed to say she wanted to dance again, even to Penny. When someone you love already has the job of your dreams it's pretty mortifying to admit how much you envy them. Penny's eyes were drooping anyway. Claudia knew she could move on without answering the question.

'I think I'll go home today,' she declared.

'You don't have to leave, I like having you here.'

'I like it, too. I couldn't have got through this last week without you.' She really couldn't have, and the thought of going back to her flat filled her with dread. But she had to, so moaning wasn't allowed.

'Don't say sweet things because I'll throw up on your face,' Penny mumbled with a smile.

'I need to go back, have a sort out, be a grown-up. I can't wear your underwear for ever.'

'Don't forget to be at Winter Wonderland for eleven, though.'

Claudia glanced at the clock: 9.30. She looked blankly at Penny, who prompted: 'Your blind date.'

'Oh no, I can't do it. You have to cancel.'

'Noooooooooooo.'

'Penny, look at me.' She pulled at her half-in, half-out remnant of a ponytail. She stretched open her bloodshot eyelids with her fingers.

'Shh, don't shout,' begged Penny. 'Go and have a shower. If you still feel rubbish when you come out I'll cancel for you.' She pulled down the eye mask from her forehead, and lowered her head to the counter.

Claudia emerged twenty minutes later, steam-cleaned and wrapped in a soft John Lewis towel. Her body felt a little better, but her mind was still crashed and burnt at the side of the road.

She checked her phone, which she'd left on silent. Wow. The count was up to six messages and three missed calls since last night. All from Nick. All ignored.

What was he so desperate to say? *I'm sorry, I just don't think about you like that?* She itched to read the texts but was in no rush to hear that little gem. *Go away, go away, go away.*

Maybe she could read one. Her heart thudded as she opened the first one, dated at one a.m.

Claud, I'm so sorry the evening ended like that.
Can I come and see you in the morning?

No.

She opened one from 4.17 a.m.

> Are you asleep?

She opened the latest, sent at 9.32.

> Sorry to sound like a soap opera character, but we need to talk a bit, please.

She swiftly hit 'delete' on the whole batch.

'How are you feeling?' asked Penny, coming out of her room looking even rougher than before.

'Like crap, with crap on. Can you cancel this blind date?'

Penny nodded, picking up her phone. 'You might want to put some clothes on by the way, you rudey nude. Nick's on his way over.'

Claudia froze. 'Now?'

'Yeah. Is that okay?'

'Sure ...' Claudia dived for her suitcase and pulled out some jeans and a big pink woolly jumper. This would have to do. 'You know what?' she said, injecting brightness into her voice. 'I think I will go on that date.' Penny lowered her phone. 'You're right, it'll do me good. It's getting late, though, so I'd better shoot off.'

She frantically lobbed some items into her handbag and zipped up the suitcase, pushing it against the wall. 'I'll pick this up later, or tomorrow, whatever.'

She pulled on her flat brown leather boots and ran a brush through her hair.

Taking a look in the mirror and recoiling, she quickly rubbed on some tinted moisturiser and added a sweep of mascara.

Penny handed her a slip of paper and yawned. 'Okay, cool. This is his number. His name's Eddie. He's going to meet you by the Ferris wheel.'

'Ferris wheel, got it.' Claudia gave her friend a quick one-armed hug, her heart pounding at the thought of running into Nick in the corridor. 'Thanks again for looking after me. I'll do the "Single Lades" routine with you at the wedding as a thank you.'

'Cool!'

Claudia hurried out the door. *Go, go, go!*

'Eddie's pretty easy to spot, by the way,' Penny called after her. 'He's quite short.'

The endless lush grass of Hyde Park had been sprinkled with an icing-sugar frost, which melted under Claudia's steps, leaving a trail of vibrant green footprints. The cloud was low today, a thick pale grey, and the air was heavy. It felt like snow was coming.

Claudia trudged her way across the park, head pounding, mind stuck on a loop showing re runs of last night's episode of *What Claudia Did to Cock Everything Up*. She had relived the moment so many times she was now

100

embellishing it. She leaned forward for a kiss, Nick shrieked 'URGH' in her face. She leaned forward for a kiss, Nick bolted and threw up over the balcony.

Why had he led her on? She may have been drunk but she wasn't crazy; he'd been flirting right along with her. Did he think it was just a game?

Of course he didn't, stupid, that wasn't the Nick she knew.

He'd always been flirty; maybe she just read too much into it this time and that's why Nick had backed off.

She stopped in her tracks, long lengths of the park stretching away from her in all directions. Her mind was suddenly wiped clean of everything but a single thought that had to be given life.

What was really bothering her here? Was it the embarrassment of rocking a friendship or the pain of being turned down? The little stab wound in her heart told her it was more than just a bit of drunken mortification that she'd be over in a week.

Did she *like* Nick?

No, the wound must be from Seth, and it was just aching because she had been rejected again. The fact that this had happened with Nick was just bad luck. She started walking.

She missed Seth. She missed the constancy of having him in her life. Back when things weren't so confusing.

But she didn't want to miss him any more. She had to get over it.

Going cold turkey on Seth was hard, hard work. But it was the best thing to do; it was helping. Time heals …

'Oh shut up, you miserable old loner,' she muttered to herself as she drew near the fair. She was so sick of herself this morning.

Claudia entered the Winter Wonderland section of Hyde Park, which was already alive with piped music, neon lights and crowds of merrymakers. She trudged past the fairground rides covered in thick fake snow towards the Ferris wheel. Her eyes scanned the crowd for Eddie.

She thought she spotted him. It *must* be him.

He was dressed in a woolly Jack Wills jumper and Wayfarer shades, with coiffed hair, short legs and a bored expression on his chiselled cheeks. Claudia cursed Penny and all she stood for.

It could be worse. She could be at Penny's making excruciatingly awkward small talk with Nick.

Claudia approached Eddie and caught his eye. 'Eddie?'

Eddie turned *his* to face her, and she could feel his eyes giving her the once-over behind the shades. 'Yah. Camilla, right?'

You're an idiot. 'Claudia, actually.'

'My mistake. You look like a nice girl.' He moved to the left. 'These are my parents.' He motioned to an overdressed middle-aged couple standing behind him, shrinking in fear from the dirty tourists.

Whaaaaaaat?

'Um, okay ... Hello.' She bobbed her head at them. They kind of smiled back at her.

'I'm fammed,' Eddie declared. 'Shall we hit those food stalls and have some nosh?'

Sticky baklava was the last thing Claudia's delicate stomach wanted, but as they started walking towards the stalls she became less concerned about her hangover and more about the parents who were coming along for the ride.

'Are your parents visiting for the weekend or something?' she asked Eddie, lightly.

He threw Claudia a quizzical look. 'No. We live in Richmond.'

'Together?'

'Yah. My father's a surgeon. We have just the most incredible mansh, I'd be a damned fool to move out, don't you think?'

You don't want to know what I think, Claudia thought.

'So, Claud,' Eddie said. She cringed. She didn't like him calling her that; it sounded too familiar. 'Tell me why you're single. You're a pretty thing, what's wrong with you?'

Claudia looked at him, aghast. She turned to the other side to see his parents staring at her, also waiting for an answer. 'There's nothing wrong with me!' she protested. 'I'm lovely!'

Eddie laughed, a short, sharp 'Ha!', and ran a hand

through his hair. 'Cracking answer. Tell me why your last relationship ended. You weren't a nag, were you? I bloody hate nags.'

'Bloody off-putting,' piped up Eddie's father. His mother's calm exterior cracked minutely.

'It ended because I cut his balls off with a pizza slice.'

They didn't hear her; all three of them were drifting to a sauerkraut stand and making disgusting orgasmic sounds together.

'Uhhh, Claud.' Eddie beckoned her over, his mouth full. 'Try this.'

He thrust a plastic forkful of the fermented cabbage under her nose. The vinegary sour smell caused her stomach to heave. 'No, thank you,' she squeaked.

'Dear, you must eat,' said his mother, without smiling. She had the jawline of a T-Rex.

Who was this patronising woman, telling her to eat as if she hadn't had a meal in days? As if she were *her* mother?

'I do eat! I ate about two hours ago.' *And by the way, why are you here?*

'Didn't you know there would be food stands here?' she scolded, penetrating Claudia with a sharp, black stare that made her want to run away. 'They've laid out a traditional European Christmas market and you've already eaten?'

She was being told off . . .

For the first time in a very long time Claudia had a fleeting sensation that she was glad her mum wasn't like this.

Zero tellings-off was better than this kind of interrogation, surely?

'The world is your oyster: you're more than welcome to eat anything you want.' Claudia gestured to the row of huts, her patience waning.

'What exactly did you eat two hours ago?' the mother pressed.

Claudia turned to her 'date'. 'Eddie. Fancy playing the coconut shy with me?' She marched off towards the fairground games with Eddie and his short legs struggling to keep up. She had no interest in lobbing balls at defenceless coconuts. As far as she was concerned, this date was already a ridiculous waste of time, but for as long as she could stretch it out she could keep the demons of Nick and Seth at bay.

After a couple of unenthusiastic games Claudia tried, but failed, to edge away from Eddie, who was having the time of his life winning cheap-looking reindeer toys for his mum at the ring-toss and revelling in his parents' praise at what a clever manly man he was. He jogged after her.

A nearby craft chalet had garlands of dried oranges, limes and cinnamon hanging from the ceiling. The aroma calmed Claudia, even stilling her churning insides.

'What a foul smell,' Eddie guffawed. 'Yuk, why would anyone want their house to smell like the kitchen? Do you know what my favourite smell is, Claud? Jägerbombs.'

'Not the smell of money?'

'You're a riot, you know? But actually, that's *so* true.

There's a certain ethos that goes along with having money, don't you think? Do you have money?'

'Yah, *plenty*,' Claudia answered. The hut was filled with intricate three-dimensional scenes carved from the palest wood – Santa's grotto, the Bethlehem stable, reindeer in the woods – each with a tea-light hidden within, whose heat caused the tiny figures and animals to move around the scene. They were enchanting.

Claudia stopped in front of one in the shape of a hollowed-out Christmas tree. Inside was a miniature ice-skating girl, spinning round in happy circles. Dancing for ever. *She's like me.*

She watched the figurine, her mind drifting. It wasn't just Nick who Claudia was putting off. She also had a decision she needed to make for Greg, the director of the Royal Ballet.

Writing a behind-the-scenes book wasn't what she wanted. She wanted to be a ballerina. That was her dream, the only ambition she'd ever had. But if she still wanted to be a ballerina that badly, wouldn't she have done something more towards it by now?

She watched Tiny Claudia as she spun in the tree. What a simple, joyful life. *You're jealous of a wooden toy now?*

So maybe it was too late to be a ballerina; maybe that ship had sailed. But this job offer was hardly the next best thing. Was working in a dance shop the next best thing? No, though she didn't mind it. The people were nice. But as it turned out, so were the ballet company. Claudia wondered how long she could get away with putting off the decision, and decided it certainly didn't have to be made today.

'I'd slap someone in the face if they got me one of these for Christmas,' Eddie piped up. She'd almost forgotten about him. 'Imagine hoping for Google Glass and getting one of these – ha, ha, ha.'

'These are gorgeous. Why are you such a moron?' The hangover was wearing her tolerance thin.

Eddie sidled closer. 'You're a feisty one, I like it. Yes I do.'

Time to rescue tiny Claudia and take her home. Something brand new and all hers for the flat full of shared things.

She bought the little skater and a sweet-smelling citrus garland as well, which she spitefully carried between her and Eddie as they made their way back over to the ring-toss where his parents stood, carefully not touching anything or anyone. As much as she was ready to go, and as much as her head still pounded under these oppressive clouds, she couldn't bring herself to be rude and just walk away without a goodbye. It's not like they were bad people, just a bit . . . socially inept.

'Eddie, I have to ask you something,' she said, with as much pleasantness as she could muster. 'Why did you bring your parents along on our blind date?'

Eddie shrugged nonchalantly. 'I wouldn't date a girl who

107

didn't get on with Mummy and Father. If they join us at the start it saves a lot of wasted time, don't you think?'

What a romantic. Claudia would have laughed if she didn't feel so utterly drained.

'Right,' Eddie said, looking at his watch. 'We're going for a light bite at Claridge's now.' He motioned to his parents.

'Okay.' Unexpected. She was done with this date, she didn't have the energy to draw it out any longer, but she *had* always wanted to go to Claridge's. What to do . . .

'So it's been great. *Rally, rally* great. Here's my card if you want to hang again at some point.'

Oh. Decision made then. 'Thanks.' She took the card and surreptitiously glanced around for a bin.

'You truly are quite pretty,' he schmoozed, moving closer and tucking her hair behind her ear. He leant over and she turned her face, catching the eye of his father, who gave her a curt nod of encouragement.

Eddie gave her a lingering kiss on the cheek while she steadied her breath to quell the nausea. He stood back. 'Ah. Bugger. Mummy? Have you got a tissue?'

'What?' Claudia asked, touching her face. She looked at her fingertips, which were covered in blood.

Blood. For crying out loud!

She snatched the tissue Eddie was holding out for her. 'Sorry about that, I'm rather prone to nosebleeds.'

'You had a *nosebleed*. ON MY FACE.'

'Yah, soz.'

She scrubbed her cheek and handed him the bloody tissue, then spat on his card and used that to wipe off any remaining traces of his DNA. It was time to go; she was *this close* to vomiting on him.

Claudia bade Eddie and his parents a quick and cordial farewell for ever and walked away through the Wonderland. She furiously shot a text off to Penny:

> He brought his parents and had a nosebleed on
> my face. FUTURE HUSBAND FOUND.

Her phone bleeped immediately, with another text from Nick that she didn't want to read, so she stuffed it back into her pocket.

So, date four of December had been about as successful as the other three, she thought bitterly.

Date two was nice. But she didn't want to think about that. About Nick.

Rounding the corner, she found herself in front of the Ferris wheel again. Slowly turning, lit up by calming icicle-blue bulbs, it looked gentle, like it would be peaceful to float in the sky all on your own.

A little fresh air might do her the world of good.

Claudia paid for the ride and waited in the queue for her turn to board. She stared fixedly at the criss-cross patterned ski jacked of the person in front, counting the boxes, ignoring her churning tummy.

Finally she boarded, sitting on the metal seat with an

audible 'ahhh'. Sitting. This was already much better than walking, eating, blind dates, odd parents and other people's blood.

She closed her eyes.

The wheel moved with a jolt that Claudia wasn't expecting and her seat swung gaily back and forth. Her eyes shot open and her insides danced like they were at Mardi Gras.

The big wheel was edging upwards and Claudia's feet dangled a metre or so off the ground. She clasped the sides of the seat, holding tightly and begging it to stop swinging.

She soared higher. Winter Wonderland stretched in front of her, a river of multicoloured lightbulbs and snow-covered sheds. Children were laughing and point-ing up at the Ferris wheel, gagging to get on. She was gagging to get off. Literally.

'No,' she whispered. 'This is fun, I'm having an adventure.'

Higher she went, her view of the beautiful hotch-potch rooftops of London widening. The seat was jiggling and shimmying at high speed while the wheel edged excruciatingly slowly around. 'I feel sick,' she moaned pitifully to the city.

Claudia felt the nausea rising. No. No, no, no, not here. She took a deep breath and exhaled slowly. She scrunched her eyes closed. She wasn't swinging, she definitely wasn't swinging, and she certainly wasn't sixty metres up in the air. *It'll be over soon. Breathe innnnnnn, breathe ouuuuuuut.* She just needed to last a little longer. She could puke all she wanted over the length and breadth of Hyde Park, if only she'd hold out that little bit longer.

She felt the sweats coming.

No.

A guttural cough escaped and she stayed very still. Was that it?

Her breathing was shallow, like she was afraid to make too much noise and disturb the monster that paced around her stomach. Her face felt like someone was pushing a hot, damp sponge through it from the inside, and her breathing quickened.

No, please, no.

I'm at the top, was her last thought before her body instinctively flung itself to the side of the seat.

Out it came. Out came the snowballs, the mulled wine, the torture. Raining down the full diameter of the Ferris wheel.

Claudia slumped back in her seat, clammy, spent, tears dripping from her eyes. She didn't want to see the view any more. She just wanted to go home. She leant her heavy head on the bar while the wheel slowly brought her back down to Earth.

Claudia opened her eyes and stared up at a white canvas roof. A woman's head popped into her line of vision. She had big, curly red hair and rosy cheeks. This is what Mrs Claus must have looked like in her younger days.

'Hello,' Claudia rasped.

'Ooo hello,' said the lady. 'Let's get you a glass of water.'

Claudia pushed herself up onto her elbows and had a good look around. The medical kits, wheelie beds, St John Ambulance logos and general hubbub hinted that she was in a medical tent.

'You're in the medical tent, my love,' said Mrs Claus, coming back with a plastic cup of tepid water. Claudia sat up. Yuk. She tasted like vomit.

Mrs Claus shone a torch in Claudia's eyes that made Claudia want to wail like she worked in a Dickensian workhouse. 'How are you feeling? Do you remember what happened?'

Shame seeped into Claudia's consciousness. 'I threw up on the Ferris wheel ... '

'That's right, my darling,' said Mrs Claus, strapping the cuff of a blood-pressure gauge around her arm. 'Then you had a little faint. Very delicately, mind, all curled up like a kitten.'

'Did I get anyone?'

'With the vomit? Not that I'm aware of, my darling. I didn't see anyone throwing a paddy when they called me over.' She stood. 'Now, I'm just going to pop outside to buy a few choccie biscuits from one of the stalls because we've run out, and we need to up your sugar intake a little. Will you be okay on your own for a second?'

Mrs Claus exited the tent, pinning the door flap wide open. Claudia lay back down and looked out at Winter Wonderland. In her drowsy haze she felt removed from the situation, like she was watching through an advent-calendar window. Outside her little world – of both medical tent and herself in general – people were happy and carefree. Christmas magic whirled around them, excitement building as they counted down the days.

I want to feel like that, Claudia thought with the tiniest glow of clarity. She *would* feel like that. She was going to embrace Christmas in London and all it had to offer. There were a thousand festivities taking place in the capital this month that Seth would never have enjoyed with her, but Seth was gone. And she wouldn't let it drift by for another year; she was ready to feel some Christmas magic again.

She was ready to feel at least some kind of magic again. The only person to get her out of this rut could be her, and she was determined to buck up, stop feeling sorry for herself and make her own excitement. In a way, she'd thrown up her old life. Now it was in with the new ...

Her phone rang and she reached into her pocket, still gazing at the festivities outside the tent. She answered it without looking at the screen.

'Hello?' she mumbled.

'Claudia!' Nick's voice rang with surprise and glee.

Balls.

'Mmm,' she grunted.

'Where are you?' She heard a rhythmic clack-clack-clack in the background.

Her fuzzy brain couldn't muster up the anger or bitterness she wanted to project at that point, giving way to that irrepressible feeling everyone gets when they feel poorly – a cry for comfort. 'I passed out.'

The clacking stopped. 'What? Where are you? Are you okay?'

'Yeah, I'm okay. I'm at Winter Bloody Wonderland. I puked down the Ferris wheel.' A small, breathy laugh escaped her. What a day.

'I'm coming to get you. I'll take you home.'

'No!' Claudia cried, propping herself up on her elbow. She felt wobbly.

'Claudia—'

Claudia lay back down. Maybe she would quite like someone to take her home. She still felt a little woozy. 'Can you send Penny?'

'Penny's asleep face-down on the sofa. Man, she looked rough.' The clacking started again, this time faster. 'I'm already halfway to yours with your suitcase.' Ah, the clacking; it was her suitcase being dragged over the paving slabs of West Kensington. 'Now where exactly are you?'

She'd have to feel bitter and angry another time. 'I'm in the medical tent,' she relented. 'Thank you.'

Where are those chocolate biscuits when you need them?

Twenty minutes later Claudia was sitting up on the bed, four Penguins in her stomach and a Styrofoam cup of strong tea in her hand. Mrs Claus was chattering on about the various disasters she'd encountered since being with St John Ambulance, which strangely was making Claudia feel better by the minute.

' . . . and his finger came clean off! All because of an ice-lolly stick!' Mrs Claus chuckled, munching on a Penguin of her own.

Now that the nausea had wandered off, those damned butterflies were flittering back. Claudia wasn't sure what she was going to say to Nick. They couldn't just brush this under the carpet, but she was in no mood for a heart-to-heart right now. At least she'd wiped the sick off her chin with one of Mrs Claus's handy wet wipes.

A skinny man wearing a crisp white shirt with the St John Ambulance logo stuck his head in the tent. 'Have you got a mo?' he asked Mrs Claus. 'We've got a mum having a flap about a little lad who's eaten too much candy floss.'

Mrs Claus dusted the crumbs off her and gave Claudia a last warm smile. 'You'll be fine now, lovely, but no more rides today, okay?'

'Thanks for looking after me, and for the stories.'

'Oooh, you're welcome. You're good to go. Your emergency contact is on his way.' She pottered outside.

Emergency contact?

Claudia stood, stretched and walked to the door of the tent. She spotted Nick immediately, striding over the frosty grass towards the tent, dragging her giant pink suitcase behind him.

Her heart leapt and just for a second she forgot she was angry and hurt, and wanted Nick – her faithful and, actually, incredibly hot Nick – to come on over and sweep her off her feet.

But he wasn't looking at her. He was staring off to his left with hostility.

Claudia followed his gaze.

Also striding over the grass towards her, a look of amusement on his face, was the last person Claudia expected to see.

Seth.

Oh crap.

Date Five

The South Bank

'What the hell are you doing here?' Claudia spat just before realisation dawned on her. Her donor card. The St John Ambulance woman must have looked through her wallet while she was passed out and called Seth to come and pick her up. 'You're my emergency contact . . . ' Well, that was embarrassing.

'Also known as your knight in shining armour, at your service.' Seth oozed self-importance.

'I've got her – you can go,' Nick said, his face set in a glare she rarely saw. The two men had never warmed to each other, Nick insisting that Seth wasn't good enough for her and Seth grumbling about Nick being too touchy-feely with his girlfriend. They had reluctantly fallen into dormant frenemy territory, but today the volcano looked close to erupting.

'That's all right, Nick, I'll take her home.'

'No, you won't.'

'Nick.' Claudia stopped him, she could handle this. 'No, you won't,' she said to Seth.

'How are you feeling, sweetheart?' he charmed.

'I'm just fine, let's not "sweetheart" each other. I didn't know the nurse was calling you. You can leave.'

'Claudia asked me to come,' said Nick with a smirk.

'Good for you, but I'm not going anywhere just yet.'

'She wants you to go.'

'*Nick.*' Claudia shushed him with a fierce look and turned back to Seth. 'Since you're here, let's catch up. How's your girlfriend?'

'She's not my girlfriend; I just met her that night. Nothing happened.'

'Things were happening from where I was standing,' she flashed. Still, it was nice to hear; she hadn't reached indifference yet.

Seth lingered closer to Claudia, giving her his *I'm sorry* smile which just happened to be his *I'm hot* smile as well. Her eyes traced the shape of Seth's lips and curve of his teeth, the length of his stubble, exactly how he always was. 'I was upset, just trying to replace your sexy self, but how could I do that?' he said.

'Yeah, how could you do that?' asked Nick.

'I was a bit pissed, and I was upset. I didn't want things to end like that.'

'Neither did she, but she didn't run into someone else's arms.'

Apart from yours, thought Claudia. She would bet her life savings Nick was thinking the same.

'Nick, mate, I don't remember you being there, so do

you want to give us a bit of space?' Seth asked, his jaw set in a tight line.

Nick responded by putting a heavy arm around Claudia's shoulders. She felt herself blush, acutely aware of the smell of Nick's shower gel on his skin, and the warm tickle of the wool in his jumper. Despite the frost, Claudia was blistering in the heat of both men, feeling heady at having them so close. If this were a fiery Latin dance, Nick would have just spun her into him like her body was not her own.

Claudia felt herself losing control of the situation. 'Go back to wherever you're staying at the moment,' she said to Seth, shamefully hoping he wasn't at a woman's.

'I'm just at Paul's. Don't be mad, Claud, this is a good thing, a bit of time apart. We can still be friends, we just won't sleep together any more. No change from usual, hey?' He laughed and then had the decency to look embarrassed.

'Wow, I am just getting used to you being gone, and when you say things like that it makes it much easier.'

'Great apology, *mate*. Now, she's had enough drama for today, I think.' Nick moved forward, putting himself in the space between Seth and Claudia. 'Time for you to leave.'

'That's all right, *mate*, you can get going. I'll look after her; I know what she needs.'

'You know what I need?' cried Claudia. 'You have no idea what I need, that's the whole problem! All you seem to think I *need* is your willy. Trust me, no girl *needs* a willy.'

'Say it isn't so!' Nick quipped, then composed himself and returned to looking severe.

Seth leant round Nick, a concerned look on his face. 'Sometimes you needed my willy, though, didn't you?'

'I don't need it now. And I don't need you, I have Nick.' Claudia's insides palpitated when she realised what she had just admitted. Her eyes flicked to Nick, and when they met his she looked away quickly. Her throat was dry. 'I mean, not for that.' She was so embarrassed.

'I'm going to take her home,' Nick said to Seth, without a smile.

'I'll take her home,' he replied.

'No, you won't.'

'Mate, all due respect, but I can go to my own house.' 'WHY DON'T YOU GO AND ROLL AROUND IN THE PILE OF SICK I LEFT BY THE FERRIS WHEEL INSTEAD?'

Both men, and a handful of merrymakers passing by, fell silent and gawped at her. Perhaps not the classiest thing to have said, but she felt she'd got her point across.

Her head cleared. Nothing like the remnants of a hangover, a puke and the overwhelming urge to kick someone in the nuts to snap you back to reality. 'I'm not a toy, Seth. You can't dump me, hook up with another girl, not even stand up for me in front of her and then come back a few days later, standing all close, calling me sexy, trying to keep me interested. Well, I'm *not* interested. Get away from me.'

She shrugged out from under Nick's arm. She hadn't forgotten how she'd been a puppet on a string for him last night, either. He was protective *now* – arms around her *now* – but he had shot her down only hours ago. 'And you, get off . . . I'm not your girlfriend.' This three-person tango had to end.

Claudia didn't really want to be around either man, but was still a bit jelly-legged and, annoyingly, would appreciate some company on the walk home. Nick was the lesser of two evils.

'You're right babe, I'm sorry.' Seth tried to hold her arms but she spun away.

She faced Nick yet couldn't look him in the eye. 'Please will you walk me back?'

She started off before he could answer, and the two of them stamped across Hyde Park, Nick dragging the suitcase. Claudia's face was hot and pink against the freezing wind. They walked in silence, all the way back to Claudia's flat. Nick carried her suitcase up the stairs and they stopped at her door. Claudia was no longer nervous about going inside, but was anxious about being out here with Nick.

'Thank you for bringing me back. And for my suitcase.' She didn't look at him.

'Do you want to talk?'

'No. No, right now I just want to sleep.'

'Okay.' They stood awkwardly for a moment, then Nick leant down and wrapped Claudia in a big, warm, familiar hug. She sank in to him a fraction.

He spoke quietly into her ear. 'You're right here, but I feel like we're a million miles apart at the moment.' He let her go and walked away without looking back.

For the second time ever, Claudia entered her flat as a single woman. This time she didn't crumble at the photos or swoon at the breakfast cereal. This time she stacked up all the picture frames, hiding the face she didn't want to look at. She went to the back of the wardrobe and pulled out a brand-new set of bedlinen she'd bought years ago because she'd loved its bright Moroccan pinks and oranges, but Seth had refused to use. She yanked the beige-striped linen off the bed, throwing it straight into the recycling box.

As she shook the duvet into its new cover her mind twisted and back-flipped around Nick's parting words, dissecting every one. Their relationship had shifted for him too, but were they both heading down the same path? Did he want to just stay friends? Did *she* want to just stay friends, if it really came down to it? Was she subconsciously doing something to keep the distance between them?

The bed was ready; Claudia stripped off her clothes and climbed under the cool covers. She lay on 'her' side of the bed, looking at the blank space next to her, the uncreased other pillow. She stretched her hand out and felt . . . nothing. Seth was really gone.

'You told me you'd never leave me,' she whispered to the space. 'You said it so many times. But you were telling me lies. And now I'm lonely.' Some tears came and she let them. She felt like these might be the last, and they needed to come and not be wiped away or told to stop.

'Listen to me, Seth. Listen to me. I'm getting over you,' she choked. 'I won't keep dreaming about the life we'll never have and the things that'll never happen. You're not my maker, and I'm going to make it without you.'

She *was* going to make it.

The world seemed brighter when Claudia awoke the next morning. Although the sun was yet to stretch up over the horizon, the dawn light behind the curtains was more opal than slate. She had slept for nearly sixteen hours, and her stomach growled to complain about it.

She stepped her rested, naked body out from under her beautiful duvet and padded over to the window, grabbing her dressing gown en route. Pulling back the curtains she gasped at the street below. The entire dark grey road and all the rooftops and chimneys of London were covered in thick white snow, tinted a Tiffany blue filter by the early-morning sky. Looking up, she saw fat white flakes lazily drifting down from the clouds and she smiled. She'd made it.

Claudia pushed her iPod into its dock and cranked up her Christmas playlist. To the classic sounds of The Ronettes and Wizzard she danced her way through the flat, flicking on the multicoloured lights of the Christmas tree, rehanging some tinsel that had fallen off a picture frame, filling the expensive coffee maker they'd hardly ever used with her stash of finest Hawaiian hazelnut coffee.

'Hello, *me*,' she said to her reflection, and – to hell with the ballet – threw some amazing shapes that would have made Beyoncé snap her up as a backing dancer.

Getting through her first night alone in the flat, giving Seth a piece of her mind, allowing herself to have a good cry and leaving things a bit odd but not *too* horrendous with Nick had all contributed to lifting the gloom and making her feel like the Ghost of Christmas Present. Even better – the one from *The Muppet Christmas Carol*. She'd vowed at Hyde Park that she wouldn't let Christmas pass her by.

She wanted pancakes. Not because Seth didn't like them and she rarely made them just for her, but because *she wanted* them. She merrily mixed up a batch of her favourite peanut butter and bacon batter and fried three large fluffy pancakes. She poured half a bottle of maple syrup on the top, popped a Santa hat on her head and settled down on the sofa to watch *Sunday Brunch*.

'Single life is great!' she told Tim Lovejoy and Simon Rimmer through a mouthful of pancake, while they sampled Christmas cocktails on the TV.

Her phone tinkled with its text-message reindeer bells. 'Good morning,' she said to it as she reached into her dressing-gown pocket.

Seth. 'Go away,' she mumbled, but opened the message anyway. No more avoiding things like a big old scaredy cat.

> Sorry about yesterday. Didn't mean to upset you and be an arse. Tried to make an awkward situation lighter, but made it more awkward. You know me! Hope we can talk it through some time, when I'm not claiming territory like an idiot and you don't smell of puke xx

Hmm. 'I don't think I want to talk to you at the moment,' she said, carefully laying her phone down at the opposite end of the sofa. 'I'm quite happy talking to myself.'

Claudia was sitting cross-legged on the floor with a biro dangling out of her mouth, staring at Cameron Diaz's beautiful hair in *The Holiday*, when there was a knock on the door. She spat out the biro and pushed aside a confetti of half-written Christmas cards.

'Who could this be, eh, Claud?' she whispered, heading to the door and pressing the buttons on her huge, gaudy Christmas-tree earrings so they came alive with lights scampering over the shiny plastic. Even if it were one of those pesky men, she felt ready to handle it.

'Merry Christmas, my darling!' shrieked a petite blonde woman with a year-round tan and the pinkest of pink lipstick. Nick's mum.

'Christine!' Claudia exclaimed, enveloped in a hug doused with Ralph Lauren Romance.

'Hope you don't mind me stopping by, love,' she said, shuffling into the house and dropping her oversized handbag on the floor. 'It's jolly cold out there you know, the snow's threatening to stop all the trains but they can't stop Christine. Oooh, that coffee smells nice, mind if I grab one? Love your earrings by the way, my darling.'

Christine and Claudia were close and could natter for hours, but they rarely hung out without Nick in tow. What was she up to?

Christine re-emerged from the kitchen with two steaming mugs of coffee, handed one to Claudia and pulled a huge box of Marks and Spencer chocolate biscuits out of her handbag. She settled down on an armchair and gestured for Claudia to take a seat, too.

'How are you doing, my angel?'

'I'm okay thanks, you?'

'Same old with me, my love. Pilates is going well,

though I think the instructor has a thing for me. Looking forward to seeing you all at Christmas for the wedding. But I want to talk about *you*. I heard about Seth.'

'Yes. Not the best Christmas pressie.'

'What a little twerp he is. How are you feeling about it all?'

'I'm actually okay. I've been a bit all over the place, but think I'm coming through the other side now.'

'That's good to hear. Been keeping yourself busy?'

'Non-stop, actually. Some good distractions.'

'That's good. Any Christmas parties?'

Claudia eyed Christine with suspicion. Where was this going? 'Just the one so far, with Nick and Penny.'

'And did you have a magical time?'

'Yes ... it was *quite* magical.'

Christine was staring at her, trying to make her crack. *Plop.* Three-quarters of her chocolate-coated ginger nut fell into her coffee, after drowning by excessive dunkage, leaving Christine clutching a melting corner in her baby-pink talons.

'How's the job?' she asked, changing tack.

'It's okay. Same old. You know I don't want to be there for ever.'

'So what are you being a ninny about, then? Take the Royal Ballet job!' Christine visibly relaxed, a weight off her shoulders. She put down her mug and sat back, worn out by her outburst.

Claudia smiled. 'Nick told you, then?'

'Of course he did,' Christine said proudly. Proud of herself for getting it out of him, rather than of Nick for setting it up. 'He was all excited and chuffed with himself, banging on about making you happy and getting to work with you every day.'

Claudia munched a biscuit to hide her guilty face.

'I said to him,' Christine continued, 'won't you three get sick of each other, all day, every day? But he was adamant it would be just brilliant. Why wouldn't he want to spend as much time as possible with a girl he loves. His words.'

'As friends, Christine, *as friends*!' Claudia spluttered, a blush creeping up over her face.

'Mmm-hmm. So are you going to take it?'

'I haven't decided yet.' She really had to make her mind up. She was coming around to the idea, but every time she thought about watching them all dancing from the sidelines she couldn't help but feel a pang of loss. She was having trouble deciding if she could live like that for a year.

'So what's my son, your *friend*, up to today?' Christine pried.

'I don't know, aren't you going to see him?'

'No, I think I'd better get back home before the snow gets much heavier. You don't know where he is?'

'No,' Claudia laughed. 'We don't all have synchronised diaries.'

'Are you sure it's not because you're avoiding him?' Christine had stopped beating around the bush and was practically standing tall right in the middle of it.

'Oh my, he told you that too?'

'He didn't have to. I called him last night and he was such a Mr Mopeypants I knew something was wrong. Especially when he said he didn't know what you were going to do about the job. You three know everything about each other.'

'It's quite complicated.'

'Was he mean to you?'

'No.'

'Did he stab you in the back?'

'No.'

'Did he side with Seth?'

'No!'

'Well make up with him, won't you, love? He's usually such a happy thing at this time of year, I hate seeing him wallowing about. I'm sure it's nothing that can't be fixed over a Sunday roast.'

Christine slurped the rest of her coffee and grabbed a few more biscuits from the box before heading to the door. 'Must dash, my love, I want to do a spot of Christmas shopping at John Lewis before I head home.'

'I thought you were worried about the snow?' Claudia teased.

Christine winked and shrugged on her coat. She

kissed Claudia on the cheek. 'Be friends with Nick again. Don't lose the people who know you the best.'

'I just lost Seth,' said Claudia.

'Pssh, Seth never really knew you. If he did he'd have loved you so much he would never have been such a prat and left. Call Nick.'

She wafted away down the corridor; such a meddler, but always right.

The snow had stopped falling and the clouds had drifted away. A brilliant blue sky domed over London and the fluffy whiteness sparkled in the sunshine. It looked like a nice day for a walk and a pub lunch. Claudia reached for her phone.

Claudia and Nick strolled along the South Bank, the only sound coming from the slushing of their feet in the melting snow. Next to them, the Thames was a proud, choppy brown and the Clipper boats whizzed up and down with the bucketloads of tourists who were descending on the city in the run-up to Christmas.

They hadn't said more than a hello since meeting ten minutes ago.

Then Nick asked, 'How are you feeling?'

'Much better, thanks.' Another few minutes passed. Under Waterloo Bridge they passed the long tables of second-hand books surrounded by brave people extracting their fingers from gloves to have a closer look. Opposite, the Technicolor-graffitied undercroft buzzed with skateboarders and BMX bikers jumping, spinning, tumbling and laughing, while Rat Pack Christmas classics blasted from a stereo. 'How cool is all this snow?'

'Icy cool,' Nick wisecracked, his face struggling with the seriousness of the mood and glee at the real winter wonderland he was standing in. He peeped sideways at Claudia and they shared amused smiles.

'So, your mum came to see me.'

'Whaaaat?' cried Nick, stopping. 'My mum is *so* embarrassing. What did she say?'

Claudia laughed. 'That you're a happy little thing at Yuletide and I'm a big old mean Grinch for bringing you down.'

'You didn't do anything wrong,' Nick said quietly. They walked further, past tourists taking selfies and teens bundling snow off the railings and hurling it at each other's heads. 'Did she really say "happy little thing"?'

'Pretty much.'

'*Mum*. I'm not little, I'm a big strapping lad.'

'Sure you are, mummy's boy.'

'I am. I'm the tallest of everyone at work. And I'm very tough and rugged and I like beer and fighting and I don't care at all about Yuletide.'

'You are quite tall . . . ' Claudia agreed.

'What am I saying? I love Yuletide,' said Nick, lunging

to the ground and scooping up a fistful of snow. He hurled it into Claudia's face.

Freezing cold and powder soft, the snow woke her senses and a shocked, reflexive laugh burst from her mouth. She shook the flakes from her hair and blinked at Nick.

'Sorry! Sorry, sorry, sorry!'

Claudia edged towards him. She stopped and rubbed her eye.

'Are you okay?' he asked, tentatively coming closer.

'I think you got some grit in my eye.' She blinked hard and backed away against the railing.

Nick took two giant steps towards her and cupped her face. Her fingers curled behind her and gripped a handful of snow. She kept her eyes tight shut for effect and because if she opened them and saw him this close again she didn't know how she'd react.

He was leaning right in, his head bent down, his fingers gently pulling on her eyelid. She lifted her arm slowly, quietly, nearly there.

Bam. She opened her eyes, saw the opening of his collar and threw the snow down the back of his neck. He leapt back from her, whooping and laughing. He danced a jig, hopping and leaping and shaking his jumper to get the snow out. 'You cheeky monkey!' he yelped.

They held up truce hands, and Nick flung an arm around Claudia's shoulder. 'Come on, woman, you promised me a date. I mean, you know, a date with a log fire. Claud – I didn't mean ...' She'd stopped and was staring up at the British Film Institute, pretending she hadn't heard. He followed her gaze.

'*It's a Wonderful Life*,' he read off the billboard. 'It started five minutes ago. Do you want to go?'

'Do you?' Claudia longed to – it was her favourite Christmas movie – but she was petrified of it sounding too date-like.

'Sure.' Nick took her hand like it was the most natural thing in the world then, remembering the implication, gave it a quick squeeze and dropped it again.

They rushed through the box office and into the theatre and settled into their seats in the dark just as, up on the big screen, the young George Bailey was scolding Mary for not liking coconuts. They peeled off their coats, Claudia being careful not to let her hot skin touch Nick and give her away. Sure, a romantic walk in the snow, an old movie and a meal could be construed as a date – especially when Person A tingled every time Person B put his big warm arm around her shoulders. But Claudia had her sensible head on; no getting distracted by runaway thoughts. She concentrated on the screen, ignoring Nick's proximity.

Claudia stood at the bar of the King's Inn a few hours later, ordering a Baileys, a Christmas ale and two turkey roasts (Nick insisted that no other roast was allowed in

December). She looked back at Nick, who was nestled in an armchair by the log fire, his bare arms warming while his jumper dried out on the back of the seat. He stared into the flames, throwing little pieces of ripped-up napkin onto the logs and watching them ignite, bobbing his head to the low melodies of Bing Crosby and Ella Fitzgerald. Behind him a huge misted-up window looked out across the Thames.

Being back on good terms with Nick felt right. Things were disjointed without him around and making up was a huge relief. Not that they'd really made up about anything as such. Maybe she should brush the whole Christmas party under the carpet for the sake of harmony. But there were a lot of feelings still churning around inside her; could she hold on to them, unanswered, for another twelve years? As she carried the drinks over Nick's eyes met hers and crinkled at the corners. God, he was attractive.

'Cheers,' they murmured, clinking glasses as Claudia sank deep into the opposite armchair.

'Less than two weeks to Christmas, you know,' smiled Nick.

'Have you bought all your pressies?'

'Some. There's one person I'm not sure what to buy for yet.'

'Who's that?'

'Just someone I don't feel I can get the usual tat for. I feel like I want to put a bit more thought in this year.'

Claudia's brow sweated. She fanned herself. 'Hot next to this fire, isn't it?' Did he mean her? *No*. She had to stop reading something into everything he said. That's exactly what caused the avalanche of snowball cocktails, the unwelcome mistletoe kiss and the vomit on the tamest fairground ride of all.

'So, um,' Nick started, 'I'm having a cracking day. Thanks for bringing me here. I feel like it makes my Starbucks date look a bit crap.'

'That was a brilliant date. It was probably my favourite date I've had this Christmas, from start to finish.' She watched Nick closely. This was the perfect time to get things out in the open. For the sake of her battered heart they had to move past this.

Just as she opened her mouth to speak Nick stood up and started swaying. Claudia cocked her ear to hear the music, just as the pub owners, evidently huge East 17 fans, cranked up the volume to the 1994 Christmas number one, 'Stay Another Day'.

Nick sang along, lifting his T-shirt to show his stomach and looking every bit the nineties boy-band member.

'What are you doing?' she giggled. 'Sit down, you maniac!'

This only made Nick shut his eyes, clench his fists and sing louder. She watched him in awe. Was this Nick telling her his true feelings?

'Fine. *Fine*.' If that's how he wanted to communicate,

she'd do it his way. She stood and joined in, swaying and warbling, ignoring the bemused looks of the other patrons.

The song ended and they fell back into their seats, flushed and topped up with Christmas spirit. But as wise as East 17's words were, Nick wasn't getting out of it that easily. She had to know where she stood. She didn't want to get the wrong end of the stick again.

'Thanks for taking me home yesterday,' she ventured.

'Of course. I'll take you home any time.' He grinned like a naughty schoolboy.

'You didn't seem to think like that at the party,' Claudia said quietly.

Nick shuffled forward in his seat and Claudia mirrored him, while intently watching the ice swirling in her glass. They leant towards each other and she glanced up and gave him a smile and a shrug. She had to know why he'd turned her down. His face showed regret, but she couldn't tell if he was looking at her as more than a friend, or the same as he always had. *What are you thinking in there?*

'Claud, it just wasn't right.'

She nodded. That hurt her heart. But it was only Nick; her *friend* Nick. She had to stop thinking it was more.

'You were raging, table-dancing, uni-student drunk.'

'Tell me about it. Tell everyone on the Ferris wheel the morning after about it.'

'I was really hoping to show you a good night, to cheer you up, but I think I went a bit overboard and got you completely sloshed.'

'You didn't do that, I did it to myself.' Claudia took a deep breath and made herself look him straight in the face. 'I thought you were flirting with me,' she said before she could chicken out. She braced herself.

'I was.'

'You were?'

'You looked so ... beautiful. I couldn't take my eyes off you. And for the first time in a long time I didn't have the boyfriend card keeping me in check.' Nick gave her a guilty smile. 'I know that makes me sound like a massive creep, slinking in as soon as you've broken up with the love of your life.'

'I hope Seth wasn't the love of my life.' Claudia smiled.

'I just took it too far and then I didn't want to take advantage of you. I'm really sorry.'

'For not taking advantage of me?'

'A little bit. But mainly for messing around with your emotions. I always want you to feel you can trust me. I'm not a total arse.'

'I know you're not. I'm sorry for flipping out at you. I *had* had a bit too much ...'

They grinned at each other, as warm as the fireplace next to them.

Nick held her gaze. 'I just didn't want it to be like that.'

'"It"?'

'The first time we kiss.' He just threw it out there. And then he looked up, smiling at the waiter who had brought their plates. He wouldn't meet her eyes again as he marvelled at the food on his plate. 'Look, chestnut stuffing.'

'Wait,' Claudia said, her heart racing. 'What does that mean, go back to that.'

'I love pigs in blankets, too. Look – we have three each!'

She knew he wasn't going to give away any more today, and she smiled down at her meal; the rich smells of tradition wafted up into her face. So they were to have a first kiss. Not 'if', though 'when' and 'how' were still a mystery. An exciting, unexpected, thrilling mystery, and she could hardly wait.

She settled in for the perfect afternoon of food, drinks and flirting that glittered with the magic of knowing it actually meant something, with a man straight off a Christmas list. Date Five may not have the grand gestures and the fancy parties, nor did it have the drama, but to Claudia it was the most exciting date yet.

Claudia walked home feeling like a teenager in a Katy Perry song. What a crazy, sometimes horrid, often exciting, weird month this was turning out to be.

Nick wanted to kiss her! She jumped up in the air

and landed softly in the snow. Her cheeks were flushed pink and the smile on her face probably made anyone walking by think she was a loon. Maybe she *was* a loon, swooning over her best friend.

'You silly mistletoe- and booze-filled season,' she whispered. 'What have you done to me?'

Her phone rang.

'Penny, merry Christmas!' she chirped down the line.

'Merry Christmas! You sound healthier than yesterday. Fancy coming over for some burnt Christmas cookies?'

'Yum, how can I resist?' Claudia took a sharp right and headed in the direction of Penny's flat.

'Brill, I really need to talk to you about something. Come quick.'

Claudia danced into Penny's flat humming Christmas carols. Penny stood in the kitchen badly spreading lime-green icing over the most burnt bits of the burnt cookies. 'Look, Christmas trees,' she said.

'They look crap. I'll take them all!'

Penny, Claudia and Nick were all fairly shocking cooks, but Penny was the worst. She always overestimated oven time and therefore everything she served was chargrilled. Unless she was trying to do chargrilled, in which case the dish would undoubtedly appear anaemic and soulless.

Claudia reached for a cookie and started sucking on it. 'What do you want to talk about? Oh my God, are you pregnant?'

'No, please, there has been a grand total of nil willies – or test tubes – near me.'

'Okay. Crikey, I nearly started packing a labour bag for you then.'

'You'd really pack my bag for me?'

'Of course. I've already planned it: your big NY Knicks T-shirt, a packet of Tangfastics, the *Twilight* books and your coral nail polish.'

'My favourite things . . .' Penny put her hand on her heart.

'So what do you want to talk about?'

Penny took a deep breath, then turned away. 'I can't.'

'What?'

'A drink first. Join me?' She poured a very large glass of red.

'No thanks, I've already had a Baileys today, I can't face any more alcohol than that yet.'

'Where'd you go for that?'

'I just met Nick for a roast.' Claudia immediately clocked Penny's 'left-out' face. 'It was a last-minute thing, and I needed to apologise for him having to drag a suitcase and a puke-covered girl home on his Saturday.'

Penny laughed. 'Fair enough. So how is he?'

'Well, loving the snow of course.'

'I bet he is. He's really cute at Christmas.'

'Mmm.' Maybe it was time to tell Penny what was going on. It would be mega-embarrassing, but it had to be done.

'Did he mention if he was bringing anyone to the wedding, by the way?'

'No, but I've never actually asked him.'

'I just wondered if he liked anyone at the moment.'

Claudia shrugged and reached for another cookie, avoiding Penny's eyes. *I'll tell her after she's told me her news. Because I'm a humongous wimp.*

'Okay,' said Penny, taking a big gulp of wine.

'Spill,' Claudia coaxed. What was all this about?

'Guess what?'

'What?'

Penny took a deep breath and covered her face in her hands. She squealed. 'I have ... Oh God, I'm too embarrassed to admit it.'

'Just say it, unleash it, you'll feel *amazing*.' She should take her own advice, she thought.

Penny giggled and fanned herself with her hands. 'Okay. Phew. I'm just going to say it.'

Claudia waited.

'I have developed the most *major* crush. On Nick!'

Date Six

The Shard, London Bridge Quarter

'You fancy *Nick*?' Claudia struggled to digest a char-coaled Christmas tree cookie and the news that both she and her best friend had a thing for the same man, who happened to be their other best friend.

Penny nodded, her eyes sparkling.

'That's *brilliant*.' *Nooooooo, what do I say, what do I say?* 'That is just ... such BRILLIANT news.' *Stop saying it's brilliant!*

'You don't mind?' Penny squealed.

YES. 'Why would I mind?'

'Because, you know, if anything happens between us it might change the dynamics a little bit.'

'If anything happens between us? You mean you and me?'

'No, me and Nick.'

Of course. Penny and Nick. Nick and Penny. Bleurgh. She'd been spectacularly pipped to the post. Claudia violently sawed a cookie in half with a carving knife. 'So, um, when the bloody hell did this start?'

'Quite recently really. Because of you!'

'BRILLIANT.'

'You know I've always dated hotties with zero personality?'

'Now that's not fair, sometimes it's nice to have somebody . . . mellow. Don't rule them out yet.'

'But usually they're so mellow they don't even show emotion, or get it when I show emotion. Then when you and Seth split up and I saw how completely lovely Nick was being with you, it dawned on me: all along, here's been a good-looking bloke who's a real sweetie-pie and we already adore each other.'

'He is being very nice to me at the moment, but it's just a one-off. Usually he can be a bit of an idiot, am I right?' Was it too late to change Penny's mind? *Tell her, tell her, tell her.*

'No, he's always been lovely. But the way he's just been there for you over the past week, taking you on the date, holding your hand, checking up on you . . . swoon.'

Tell me about it. 'I know, I fancy him too.'

Penny looked at Claudia.

'HA, HA, HA.' Claudia laughed. *Chicken.* 'HA, HA, HA.'

Penny laughed back. 'I'll fight you for him!'

'You're on! HA, HA, HA.' Claudia waved the knife in the air. No, better put that down.

'Do you think he likes me?' Penny asked, looking nervous and happy and hopeful.

'Well, pffff, dunno. Do *you* think he likes you?'

'Maybe … I mean, he's always over here. And he knows how much I want a baby and he mentions a lot that he wants kids. Maybe he's been trying to tell me something.'

'Wow. So this isn't just a fancying thing, you're thinking about Nick in terms of a potential sperm donor?'

'Not just a sperm donor! It just all makes sense: I like him – *a lot* – we could be in a relationship for a bit, and then I think he'd make a pretty damned fine dad when the time's right. Which will hopefully be soon!'

This was worse than Claudia thought. This wasn't just a 'I want to bonk my bestie' situation, this was a solution to what Penny craved most in the world, with only Claudia standing in her way.

'Do you think this is a really bad idea?' Penny asked.

'Noooo.' Yes, but only because Claudia fancied Nick herself. She had three choices: tell Penny it was a great idea and watch her and Nick shack up together; tell her it was a bad idea and go out with him herself, thus being a horrible best friend and total hypocrite; or admit to Penny that she and Nick had a little sumpin-sumpin going on, breaking her trust in the friendship and pooping all over her feelings.

'I just think we're actually kind of perfect for each other, don't you agree?'

'In what way?'

'Well, we already spend every day together holed up

in dark auditoriums, so we know we don't drive each other insane, we have a lot of the same friends, we both work in the world of theatre . . .'

This was all true; she made a good argument. Penny was winning. 'Don't you reckon that if you really fancied him there would have been some kind of spark there all along? You wouldn't just suddenly like him after all these years?' As if Claudia believed any of that.

'No, I think sometimes it just hits you. Boom. He's it. He might just be The One.'

'Boom . . .'

'And he's kind, you know? I'm tired of silly boys; I really just want a kind man in my life.'

Claudia had lost Nick. Before she'd even had him.

'Plus he *is* a hottie.' Penny grinned.

Hearing Penny all excited and hopeful suddenly made it very clear to Claudia exactly how she felt. Somehow this last week had brought them closer than ever before, and she realised Nick had been there all along.

Just like Penny said.

But I want Nick to be mine, a small voice inside her said. Well, too late. She couldn't let anything happen now. She had to step aside. Her head felt tangled, so she stuffed another cookie inside it.

'You're such a good friend.' Penny broke into her sludgy thoughts. 'And I'm crap – I never apologised for that rubbish blind date I set you up on.'

I never apologised for the future father of your baby

telling me he wanted to kiss me. 'S'okay. It was ... an experience.'

'I promise I won't meddle again. I did have another one in mind, but I've learnt my lesson.'

'Another blind date?'

'Yep, Mikael, a dancer from the ballet. He's quite fit. But we do need to find you a good new man. We need to find you a Nick.'

'Mmm-hmm.' Right. Crisis mode. So Penny was going to make a move on Nick. Even if he wasn't interested there was still no way she could swoop in now. And she couldn't deal with one failed relationship and one failed start-up relationship while playing confidante to Penny during Operation Nick.

There were plenty more nice men out there. Plenty of reasons to be fun, free and single. Plenty of people to remind her that Nick – and Seth – weren't the only likeable men in London.

'Set me up on the date,' Claudia said.

'Seriously?'

'Yes, why not, set me up on as many as you like. Let the boys of London nosebleed upon my face. I do need to find another Nick. I mean, someone like Nick.'

Nick was pretty one-of-a-kind; she hadn't stumbled across another one in the last fourteen years. But it was time to look. Because what choice did she have?

Claudia raced out of Edurné's the second the clock struck three. She had no idea if he'd be there, but it was worth a try, before she talked herself out of it. She weaved through Covent Garden, salt and slush gripping on to the bottom of her boots, glancing at the mulled wine stand she and Nick had been to three days ago, and then pushed open the door of the Italian restaurant.

'Billy.'

'Claudia!' He looked up from clearing a table. 'How are ya?'

'Good, yes. On the mend. A little less drunk than the last time you saw me.'

'Just a little?'

'I mean, it is Christmas. Here in England it's tradition to start every December morning with a glass of port.'

'That makes sense. I start every day with a beer.'

'Upholding one's culture is very important.' They looked at each other. Billy passed Claudia a breadstick. *Say it. He's nice. Nick's gone.* 'Billy. What are you up to tomorrow?'

'I'm working the evening shift, but free as a bird all day.'

'Do you want to do something? Hang out? Like a date? Or whatever?'

'A date? Sure, that'd be ace. I'm gagging to find out what happened at your showdown with Dickhead.'

'Not much to tell—'

'Don't spoil it – tell me tomorrow.' He gasped. 'Mate, can we go to the Shard?'

'Sure!'

'I haven't been yet, and don't you reckon London'll look pretty awesome from up high in all this snow?'

Claudia and Billy arranged to meet at ten o'clock the following morning. They swapped phone numbers and she scarpered.

She had a strange feeling in the pit of her stomach. It was a little bit horrible. Like sadness churning with guilt and too many cups of tea. Billy was lovely, but setting herself up on another date didn't have the empowering, moving-on feeling she'd anticipated.

Too late now. The sixth date of Christmas was fixed.

It was ridiculous o'clock the next morning when Claudia met Penny outside her house for their first-ever run together. Penny had latched on to Claudia's quest to be a sexier lady, and the two of them vowed to become better versions of themselves over the winter, beating the swimsuit-season gym lock-ins come March.

It was lightly snowing, and still dark enough that Christmas-tree lights sparkled merrily through people's windows, turning the street into a wide, glittery tunnel.

Bloody hell it was cold. Claudia hopped on the spot

while she waited for Penny to stretch. They took a few preliminary strides and Penny's foot shot out to the left. She gripped a railing and smothered a snort of laughter.

'Shh! Claudia giggled, her own feet slipping on the icy pavement. She flailed about until she was spooning Penny against the wrought iron.

'Shall we just walk today? We can be fit and healthy when the snow's gone,' Penny whispered.

'Yep, let's just do bikini bootcamp next summer and forget this nonsense for now.'

They clutched each other's hands and made their way down the road and into Kensington Gardens, which wasn't quite so hazardous, and where they could talk without waking anyone up.

'I have something hilarious to show you,' said Penny, pulling out her iPhone. She held it up for Claudia to see.

On the screen was the ugliest baby in the world. Claudia felt bad just thinking it, but it looked like a greying old man with stubble rash and teeny evil eyes. 'Who is *that*?'

'Isn't it grim? It's an app where you can merge people's faces and see what their baby will look like. This is me and Nick!'

A minute ripple of a thought went through Claudia's mind, which she shooed away immediately. *Naughty thought. It's not a good thing that they might have unattractive babies.*

'But you're both so good-looking. Like, in real life.'

'Fingers crossed it's just a rubbish app. Look, this is me merged with you.'

'Why do we have two foreheads?'

'I like to think it's because our babies would have such enormous brains.' She put her phone away. 'So I was thinking about Nick.'

'Evidently.' *Me too.*

'Claud, how am I actually going to do this? Should I just tell him how I feel? Should I start flirting?'

Claudia began doing lunges as they walked, to warm herself up and hide her big, petulant bottom lip that was sticking out at having to give advice about this. 'I don't know. Maybe before you do anything you should scope him out and see if he has any feelings for you. That way if he hasn't you won't feel silly.'

'You're right. You're good at things like this. Maybe you could ask him for me?'

Damn it. 'No, I really don't want to.'

'Pleeeeease. You see him so much at the moment, you could easily just slip it in.'

She couldn't refuse. Penny had done so much for her in the last week, and she had no idea how big an ask this was. Though her heart felt like it was tearing apart, she had to be a good friend. 'Fine,' she mumbled.

'You're the best! Just think, in a couple of weeks Nick and I could be *dates* to Emma and Ellie's wedding! Can you imagine everyone's faces? It would be the funniest thing.'

'Wow, that *would* be funny.' Claudia reached up and gripped the end of an overhanging tree branch. 'Just like this.' She let go and it twanged back, a waterfall of snow cascading onto Penny. Claudia ran away laughing her head off, with Penny not far behind her.

Claudia and Billy pressed their noses against the toughened glass at the top of the Shard, a thousand feet above the city, and looked down at the snow-covered model village far below.

'What's that one?' asked Billy, pointing to a black and white high-rise that stuck out above the surrounding buildings.

'Um, I think that's the Ministry of Defence's James Bond-themed simulation training centre.'

'Cool. And that one?' He pointed to a blue, glass-fronted building on the edge of the Thames.

'That's the corgi hotel, for when the Queen goes on holiday.'

'You're such a good tour guide,' Billy marvelled, amused.

'Maybe *that* could be my new career ... What did you do back in Australia?'

'I was a dive instructor on a Barrier Reef catamaran off Cairns. I'm such a cliché, right?'

'Nothing wrong with being a cliché if you have a dream job.'

'I loved it: being outside all day, hanging out with the fishes, seeing people's eyes bulge through their masks when a reef shark swam past.'

'Do you have a favourite memory?'

Billy was thoughtful. 'I do, actually. There were these two backpackers, girls, utterly down in the dumps because they'd been bitten to shit by bedbugs in some crappy hostel. They were hot and itching like hell and it was proper wrecking their trip. I took them in the ocean and the minute their bodies hit that cool water and they dropped their heads under the surface and saw all these parrotfish, like, conga-lining around them, their faces just lit up. They had the best time and totally came out of their shells. They told me it saved their trip.' He smiled and shrugged.

Claudia melted.

'You're the first person in the UK to ask me that question, you know.'

'Well, more people should, because it's a winning day-at-the-office story. The Barrier Reef is my friend Penny's dream holiday destination.'

'Yeah? She should definitely go.'

'Maybe you could take her on your next trip back.'

'If she's cool like you, consider it done.'

An Aussie dive instructor had just called her 'cool'. She felt like running to the shops for Sun-In and a surfboard. She couldn't wait to tell Penny. 'Weren't you scared to give it up and come to England? It's a bit rubbish here sometimes.'

'Nah, it's rubbish everywhere sometimes. And one day I'll probably go back to Oz. But you can't stay put doing one thing for ever, just in case the next thing isn't quite as good. Especially if that thing is something you know you want to give a shot.'

'You're so wise.'

'Wise? Ha!'

'You are. I know we don't know each other brilliantly, but you're strangely insightful.'

He blushed, just a touch. 'Thanks. Maybe I just always reckon I know what's best!'

Claudia and Billy took the stairs up to level 72, open to the sky above, where the freezing wind whipped her hair about like a candyfloss machine. They huddled into a corner and resumed their sightseeing. Billy squashed her against the glass and stood close, sheltering her from the wind. His tanned hand rested on the glass next to hers, snow-white.

'What's your dream holiday destination?' he asked.

Anywhere with Nick.

Gah! Where did that come from?

'It's a bit sad, but it's actually somewhere I've already been. Penny and I went to Greece when we were twenty-two and we just had the best time ever. It wasn't about boys or work, but about me and her and dancing and cocktails and having an adventure. So my dream holiday would be to go back there and recreate that trip.'

'You're one to hold on to the past, aren't you? Not being a dick, just, you know, *insightful*.' He grinned. 'Don't live back there, just hold on to the ace memories that make up your life. Then create as many new ones as you can. Bloody hell, I really am wise. I think I'm gonna sack this all in and bake fortune cookies.'

'Create new memories,' Claudia murmured. Time to be courageous. She turned in his arms, trying to block the image of Nick's face, his eyes, his smile. She studied Billy. Could she kiss someone else? This was bigger than getting over Nick. This would be her first kiss since Seth. The only other lips she'd have touched in more than five years. *Get over the past*. She exhaled and edged closer, feeling the heat of Billy's body through their thick layers of winter coats.

Billy was watching her, a shy smile on his face. He seemed in no rush, like he was telling her to take as long as she needed. Claudia put her hands on his chest and raised herself up on tiptoes. She thought of how close she'd been to kissing Nick at the Christmas party. Would things have changed if it had actually happened? Would she be here now?

Claudia tilted her chin up and Billy sank his face down to meet her. They kissed, lightly, affectionately. It lasted no more than a few seconds and then they slowly pulled apart; staying close, their foreheads touching.

'That was a bit shit, wasn't it?' whispered Billy. Claudia pulled back and burst out laughing. 'What are you thinking, Sheila?' He grinned.

'You really call women "Sheila"?'

'No, just threw it in there to break the tension.'

'Um, I was thinking . . . It wasn't *shit.*'

'Yes it was, you bloody liar!'

She hadn't felt a thing, not a single spark. 'It was like kissing a brother.'

'Safe to say the stars won't be aligning for us.'

'They can't even be bothered to get out of their armchairs.'

'Lazy stars. It's a shame, eh? You're awesome, and pretty as hell by the way, but you and I are just not destined to be more than friends.'

It *was* a shame. Billy was a great guy. But now she knew two things for sure.

One: she didn't just like Nick because he was being nice to her and she was rebounding. Billy was just as yumtastic and she couldn't even sweat a palm for him.

Two: there really are other good catches in the world. And she'd be okay when the time came.

'Right, listen,' Claudia said. 'That was just a friendship induction that I put everyone through, don't go thinking you're special. Now let's get back to work. What do you think that building is?' she pointed towards Canary Wharf. Billy laughed and shoved her out the way to get a better view.

Claudia listened to him babble on with some nonsense about Henry the Eighth's office block. *Okay Nick, I'm going to have to step my game up to get over you.*

❄

Claudia arrived home mid-afternoon and flicked on the TV. One of the channels was halfway through *Love Actually*, which was tempting, but she had a phone call to make and something she needed to ask.

'Hi, Dad.'

'Hello, my darling, this is a nice surprise.'

'What were you up to?'

'Um, well, *Love Actually*'s on TV, so I was giving that a go. I don't like that secretary of Alan Rickman's much.'

'I don't like anyone who's mean to Emma Thompson.'

'Me neither.'

'Shall I call you back when it's finished?'

'No, no, I've paused it. Chatting to you's much more fun.'

'Thanks.' Claudia hoped she wasn't about to make her dad sad, dredging up the past. 'I have a question.'

'Go for it.'

'Can I ask ... how did you get over Mum?'

'After she left?'

'Yeah, but I don't mean how did you react straight after she moved away; I know you were probably angry and hurt, but, like, how did you actually get through knowing that you couldn't be with the person you loved ever again?'

They didn't talk about this stuff often. Claudia knew her dad felt like he'd failed her when he and her mum had divorced. Claudia's mum had never really been your typical mum. She was a free spirit, if you were being polite. A bad mother if you weren't. She was an adventurer, and getting married and having a baby was an adventure. But the aftermath wasn't. She loved Claudia, but traditional motherhood bored her. Joe always had to be the bad cop, because often her mum would be the one encouraging Claudia to take the day off school or to go to parties she was really too young for. Claudia saw how difficult it was for her dad so tried to be a good child. He was drained by trying to keep the family together when it was painfully obvious her mum was itching to fly away. And one day she did. She now lived in New Zealand, and Claudia saw her about once a year.

'Oh honey,' said Joe. 'Are you thinking about Seth?'

No, I'm actually thinking about Nick. 'Yep.'

'To be honest, it did take a long time. I kept reminding myself of the fact that it wasn't working while she was around, therefore her leaving wasn't the world's biggest disaster.' He paused. 'But it still felt like that, for a long time.'

Poor Dad. 'What helped you through it?'

'You did.'

'Me?'

'You were my crutch, which wasn't fair on you, but you helped me see that the, um, love of one person is not the be all and end all of life. If it finishes there are other people who you can pour even more of your love into.'

'Dad, *you* were *my* crutch.'

She heard a foghorn of a nose blow. 'I'm sorry Seth's gone,' Joe said, coming back on the line. 'It's really hard, but you've got me, Penny, Nick and lots of other people. And you'll have a whole big heartful of love to share with someone new when they come along. I sound like a right hippy.'

Claudia laughed.

'Another thing I did was think, right, if I can't have one thing I want – i.e. your mother – I'll look into getting something else I want. Not calling your mum a "thing", of course. I'd spent a long time trying to make her happy and keep her interested, so I decided to do those things for me. My dreams weren't as wild as hers – in fact my biggest dream was just to hang out with my pre-teen daughter and keep her out of harm's way! But it was a good excuse to try a few hobbies. That's when I started playing the keyboard, you know. I can still only play "Chim Chim Cher-ee", but I gave it a go. And more importantly, I followed my little ambition to open a fishing shop. Some called me crazy, doing that in the middle of Surrey, but I didn't do too bad, did I?'

'Best fishing shop in all of the south,' agreed Claudia.

Her dad had sold his business a couple of years ago, after a successful decade and a half.

'I know it feels like a monumental task to get yourself happy again, but there are lots of opportunities out there for excitement, I promise you.'

First Billy, then her dad; who would be Claudia's third wise man this Christmas?

'Christine called me, by the way,' she said

'Did she now?'

'She told me Nick's offered you a new job. It sounds good. What do you think?'

'I really don't know. It does sound good, but . . .'

Joe waited. 'All right, Miss, here's a question for you: what do you want to do with your life?'

'Well, my dream job has always been to be a dancer.'

'I know, but you haven't done anything about that for twelve years.'

Claudia felt a twist of shame. 'I know, Dad, I know I should have done something sooner. I feel like an idiot for letting it all slip away.'

'I'm not having a go, love, I'm just saying that if that was really still your big passion you'd have had more drive to keep going with it. I know you'll always love dancing and everything about it, but maybe you need to have a big hot chocolate and a good think about what you'd really like to do with yourself. Just because you had a dream a decade ago doesn't mean it has to be the same one now.'

'Mmm. I've been thinking the same thing lately.'

'Do you want me to come over and bring you some marshmallows for that hot choc?'

'No, Dad, this is London, there's a twenty-four-hour Tesco on every corner.'

'Okay.' He sounded sad.

'But I could bring some to you. Maybe we could have that hot choc together? And I'll pick up dinner on the way.'

'You don't have to do that, my darling, it's a long way and you're a busy girl.'

'I want to.'

'In that case, can we have fish and chips, please?'

❄

'MERRY CHRISTMAS!' Nick boomed, banging open the door to Edurné's the next day and standing in the entrance, arms out, in the ugliest Christmas jumper Claudia had ever seen. 'How awesome is my jumper?'

'It's so awesome,' Beth fluttered.

Why did he have to always look so attractive? She'd obviously caught something off Beth because that smile now made her weak at the knees. *Pull yourself together.* 'Hello, what are you doing here?' Sensible conversation only, no flirting allowed.

'Two reasons. Firstly, I want to offload these.' He dumped a Tupperware box of the burnt Christmas tree cookies on the counter. 'Penny gave them to me and they're God-awful. Secondly, I'd like to take you to dinner tonight, please.' He stood close and grinned down at her. She held herself back, no touching, but couldn't help smiling back at him. He was infectious.

Tonight Claudia was meeting Mikael for a drink at nine. She wasn't looking forward to it much, but her moving-on resolutions wouldn't let her back out. But spending time with Nick was much more appealing. And they were still friends. Maybe this would be a good time to put a cap on anything else before it was too late.

'I can do an early dinner. Just somewhere casual.' *Not somewhere romantic.*

'Excellent. Let's say that barbecue place around the corner. Six-thirty okay?'

'Yes please. Will you be wearing that jumper?'

'Yes.'

'Good. I'm going to wear two ginormous Christmas stockings.'

'And nothing else? Bloody hell!'

'You wish. Get out of here, we're very busy and important.'

Nick headed for the door, then turned back at the last minute. He locked eyes with Claudia and jabbed a finger in her direction. 'You're mine, stockings girl.'

He swept out of the shop and into the blizzard that was picking up outside. Beth faced Claudia with the look of someone who'd been dragged through an emotional hedge. 'Ohmygod,' she mouthed and fell into a lust-induced faint against the counter.

Claudia knew it was wrong, but in that moment she was *so* his.

This is not a date, Claudia told herself as she chomped her way through sticky ribs that evening. She'd chosen the messiest thing on the menu in the hope that Nick would be revolted by her and realise how beautiful and ladylike Penny was. Then it would be over.

'For crying out loud, do you even have any idea how good you look ripping that meat off the bone?'

Argh, *fail*. 'I don't look good at all, you weirdo. Look, I have barbecue sauce on my chin,' she said, smearing some barbecue sauce on her chin. 'Penny is a much prettier eater than me, don't you think?'

'*You're* a weirdo, but that's why I like you.'

I like you so much, she silently screamed at him. Subject-changing time. 'How's your sis? Is the surgery booked yet?' Jennifer was due to go to hospital for a procedure to loosen her hip joints.

Nick's eyes lit up, like they always did when he spoke about her. 'She's doing really well, thanks. We heard about the operation yesterday – it's not going to be until the new year, so she doesn't have to go in until after Christmas.'

'She's still spending Christmas with your dad?'

'Yeah, he's much closer to the hospital, but Mum and I will travel up a couple of days after.'

'I have a present for her, don't let me forget.'

'Thanks, Claud. You get the best pressies. She loves you to bits.'

'I love her to bits, too,' Claudia said, keeping her eyes from Nick. 'And so does Penny.'

'Penny's great with her as well.'

'Don't you think Penny looks pretty in the ballet this year? I think she just glows out there.'

'Yeah, she looks gorgeous.'

'How has she not been snapped up yet? She's so lovely and she's quite sexy when she dances.' This was so ridiculous. Claudia was going to have to ask Penny to just come clean to Nick.

'You two have such girl-crushes on each other. Now, listen you,' he said, commanding her attention. 'We need to talk about something.'

'What?'

'I think we need to talk about us.'

Bugger. She desperately wanted him to tell her there was nothing between them and that he was mad about Penny. At the same time, she was also wishing him to confess his undying love for her. She waited, nibbling on fries and unable to say a word.

'I hear Penny's going to be sending you on more blind dates. So I feel it's only fair to give you all the facts up front. One: whoever she's setting you up with is a moron with no teeth and a criminal conviction for pushing over old ladies. Two: Penny has horrible taste in men—'

'No she *absolutely* doesn't!' Claudia cried, and slapped her hand across her mouth.

'And three,' Nick took a deep breath, 'I don't want you to go on any other dates.'

'You don't?' *Don't say it ... except ... I really want you to say it.*

'I know what I want shouldn't factor in, but ...'

Nick reached across the table and put a big, heavy hand over hers. Her fingers moved upwards and she laced them in with his. She stared at the physical contact. Uh-oh. Her brain was telling her to pack this in at once, while all of her senses told her this was the best thing she'd ever felt.

'But I want you to date me.'

Oh shit. Shit, shit, shit. If only he hadn't said it. If only she'd stopped him in time.

'I know we're friends and you might be thinking I'm a massive weirdo, but to be totally honest, Claud, I've always had a bit of a thing for you, and I've got to say it now, and if you turn me down that's totally fine and we can never mention it again and I'll burn all my "I Heart Claudia" T-shirts.'

'You've *always* had a thing for me?' she breathed. Prospects for Penny were decreasing. That still didn't mean she could swoop in. She raised her eyes to his collar, to the triangle of bare skin below his neck. Her heart thudded and all she could think about was putting her lips against that triangle.

'Yep. And I've been a chicken for all these years. And it's Christmas. And Seth's finally out the way – sorry.' He fake-coughed, '*Not sorry.*'

Her thumb twitched under his hand and she traced his palm with it. It was a deliberately defiant move by her hormones, which made fireworks shoot about inside her chest. *You like me. I like you. But my best friend likes you, too.*

'Claudia? What do you think?'

What did she think? That she wanted to touch him, to grip the hand she was stroking, to jump over the table and onto his lap and kiss the hell out of him. But she had better not. *STOP.*

She looked up and into his nervous eyes.

'Don't make me sing Mariah at you,' he smiled.

Penny was always there for her. Always looking out for her. And she had her heart set on Nick, and on having a baby with him, and him being the key to making her dreams come true. The thought of it being her that took this away made Claudia feel wretched.

'Claud, how do you feel?'

She sighed, feeling all the sorrow in the world and opened her mouth to turn him down. What else could she do?

'Nick . . .'

'Hey, guys.' Nick and Claudia snatched their hands apart as if the sparks between them had lit a flame. Next to the table, a quizzical look on her face, stood Penny. 'What's going on?'

Date Seven

The Ice Rink at the Natural History Museum, Kensington

In a matter of seconds Claudia had wiped clean the shock and painted a thick layer of imaginary cover-up over her guilty face. She dragged on a smile. *Nothing will show.*

'Hi, Penny,' she said, and then turned straight to the girl at her friend's side.

'Hi, I'm Claudia. I kind of recognise you: do you guys work together?' she babbled, her heart thudding, desperate to distract Penny from the situation.

'Yes – I'm a physio at the Company. I'm Jada.'

'Well it's so good to meet you.'

'You too, Penny was just telling me that you and I might be working together soon.'

'I don't think I need a physio. Because of the *Insanity* workout? To be honest, I haven't exactly stuck to the regime . . .'

'No, I mean backstage, at the Royal Ballet.'

'Ah, of course.' *Plonker.* 'Yes, that might happen, maybe . . . By the way, Penny, you look lovely.'

'Thanks.' Was Penny looking at her strangely? Did she know something was going on? 'So what are you guys doing here, all alone?'

'Well,' started Nick with a big grin on his face. 'I was just telling Claud—'

'We were just having a good catch-up and telling jokes and things,' Claudia jumped in lamely. 'But I am *full*. I think we should get the bill.' She smiled at Nick who looked baffled, as if he were trying to figure out a difficult answer in a pub quiz.

'Stay for a little bit. Jada and I are just grabbing a milkshake – they're so good here. We'll join you.' Yeah right, she was totally saying 'We'll keep an eye on you'. 'Hi, Nick.' Penny gave him a warm smile and lashings of eye contact. Claudia's insides tightened.

'I remember you from the Christmas party, Claudia, you were pretty hammered,' Jada teased.

'Yep, that was me.'

'Before you fell off that table you were killing it in the dance-off. Sorry, Penny, but I think Claudia won that.'

'No way, I didn't win anything, Penny deserved to win,' Claudia insisted.

'It's okay, I accept defeat. I am second best.'

'No, you're not, you are *not* second best. I'm not taking anything away from you.'

'I believe you.' Penny looked at her directly, but Claudia couldn't hold the eye contact.

Saved by the waitress: 'Can I get you ladies anything?'

'Yes, please, can we get four chocolate milkshakes?' Penny grinned at the group.

'Actually, do you have eggnog?' Nick asked. The waitress nodded. 'Get in! Can I have eggnog instead please?'

'Ooo, me too, I've never tried it,' cried Claudia. 'No, hang on, I *will* have a milkshake, if Penny says they're good. She knows best – this girl has amazing taste,' she told Jada.

'Have eggnog, have whatever you want, my treat,' said Penny.

'Um ... no, I value your opinion and your feelings as a friend.' *Okay, stop it.* She was desperately drowning her guilt under a waterfall of gushing hero-worship, and all three of them were starting to look at her strangely.

'Well, thanks.' Penny laughed it off. 'Now come on, what are you two up to? What's the big secret?'

There was definitely an edge to her voice.

'We had some terribly important things to talk about,' said Nick. Claudia widened her eyes at him. *Please don't say anything, please.*

Suddenly Penny visibly lit up, and she leaned in to Nick. 'Important things, huh? Sounds ... important. Life-changing.'

Oh, Penny. How could Claudia tell her that no, she hadn't been about to ask if Nick liked Penny, because she already knew the answer? Claudia tried to pull Penny's attention away, but she was staring at Nick like a teenager at a One Direction concert.

Where had those lusty eyes come from? Was it the procreation hormones zipping around Penny's body that made her sumptuous and predatory? Claudia tried to imitate her expression but Nick glanced over and caught her. The shame.

'Have you talked about these *things* yet?' Penny pressed Nick.

'We were just getting to it.'

Penny turned to Claudia, all of a sudden her eyes glittering full beam and struggling to control an enormous grin from taking over her face. 'Shall I go?'

'No, stay, please stay,' said Claudia. *Coward.*

The milkshakes and eggnog were delivered and Claudia focused on the cold, creamy liquid. She took a massive, noisy slurp through the fat straw and looked up to see Penny smiling at her.

'Claudia, you look stunning tonight, you're glowing.'

'Glowing? No. It's really hot in here and I'm totally dressed for snow. It's just sweat.' *And nerves and fear and panic that you'll see through me and find out what a betraying harlot I am.*

'No, you just look happy, like you have your sparkle back. Like somehow you've got over the worst of Seth.' She stared at Claudia for a moment then turned to Nick. 'Doesn't she look gorgeous?'

'I'd do her.'

'Nick! Oh my God, sorry, Jada.' *Sorry, Penny.* He was chuckling, no idea he was piggy-in-the-middle to two romance-starved women.

Claudia polished off her milkshake in record speed and stood, pulling on her coat. 'I'm sorry, but I have to go. It was good to meet you, Jada.' She pulled a twenty-pound note out of her purse.

'You're going?' Nick said. 'Shall I come with you?'

'No, you finish your eggnog, I have ... plans.' *Please don't say anything right now, Penny.*

'Yes, you're meeting Mikael!' said Penny.

'You're meeting Mikael?' Jada fanned herself.

'You're meeting Mikael?' asked Nick.

'Woo-wee, you're in for a treat, he's HOT,' said Jada.

'He's not that hot,' grumbled Nick.

'I don't think he's that hot,' said Penny, smiling at Nick. 'But Claudia will – she could use some male model right now.'

'He is *so* not a male model; he's all lanky and stupid,' Nick sulked.

Claudia stood there awkwardly. She hated leaving things like this, but it was easier to run away than have the rest of 'the talk'. 'I said I'd be there ... I better go.' She apologised with her eyes and hoped with all her heart that Nick understood.

He handed the twenty back to her. 'You don't have to pay, I've got it.'

'No, it's fine.' Penny and Jada were watching them. 'It's not like this is a date or anything.' She hated saying it; she knew it would hurt Nick but she had to make sure Penny knew.

'Right.' Nick went back to his eggnog.

She said her goodbyes and turned to leave, feeling wretched. He must hate her.

'Wait, Claudia,' said Nick. She turned back. He was holding out his glass with a gentle smile. 'Before you go, you have to try some eggnog, otherwise ... Christmas won't like you any more.'

'You are not a ballerina.'

Claudia turned on her stool in the crowded pub and smiled at the tall Romanian glowering down at her. His arms were folded and his square-cut features were so still Claudia wondered for a moment if he was posing for an imaginary perfume advert.

'No, not any more.' She held out her hand. 'I'm Claudia.'

'No, I can see you are not a ballerina. Your body is not like a ballerina. Penny said you are a ballerina.' He ignored her hand and sat down on the stool opposite with a sigh. 'Oh well. I am Mikael. You know that, of course. You have seen me in *The Nutcracker*, I hope.'

Why am I here? 'Yes, I saw it last week. Penny was fantastic, as graceful as always.'

Mikael waited.

'And my friend Nick …' *He's lovely. He's much hotter than you.* 'He built such amazing set pieces.' Claudia took a slow sip of her drink, admiring the gold foil garlands strung around the pub. She could feel Mikael's steely eyes willing her an early death.

It was too awkward; she caved.

'And you were great.' She loathed herself. She didn't even remember him.

'Yes,' he agreed. Having got what he wanted he asked with minimal interest, 'And you do what?'

'I work in Edurné's, the dancewear shop in Covent Garden.' Mikael shrugged. 'You don't know it? I'm surprised. It's very popular; all the *best* dancers go there.' Ha.

'Of course I know it, but I don't remember the shop assistants.'

Well played, Mikael. Nope, no more wasting time on rubbish dates. Being single was far more desirable than being put through this. She gulped the rest of her cranberry juice and was about to make her excuses when the last person she wanted to see walked in.

'All right, sexyyyy?' Seth boomed across the pub. He was wearing a Santa hat and had glassy eyes, and he gave Claudia a pat on the head, his hand slipping to her right boob, as a greeting. He looked from Mikael to Claudia and back to Mikael. 'You're handsome.' Mikael nodded.

Seth leaned over the table and winked at Claudia, his beery breath filling her face. He became serious. 'Claudy. I miss your body in the mornings. You look lovely first thing, pottering about in the nod, doing your make-up.'

Claudia was stunned. Where had that come from? Seth never said such nice things. Ever.

Seth stood back upright and turned to Mikael. 'She's awesome, mate. Fantastic in bed too, when she'll give it to you. She does this thing—'

'SETH!' For just a millisecond she'd believed he might have changed. She grabbed her coat. 'Thanks, Mikael, it's been a riot.'

Seth nudged Mikael. 'Just don't expect it too often. Her sex drive's got an expiration date!' He snorted with laughter and Claudia shoved him out of her way. She tumbled from the pub and into the busy night. The Strand was heaving with Christmas-party revellers and joyful theatre-goers, all sparkly dresses and slipping heels on the icy pavement, causing whoops and squeals to peal out across the West End.

'You're such a shit.' She said it aloud, banging her fist on a brick wall. 'You're both such shits.' What an evening; constantly walking on eggshells. If she could have anything in the world right now, anything at all, it would be for everyone else to disappear, so she could just be alone with the one person she knew she had to forget.

'Santa Claus is Coming to Town' blared out of her

coat pocket and she pulled out her phone. And there he was: Nick. Perfect. 'What?'

'What?!' he yelled back, surprised.

'What, Nick?' A sniffle escaped. Damn it.

'What's wrong? What happened?'

A heavy breath escaped her and whirled about in front of her face in the frosty air. She was getting very tired of covering up her feelings. 'I just ... don't want to be on a blind date right now.' She knew what she was really saying here. Did he?

Seconds passed. She couldn't speak any more. She willed him to say something that would make everything fall into place, but what could he say?

'Where are you?' he said quietly.

'Trafalgar Square.'

'I'm coming for you.'

'Meet me at the Christmas tree?'

He hung up and Claudia slowly lowered the phone. What was she doing? This was dangerous. Dangerous, friendship-rocking, friendship-breaking territory. She made her way to the capital's biggest tree, twenty metres tall and adorned with a night-sky of white fairy lights. She hugged herself against the wind chill and let the softly piped carols blow away the horrible non-date. *Silent night, holy night.*

Minutes later, strong, warm arms spun her round and enveloped her in one swift move. She pushed her face into Nick's chest and breathed him in. He smelt of

Hugo Boss and hot chestnuts, his torso as warm as a log fire against her nose. She peeled herself back enough to glance up at him.

He smiled, breathing heavily. 'You're such a cry-baby at the moment,' he said tenderly.

'Why are you panting, you big pervert?'

'I ran, of course.'

Of course.

It was unspoken, but their feelings for each other were as loud as Big Ben. Claudia rose up on her tiptoes and pressed her forehead against Nick's mouth. He kissed her, his breath tickling through her hair.

All is calm, all is bright.

Eleven o'clock the following night and Claudia was outside the Opera House on her own – again – looking like a right lemon. She could have gone inside, but then she might have run into Penny – again. This way she could stare at the door like a total stalker and grab Nick as he came out.

Last night she'd walked away from him with an 'I'll have an answer for you tomorrow.' It was about as late into tomorrow as it could possibly be. As much as she adored putting stuff off, he was too big a part of her life to leave hanging; it wasn't fair.

She still hadn't decided what she was going to say to him, though.

She could tell him she had feelings for him but so did Penny, and for that reason they couldn't be together. At least not until Penny was well and truly over him.

Or she could tell him she didn't have feelings for him, which they both knew was a lie, and force him to move on. She wouldn't say a word about Penny being the reason behind her actions, and maybe Penny would just be able to spark his interest. That way she could keep Penny as a friend, but where would it leave her with Nick?

'Your life is a mess, sort it out,' Claudia said quietly to herself. She put her game face on and was about to stride into the building when she heard a familiar shriek.

'Claaaaaaudia! Hello, my darling!' Christine was descending the steps in a long baby pink satin gown, accompanied by Penny in full costume. It was a beautiful sight, if an unwelcome one at this moment.

'Hey, Claud, what are you doing here?' Penny grinned.

'*Hello*! Lovely!' said Claudia. 'I'm just, um, I heard you were coming tonight, Christine, so I thought I'd come and say hello.'

'Twice in one week, I'm such a lucky girl.'

'Twice? Have you ladies been hanging out without me?' scolded Penny.

'This one needed a bit of sense knocked in to her about my Nick. I am pleased you two are back on friendly terms.'

SHUSH, WOMAN.

'When were you not on friendly terms?' Penny looked at Claudia, confusion washing over her face.

'She just means, you know, when I was avoiding men after Seth.'

'It was that Christmas party that did it,' teased Christine, winking at Claudia.

'What happened at the party?' asked Penny.

'I think Nick might have got a bit caught up in the moment, nearly turned our Claudia into the one that got away.'

Penny frowned at Claudia. 'I didn't know anything about this.'

'We just had a disagreement about something. It's over now.'

'Or is it just beginning?' Christine chuckled. 'He's been back to his happy little Christmas Elf-self since he got *you* back.'

'I didn't know anything was wrong. You two have seemed super-cosy over the last week, practically dating—'

Claudia's mouth was dry as she watched Penny's penny drop. The two girls stared at each other, Claudia with panic and regret and that horrible feeling when you've royally messed something up, and Penny with clarity and hurt.

Claudia saw Penny's eyes fill up with tears and in that moment she'd never felt worse, even after all the crap she'd been through in the last week and a half. She was supposed to always mop up those tears, not cause them.

'Christine,' Claudia said quietly, 'I just need to have a chatter with Penny for a mo. Do you mind if I steal her away?'

'Of course, angels, girl-talk time. I'll go and buy a programme, and maybe another brandy.'

Claudia and Penny crossed the street in silence and sat down next to the Young Dancer statue. Claudia didn't know where to start.

'You and Nick: are you together?' Penny whispered, a line of black eye make-up dribbling down each cheek.

'No, no we're not, we're ... um—'

'What? Spit it out. Tell me what's been going on behind my back.'

'Nothing's happened.'

'Something's happened, I can see it in your face.' She looked really mad. She was giving Claudia the look she gave her ex-boyfriends, but this time with additional pain laced in.

'I promise you, nothing has happened. Nick and I ... we've got weirdly closer over the last week. He's been so attentive – just like you said – and there have been some sparks. Just tiny ones. But as soon as you said you liked him I knew I had to back off.'

'Have you two kissed?'

'*No*. Penny, there's no way I would do anything to hurt you.'

'But what about before you knew how I felt? What

went on at the party? What did Christine mean by "Nick got caught up in the moment"?'

'It was me that got caught up in the moment.' Her actions still made her cringe to think about them. 'I was drunk and felt something, and tried to kiss him but he wasn't having any of it.'

'Then what happened?'

'Then I spent a miserable thirty-six hours stewing over everything, questioning mine and Nick's whole relationship. I couldn't stop thinking about him, and finally we talked it out over that Sunday roast.'

'And?'

'And then I came over to yours, and you told me how you felt.'

'Why didn't you just tell me you liked him?'

'Because I was a total chicken and you seemed to like him for a more proper reason than me. You wanted his baby.'

'I don't want his baby if he likes you.'

'But I didn't know for sure he did like me then. I thought I might have just been reading things wrong; a bit desperate after Seth.'

'Don't play the Seth card.' Ouch. 'So now you know he does like you?'

'Yes. He told me last night.'

'At the dinner?'

'Yes.'

'So he was the reason you looked so over Seth?'

Claudia nodded. 'Seth who?' she deadpanned.

'How did it make you feel? When he told you?' Penny sounded so blue.

Claudia considered the question. 'Relieved that it wasn't only in my head, peaceful, happy. But also it killed me because I'm scared of losing you.'

'You must have thought I was such an idiot, swooning over a guy who liked you instead.'

'No, I didn't – I don't – think that at all. It just all got really complicated and I was trying to be a good friend and I'm an idiot and I messed it up and more than anything I just wanted you to be happy. So I came here tonight to tell him—'

'To tell him what?'

'I'm not sure yet. But it would be based around nothing ever happening between us.'

Penny looked away and over at the Opera House. She lapsed into silence for some time.

'I'm really sorry, Penny.'

'Well there's no point in telling him nothing can happen between you.'

'What?'

'If you like each other, he's obviously not going to want to go out with me. You do like him, don't you?'

'Yes.'

'Just don't tell him about my little crush.'

'No, Penny, I'm not going to go out with Nick with you feeling like this, you'll hate me for ever.'

'Don't be a dick, of course I won't.'

'You won't?'

'No.' She let out the most ginormous sigh. 'To be honest, thinking about it, maybe I just fancied Nick in the way you fall head over heels for the leading man in a rom-com. *Because* he was so devoted to *you*.'

'But you're still crying.'

'That's true, but that's because I've lost something I never had, not because of something you've taken from me.'

'How are you such a good person after all of this? Why don't you hate me?'

'Because if I hated you no one would do the "Single Ladies" routine with me at the wedding next week.'

'We can do that routine to every song they play if you want to.'

Penny laughed. She fanned her eyes. 'Do I look horrendous?'

'Never.'

'Look at me, the ballerina crying next to the statue of the ballerina. I feel very dramatic.' At that moment, wispy snowflakes began to fall. 'Oh!' Penny cried. 'This is even better, this would make a great photo.' She ran her fingers down her face, spreading bigger, thicker streaks of mascara. 'How's this? Do I look incredibly dramatic now?'

Nick crossed the road. 'Right, who's dumped my mum? You know she'll wander over to Dreamboys. Penny, what's wrong?'

Penny smiled and wiped her eyes on Claudia's coat. 'I'm just really upset for Claudia because she's going to have to see your willy.'

'She is?' Nick looked pleased as punch.

Claudia was unendingly grateful to Penny for not blowing up; there was literally nothing she would not let her friend do or say at this moment. So Claudia simply chuckled and shrugged at Nick. 'Maybe.'

'Okay,' she sighed. 'I'm going to leave you two to have a much-needed chinwag.'

Penny heaved herself up and Claudia draped her in a hug. 'If you need a drink, I know someone in that restaurant who's very good at cheering up sobbing Brits.'

'A drink would be perfection.'

'Ask for Billy, and tell him to put it on a tab for Claudia. I'll go in and pay it tomorrow.'

'A boy, hey? Even better.' Off Penny went into the restaurant, leaving Nick and Claudia grinning at each other in the snow like a couple of penguins.

'Is Penny okay?' Nick asked.

'She's ... fine. She just gets emotional sometimes. About having a baby and stuff.'

'She's going to make such a good mum. I hope she finds her answer soon.'

'I think she will.'

Claudia shuffled on the spot, not knowing if she should go to Nick or wait for him to come to her. All her rehearsed scenarios, of *I like you, but* and *I don't feel the same way* were no longer relevant. Now she had to tell him she liked him.

She had to tell a BOY that she FANCIED him.

She was *this close* to stealing Julia Robert's 'just a girl' speech from Notting Hill when Nick stepped a little closer and ran his fingers through her hair, and her entire nervous system disintegrated.

'It's snowing,' stated Nick. 'As much as I like you, I don't want you to see my willy now.'

'I guess I can wait a little, as much as I like you.' There. She'd said it.

'You do?'

'Um, quite a lot.'

'Well then, bestie, can I take you on a date tomorrow? An actual date, that you *agree* is a date?'

Claudia suppressed the urge to take off all her clothes and streak with happiness. Instead, she concurred to go on her seventh date this Christmas. How things were changing.

'Let's do this,' said Nick. 'And because it's a real date, I can feel you up, right?'

YES. 'No you can't. Just because we've had a thousand years of getting to know each other doesn't mean you can skip all the traditional dating stuff. All the romantic stuff.'

'Fair enough, traditional dating it is.' He leaned into her, their smiles centimetres apart. She didn't dare move her face. 'So I guess that also means no kissing on the first date.'

He stood back with a grin but this time she didn't mind him pulling him away as much. This time she was breathless.

Nick had gone back into the Opera House to find his mum, so Claudia stuck her head around the door of the restaurant. Penny was perched at the bar, bathed in soft light, her tutu falling over the edge of the stool. Next to her was a large glass of wine, along with a pile of balled-up napkins smeared with make-up. From where Claudia stood, she was relieved to see that Penny's face was scrubbed clean and happily animated. Billy couldn't take his eyes off her; he looked enthralled.

'Did you see sharks?' she was asking.

'Yep.'

'Did you see wrasse?'

'Yep.'

'Did you see rays?'

'Yep.'

This could go on for a while. Claudia smiled and left without a word.

Claudia heaved the second boot onto her foot and tugged at the laces with all her strength.

'You know, that might be easier if you took those whopping ski mittens off,' said Nick.

'Are you insane? It's freezing. I can't believe you're standing there in a T-shirt.'

Nick put his hands on his hips and struck a model pose. 'This is what happens when you're tough and manly: snow doesn't affect you.'

Claudia stood up and the two of them clomped out of the marquee to the ice rink, behind which loomed the ornate façade of the Natural History Museum. It was an extremely cold, bright-blue day; the kind of day that feels like peppermint mouthwash is being vaporised out into the air.

'You can skate, right?' asked Nick.

'Yeah, I used to do it all the time. You?'

'Nope, not a bit.'

'What? Why did you suggest ice skating?'

'Because it's festive, it's one week to Christmas, we've never done it together, you've certainly never done it on a date and, frankly, if it means I get to spend a couple of hours holding on and accidently bumping up against you it sounds like a pretty good date to me.'

'In that case, this was a very good idea.' As Nick took her paw and grinned down at her, Claudia couldn't have been happier. How had things worked out so perfectly? She couldn't take her eyes off his yummy bare arms, and so slammed into the wall of the rink.

'Are you okay?' he laughed. 'What's wrong with you?'

'You're what's wrong with me!' Had his arms always been so defined? *Of course they have. Get a grip.*

They stepped onto the ice and Claudia spun in a smooth circle. By the time she was facing Nick again he was spreadeagled, leaning over and holding the hand of a large bald man.

'Is this one yours, love?' the man asked.

'Yes he is,' Claudia said proudly, extracting Nick's hand and holding it in her own. 'Nick, look at me, up here.' He raised his torso up and gave her a huge grin.

'*I'm skating!*'

'Well, kind of.' She towed him along, her skating backwards, him sliding, feet still, body and arms stretched out in front of him.

'It's very hot that you're so good at this,' he called to her across the distance.

'You can do it too, come on.' She guided him into an upright position but he stayed gripping her hands.

They slid in close to each other until their bodies touched. Claudia raised an eyebrow at him. 'No rewards yet, mister. You have a lot more work to do to impress me out here.' She whooshed backwards and beckoned for him to follow.

Nick thud-thud-thudded across the ice after her. Claudia's laugh caught in the wind. 'You're like a yeti; stop picking your feet up.'

'Look at me, Claud – look at me. I am Phillip Schofield!'

She zipped back past him. 'Why are you Phillip Schofield?'

'He dances on ice. Like I'm doing.'

'He presents the TV show, I don't think he joins in—'

'You're such a bloody liar, Claudia, don't you ruin my dream. I AM PHILLIP SCHOFIELD!' he shouted, whizzing past her in a straight line, fists in the air, and landing with a thwack against the barrier.

Claudia slid in next to him. 'I have to ask you something. Are you nervous at all?'

'Nervous? Of you? You're not scary.'

'Of . . . us. Of our first date. Of things to come.'

'I'm not nervous.'

Claudia took a breath and whooshed away. She skated as fast as she could, ducking, spinning, unable to keep the smile from her face. The booming bass of the pumped-out Christmas music reverberated through her, and though it wasn't traditional dance, in her heart she was dancing like no one was watching. On the ice she was free, and couldn't remember being this happy.

The rush gave her cheeks a glow and a confidence she'd all but lost recently. She whizzed close to Nick, pulled off a mitten and trickled fingertips down his arm as she passed. He tried to grab her but missed.

She circled him and took his hands, spinning him in a small circle with her. She tilted up her chin until their lips were close, then she spun him hard and he whirled around, laughing.

'You're killing me, woman.'

'You said you chased me for years, you can't handle a little longer?'

'No. Come here and kiss me.'

'Nope. What, do you think you can stop trying now you've got me on a date?'

'I've got you on four dates, five if you count the dinner when Penny showed up. So yeah, I think I've put in all the effort I need to.'

Claudia laughed just as the voices of Tom Jones and Cerys Matthews rang out across the rink. Nick was improving, and the two of them skated laps, bellowing the words to 'Baby, It's Cold Outside' to each other in their loudest, most God-awful singing voices.

'You,' Claudia panted, as they swirled to a stop in the centre of the rink. 'You make me happy.'

'You're all right, too.' Nick put his arms around Claudia, causing her legs to wobble.

'Excuse me, I thought we said no kissing on the first date,' she whispered.

He moved closer and her legs gave way. She stumbled on the spot and Nick held her tight. 'You know we'll both go if you do,' he said.

She just needed a few more minutes to prepare, this was a *big deal*. She ducked and slid out from under his arms and skated away.

'Don't make me throw you down and do you right here, because I will and it's cold, and the ice'll make your hair frizz up like you hate,' Nick yelled, following her.

Claudia took a deep breath. Time to stop being a chicken. This was going to happen. She was dying for it to happen. She stopped and spun round.

Splat.

Nick hurtled into her and they both sprawled on the ice. Nick lay on top of her, simultaneously laughing hysterically and screaming in agony, pointing at his leg. 'Pulled ... muscle ... can't move ... owwwww.'

Claudia laughed and shrieked under the weight of him.

'Hey – get off that girl!' she heard someone shout. 'I heard him threaten her – he said he was going to throw her down.'

Claudia turned her head but couldn't see through her blurry tears of laughter and couldn't force any words through her guffaws.

Nick was trying to prop himself up on his elbows to take the weight off her, but they kept slipping on the ice, slamming his body back down and only making their laughing fit worse.

Suddenly she was released as Nick was hauled off her by two men in red jackets. She lay panting, staring at the sky. Well that wasn't how she'd expected her first experience of Nick on top of her to be. She kind of liked it, though.

She sat up, waving away the hands that reached for

her. She turned her head to see Nick getting a stern telling-off from the stewards outside the rink. He was gesticulating wildly, his face flushed, whilst trying to shake the pain from his leg.

As she got her breath back, the ice soaking through her jeans to her knickers, she saw two police officers approach Nick. What was going on over there?

Oh no. They each took one of Nick's arms and started leading him away. 'Where are you taking him?' she called. They didn't hear. Nick looked back at her.

She struggled to push herself up, but the second she dug the blade of the skate into the ice a shooting pain burst from her ankle and sent darts up her leg that brought tears to her eyes. Her old injury.

Nick was being taken away by the police; she had to do something.

But the pain was *intense*.

Claudia couldn't get up.

Date Eight

St Paul's Cathedral, City of London

Claudia leaned against the crutches, tittering to herself. Any minute now, any minute ...

The doors to the police station opened and out Nick sauntered, rubbing his eyes, his T-shirt crumpled and his bare arms looking very sorrowful in the late-afternoon shade. She hopped forward. 'Nick—'

'Whoa – what did I do to you?' He raced over, mortified.

'I think it's broken,' she squeaked, her eyes beginning to water with the pressure of trying not to laugh. Nick dropped to the snowy ground and tenderly held her foot like Prince Charming.

She burst, a huge 'PAH-HA-HA' escaping her. She was crap at playing tricks. 'I'm sorry, it was a joke, I don't need these at all.' She put the crutches down, mopping her eyes. God, she was funny.

'What? So you're okay?'

'I'm fine.'

'But you're not standing properly. Did I hurt you?'

'Nope, nothing more than a mild sprain, as confirmed by medical professionals.'

'I don't understand what's going on! How the world has changed since I've been in the slammer.' Nick scratched his head. 'Why did they give you crutches?'

'They didn't, Penny had these lying around. I thought I'd trick you.'

'Penny is such a hoarder, and you're such a wannabe Ashton Kutcher, but you always laugh three seconds into a prank. Is the ankle support fake?'

'No, that's real, but honestly it's no big deal.'

'I am a crap date. I'm really sorry.'

'Stop it, I had the best time.' Despite everything, she really had. When she couldn't get up there'd been a whole commotion of stewards and burly men who'd helped her off the ice, and after a little flexing and a quick check by a first-aider, followed by a very unflattering amount of cankle-swellage, Claudia had been sent on her way. But not before she demanded to know where Nick had been taken.

She'd called the police station, insisted that of course she wasn't about to press charges, and they'd told her he was being held but would be out later that afternoon. She'd hobbled her way over and waited, and Nick had called her about five minutes ago to say he was on his way out.

'I'm going to make it up to you,' said Nick. 'I'm working this eve, but tomorrow night let's do something much more low key and I will treat you like a princess. No, better, because that's a bit cheesy. Like one of those queens that people carry about in the air. No! Like a Christmas fairy. No . . .'

'Treat me like you did this morning, I liked it. I don't mind a little rough and tumble.'

'Good to know.'

Claudia reached into her bag. 'I brought you a jumper.'

He unravelled the bundle to reveal a large black hoodie with 'Fat Willy's Surf Shack, Newquay' emblazoned on the front in neon letters. 'Claud, this is obviously a big stinking man's jumper. I can't wear Seth's old shit, it's too weird.'

'Hey, that's *my* hoodie. Shut up and put it on or I'll march you straight back into that station. So what happened with the police?'

'Well,' said Nick, pulling on the hoodie, 'prepare to go weak at the knees because you're now dating a member of the criminal underworld.'

'They didn't *arrest* you? You didn't do anything!'

'Okay, they didn't arrest me, but I did get a caution.'

'For what?'

Nick smiled sheepishly. 'Threatening behaviour, assault and, um, indecency in a public place.'

'What?' This was bad. But also just a little bit funny.

'Threatening behaviour because some bloke heard

me yell that I was going to throw you down. I promise that was a joke.'

'I know, and you meant it as a nice joke.' Quite a yummy joke.

'Assault because I did then throw you down.'

'You *knocked* me down; surely that means most ice-skaters should be done for assault at some point.'

'And indecency because of the, erm, writhing about and inappropriate screaming. That one really should have been slapped on both of us.'

Claudia was laughing so hard she had to grab the crutches for support. 'Did the police really say we were inappropriately screaming?'

'Yep,' said Nick, a smirk on his face. 'It's a family place, Claud, and not suitable for sex-starved teenagers.'

'Did they really think I was a teenager?' she asked with pride.

'I think they meant it more as a metaphor.'

'Oh.'

'Don't worry, you're not that withered and haggard yet.' He took the crutches from her and held out his arm. 'Come on, let's blow my dosh on a cab home for you. It's the least I can do. Then your big hunk of an outlaw has to go to work.'

'I'm glad they didn't bang you up.'

'Me too. Do you dare to go on a date with me again tomorrow night?'

'Yes please, I'm not sure how much longer I can go

without that kiss.' Urgh, saying that to Nick sounded like the dorkiest thing on earth.

Date Eight was set, and she couldn't wait to open the advent calendar door on that one.

'But if you *had* to.'

'If I *had* to …' Claudia pondered as she tugged a black strapless dress up her body bit by bit. They were standing in Penny's flat the next morning, choosing outfits for the upcoming wedding from Penny's extensive, but a size too small for Claudia, wardrobe. 'Then I'd snog Richard Madeley, marry James May and avoid Boris Johnson. But that's not fair because you know I fancy them all.'

'That looks nice,' said Penny, once Claudia had stuffed both boobs inside the dress.

'Black, though, for a wedding?'

'I think black's totally fine now, especially for a winter wedding. You'd look weirder in a floral sundress. How's this?' Penny slid on a pale silver maxi.

'Nice, but a bit too close to bridal. Next.'

Penny whipped off her dress while Claudia rolled off the LBD, freeing her flesh and nearly taking her knickers with her. She picked up a pink kaftan.

'So, is Nick now your "date" for the wedding? Is he going to be your plus-one?'

'I don't know. Neither of us were going to be taking

anyone else, but I don't want it to be "me and Nick", and then "you", I want it to be all three of us going together. Unless there's anyone you were thinking of bringing?'

'I don't know,' answered Penny vaguely. She looked Claudia up and down. 'No, definitely not the kaftan.'

'But it's comfortable.'

'It looks absurd. You look like you're only going to the wedding so you can tag along on the honeymoon.'

'Even in heels? Even if I put a belt around it?'

'No. Next.'

Penny slid herself with ease into the black strapless dress and Claudia reluctantly swapped the kaftan for a navy blue shift with a smattering of pearls. The girls assessed each other.

'Winners?' asked Penny.

'Chicken dinners,' Claudia confirmed. 'Penny, are you *sure* you're okay about Nick and me?'

'Of course, I said I was.'

'I know, but you said yourself that if you two were together it might have changed the dynamics. Are you worried about that now?'

'Should I be worried? Are you two going to get all "smug couple" on me?'

'No way, I swear it'll be like nothing's changed.'

'Then I don't mind. You don't need to keep asking me,' Penny said. 'Are you going to take the job? Now that you're banging each other?'

'We're not banging each other!'

'You will be.'

'No we won't. Gross! Nick can't see me naked. And I still haven't decided about the job.' Tick-tock, tick-tock.

'You haven't? It's only a week till Christmas. After New Year we have a three-week break and then it's back to work in the last week of January. I expect they'll want you to start then.'

'Hmm.' Claudia hated being reminded that she had a decision to make, it only made her want to ignore it longer out of spite.

'Basically, you'd have to start in a month. How much notice would you need to give at Edurné's?'

'Two weeks, minimum.'

'So what are you going to do?'

'Do I really have to make a decision soon?' *Go away.*

'If we've learnt one thing this week, is it not that you need to figure out your own feelings and get them out there – make decisions – the sooner the better?' Penny raised an eyebrow at Claudia.

'Yes,' Claudia mumbled.

'Then go home and sort yourself out.'

'I'm going to go home and sort myself out.'

'Good idea, bugger off.'

That afternoon, with her hair tied in three unbecoming pigtails in an attempt to dry it in mermaid waves, Claudia was back in her flat surrounded by holly leaf-shaped Post-its. It was very selfish of everyone she knew not to work in an office with a pilferable stationery cupboard, so that she'd actually had to go to WH Smith and *buy* some supplies on her way home from Penny's.

The obligatory Christmas movie was playing in the background, this time *Home Alone 4*, which she was refusing to give her full attention out of loyalty to Macaulay Culkin.

Claudia shook the last of the tube of glitter onto the swirly glue-writing she'd carefully scribed at the top of a large piece of black cardboard. The board was divided into three. ROYAL BALLET JOB – PROS, ROYAL BALLET JOB – CONS and DREAM JOB.

'Right, Claud, time to get serious: let's start with pros and cons.' She loved talking to herself nowadays; she was *usually* good company and *always* found her own jokes funny.

'Work with Nick and Penny,' she said, writing the same on a holly leaf. She hovered between *Pros* and *Cons*. Would they get sick to death of each other? Would everyone think she was a total wet wipe for working with her boyfriend? But then, they wouldn't really be working *together*, they'd just be milling around doing their own things, maybe meeting for cuppas. She stuck it in the *Pro* column for now.

'He's not even your actual boyfriend yet, Miss Desperado.' She picked up another Post-it. 'It's not my dream job.' Con. No – that was a cop-out and needed more breaking down. She screwed up the Post-it.

'Still won't be dancing.' Con.

'Don't know anything about photography.' Con.

'People have faith in me, that I can do it.' Pro. That was nice. She put this one at the top of the board.

'New adventure.' Pro.

'Helps get out of rut.' Pro.

'Might always feel like a bit of a groupie.' Con.

'Lots of freedom.' Pro.

'Get to build my own schedule.' Definite pro. She could work it around the new Beyoncé dance class she'd seen advertised at Sadler's Wells. Priorities.

'Will miss Edurné ladies A LOT.' Big, huge con.

'Edurné ladies just round corner for posh-lady lunches.' Hmm, pro.

'If I take it, I'd have to hand in my notice and disappoint Laura.' Urgh, con.

'If I don't, I'd have to turn it down and disappoint Nick.' That was a good reason for taking the job, which meant an extra Post-it in the *Pro* column.

She surveyed the board, and picked up another leaf. 'Exciting,' she whispered, and stuck it in the pro column.

'Scary.' She stuck that in cons. Then she pulled it back off and shuffled it over to the line separating the two. Scary was not necessarily bad. Roller-coasters were scary but fun, and you always felt brave and glad you did it afterwards. Unless it made you puke.

Food for thought. Time to move on to the *Dream Job* section.

'DANCING.' She wrote that in block capitals and put it directly under the heading.

'But not to an über-skilled professional level.' She stuck that under the DANCING Post-it. She had to face facts that it was a little too late for that.

'Fun.' 'Be my own boss.' 'Something *involved* – not on the sidelines.' Stick, stick, stick.

'Show other people how dancing can make them feel.' She thought back to how she'd felt on the ice rink, the music pumping through her body and the ecstatic happiness of spinning, twirling, letting it completely overtake you, and feeling like you're doing it *well*. It was an adrenalin rush, a sugar high she never felt anywhere else. She wanted that feeling to be part of her life.

Salivating at her DREAM JOB section, she thought of another con for the Royal Ballet offer. She didn't choose that job, it had been chosen for her. She didn't want to base her career on something someone else had decided would be a good fit.

'Not my dream job.' She underlined the *my*.

Lots of pros, lots of cons, lots of elements of a dream job to think about. Phew, that was probably enough of a step forward for today. She had bigger, more pressing and life-changing decisions to make now. No longer being the nineties – but seeing as it was Christmas – could she get away with glitter eyeshadow for her date tonight?

Nick had told Claudia she'd be picked up at six, but when she left her building she hadn't expected to see a silver Mercedes with a driver waiting for her. He handed her a note.

'Claud, sorry I can't be there in person – coming straight from work. I'll be waiting for you when you arrive. The driver knows where to go, you sit back and relax. Don't worry, he's not a murderer (he's my uncle).'

'*Bonjour*,' said the driver in a thick Cockney accent. '*Jem'apple* Dave. *Avay voo un* seat in the back.' He gestured to the car.

'*Merci, señor*,' said Claudia, climbing in.

Claudia saw something very exciting as she glided onto the leather seat. 'What's all this?'

A hamper sat next to her, filled with her favourite festive snacks: Waitrose all-butter mince pies, a Chocolate Orange, some roast turkey Kettle Chips, a flask which she opened and sniffed – gingerbread latte!, a box of Quality Street. And the Christmas *Radio Times* with a candy cane-shaped pen attached for circling TV essentials.

This was so thoughtful; no one had done anything like this for her before. It was a small gesture, but how well Nick knew her, how much thought he'd put into this. Claudia had never felt so far from missing Seth.

'Dave, have you seen all these things Nick's left?' she called to the front seat as he pulled out of the end of the road.

'He's a good lad, my nephew. Ooo, nearly forgot to give you this.' He passed back a huge plastic bag and Claudia pulled out an enormous pair of reindeer slippers, big enough to fit a man. There was another note tucked inside.

'These are mine, you can't bloody keep them, but thought you might want some comfy shoes for the journey so as not to cause your ankle any more pain. Sorry again about that!'

Claudia slipped her poorly ankle out of her tight-feeling boot and slid her foot into the big plush reindeer. She ripped into the box of mince pies and settled back to circle some Christmas TV as Dave edged through the traffic of London.

Bliss. If Nick were a set of questions in a magazine's *Is he Mr Right?* quiz, he'd be slowly ticking all the boxes.

Claudia was utterly engrossed in an internal debate as to whether to watch *Back to the Future* or *Jools Holland's Hootenanny* on New Year's Eve when she felt the car roll to a stop.

'Here we go, *madmanmoizelle*,' said Dave, opening her door.

She popped her foot back into her boot and stepped out in front of St Paul's Cathedral. 'Oh, we're here!' The columns were lit from beneath, the iconic dome peeping out above them. A dense queue of people dressed in smart yet toasty clothing snaked from the entrance around the side of the building.

The dusting of snow and smell of warm, sugary chestnuts gave Claudia the sense of being in Dickensian London. She waved goodbye to Dave, and was buying a bag of nuts for Nick when she heard him call her name.

She turned and leaped into his arms. 'You! How come you're so nice to me?'

'Hello, and you deserve it.'

This would be a good time for that kiss. But something was burning against her chest. She detangled herself and pulled away, peeling the bag of hot chestnuts from the front of her coat. 'These are for you.'

'Thanks, Claud!'

'It's nothing compared to what you gave to me, but I know you love them.' He gave her romance, he gave her adventure, he gave her happiness without her having to ask for it. All the things Seth never gave her. *Stop thinking about Seth*. She couldn't help it; the comparison left her awestruck. There *was* no comparison.

Nick took her hand and led her towards the cathedral.

'What are we here for?' she asked.

'A candlelit carol concert. Is that okay?'

'That sounds amazing. I've never even been in St Paul's; how bad is that?'

'Really? Then I hope we get in tonight. I had no idea it would be this busy.' They joined the end of the slowly moving queue.

'Did you manage to stay out of trouble today, you big crim?' Claudia teased.

'I showed a few people who was boss. And I totally nicked a spirit level from work. But I'll take it back in a couple of days. I'm just convinced my Christmas tree's wonky and it's driving me mad.'

'On a scale of one to ten, how excited are you about Christmas Day?'

'Ten times ten. But it's not just about the actual day, the whole month gets me excited. Seeing this city transform, in both looks and atmosphere, it feels like a mini-adventure every year. Do you know what I mean?'

'I do, but until this year I guess I've always enjoyed it from the outside looking in. A bit like when you watch a Christmas movie. It feels nice and festive, but it's not a unique experience just for you. This year it's like I'm *in* a Christmas movie.'

'I'm glad you feel like that.'

'Do you know this is the eighth date I've been on this Christmas?' Eight dates. That was, like, a 700 per cent increase on last year's dating record as a whole. She wasn't counting Mikael. Yes, it was technically a date but it was very short, not very sweet, and he was a knob.

'First eight of many.'

'Do you think we can keep this up?'

Nick took hold of the ends of her woolly scarf and smiled at her. 'As God as my witness, through the power vested in me, as we stand here outside the massive Pauly-Wauly's Cathedral, I vow to you that I will take you on as many dates as my humble wallet will allow.'

Claudia wrapped her scarf tails around his hands. 'And I pledge my allegiance not to be a grumpy old cow, not to refuse to change out of my pyjamas on Sundays, and not to get too outstandingly drunk, stampy and crazy with you again.'

'Actually, I'm pretty fond of grumpy, pyjama'd, wasted Claudia.'

'Okay. How about if I promise to take you on lots of dates too?'

'Cool.'

'But since you made me take back my other vow, I now no longer promise not to be stampy and crazy. So you better give me that kiss tonight.'

He smiled at her. 'Come and get it.'

The queue moved forward. *Come and get it*. Claudia's cheeks flushed pink – she needed a cold flannel.

'You come and get it,' she said shyly.

'It's up here; it's been waiting for you for years. Come and get it.'

She had no cool left, if she'd ever had any in the first place. She should just lie face down in the snow and let herself sizzle. It was the only way.

A severe-looking woman with tight curls and a ferocious bosom under her trench coat turned around. 'If you don't go and get it soon, my girl, I will.'

'Hello, how many?' asked a petite girl, stepping in between them. Claudia hadn't even noticed they'd moved to the front of the queue.

'Um, two please,' she croaked. Nick was grinning like a Cheshire cat.

The girl handed them each a small white candle with a paper bobèche to catch the wax drips, and showed them inside.

Black and white tiles swept the vast floor of the cathedral, with wide, intricately carved arches rising on either side and delicate chandeliers hanging low from the ceiling. Claudia and Nick were ushered into the end of a tightly packed pew that seemed a million miles away from the altar.

'We were lucky to get in,' Nick whispered, achingly close to her face. *Stop it, you're in church now.* 'Look, they're shutting the doors.'

'Can't people stand in that big gap at the back?'

'No, I think that's where all the choir and, um, important people hang out before they walk down the middle.'

'Have you been to this before?'

'No, but I YouTubed it.'

'So this is new for both of us? That's cool.' Claudia looked out over the sea of tiny flickering flames. 'Do you think we should have asked Penny?'

'On our date?'

'Well, how do we differentiate what will be a date and what should be the kind of thing all three of us used to do together? Won't she feel left out?' *I'm sorry, Penny*.

'You do make a good point. We won't leave her out of things, but I'm sure Penny knows that we need a bit of space to get things off the ground. Then, once you're comfortable, I won't be putting in nearly as much effort any more.'

'Me neither. I'm not even going to bother with my fancy customised undies. You're just going to get the ones that didn't even merit a bedazzling.'

'I hear those bedazzled undies are so gross they'd make Victoria spill every one of her Secrets,' he whispered to her. 'But Claud, they're your *underwear*. You can't talk about them to me when I can't have my wicked way with you. Especially in church.'

Claudia couldn't keep the beam from her face as the organ started up. Look at her, being all sexy and exciting. Nick thought she was sexy. Ha! Little did he know.

No, she *was* sexy; she'd changed this past week.

She slipped her free hand into his and they turned to watch the choir gather behind them. The lights were dimmed, and with the flickering candles and haunting melody of 'O Holy Night' rising to the rafters you could be a priest or an atheist but you couldn't deny it was a beautiful sight.

Claudia was awestruck as the choir and their sea of perfect voices glided down the nave and dispersed at the stalls. It was magical. Totally like that scene in *Home Alone* where the little red-haired girl sings the same song and Kevin and Old Man Marley are watching. It was nice to be so cultured.

The carol ended and Nick squeezed Claudia's hand. With one hand in Nick's, and the other holding her little candle upright, Claudia unfolded the carol booklet they'd been given with difficulty, then held it out for them both to see. The cathedral erupted into a joyful sing-along of 'The Holly and the Ivy'. Claudia lip-synced her way through while Nick boomed out the wrong notes and often the wrong words.

She started to giggle and soon she was shaking and red and had to stuff the end of her scarf in her mouth. Nick looked down at her with twinkling eyes.

'Come on, mime-artist, give it a go,' he whispered in her ear between carols.

'I can't ...'

'Of course you can, I dare you.'

Okay, she could do this. The organist started up again, the first bars of 'Joy to the World' pealing out across the congregation. *Come on, risk taker, this is no big deal*. Claudia was going to give it everything she had.

'JOY—' *Oh balls. Crap, crap, crap*. It was the wrong moment and she was the only one who'd started singing. The ultimate humiliation.

She heard the sniggers around her, and was pretty sure there were many more she couldn't hear further afield. Nick burst at the seams, his laughter so loud that even when the rest of the cathedral eventually started to sing it could barely drown him out.

Seeing her mortified face Nick calmed down and wrapped her in a one-armed hug, drawing her into his chest, still chuckling away. She resumed her lip-syncing for the rest of the carol.

Claudia couldn't keep her eyes off Nick. She peeped at him constantly, often finding him peeping back at her. It was a bit of an eighties cliché, but he looked mighty fine by candlelight.

She would like a snog, please. Badly. She tried to concentrate on the words to 'God Rest Ye Merry Gentlemen' but found herself licking her lips and fantasising about being pinned up against a wall with him pressing into her.

For crying out loud, she was in the cathedral that Charles and Diana were married in. Claudia expected that Diana had managed to get through the service without becoming a quivering wreck over the thought of Charles's lips.

All this standing was beginning to make Claudia's ankle a little sore. As another new carol started she shifted her weight, looking around the church.

Bloody hell. Are you kidding me?

About twenty rows ahead, on the opposite side of the aisle, was Seth. Claudia craned her neck as surreptitiously as she could to see who he was with. He was with *her*, the 'this is awkward' girl from outside the pub. The one that Seth claimed he had nothing going on with.

They were on a *date?* What a punch in the back of the head. What made her special? For a fleeting moment Claudia felt a pang for the life she and Seth never had.

Claudia looked at Nick who was merrily ding-donging on high. She tried to concentrate on the words but every few seconds her brain sent a pulse to her eyes forcing them to look at Seth and see what he was doing. Most of the time he was playing with his phone.

Damn it, Seth. She was having probably the best date ever and there he was again. Distracting her. Ruining this.

During the polite, British clapping between carols, Claudia pulled on Nick's hand. 'Are you having a good time?' he asked.

'I'm having the best time, but look who's over there.'

Nick followed her gaze. His face went stony.

Claudia tugged his hand again. 'I don't want to see him; can we sneak to the back?'

They shuffled out of the pew and tiptoed towards the

exit. They were nearly clear of the aisle when Claudia's bad ankle twisted and she slid, gasping and her coat making a noisy, flapping sound.

Nick caught her arm and swung her round, spinning them both into an alcove out of view of the rest of the carollers. Their candles blew out.

They stood in the dark, pressed against each other, Nick taking Claudia's weight as he leaned back against the wall. A thousand voices were chorusing 'Hark! The herald angels sing' but Claudia was only aware of the shallow sound of Nick's breath against her face, causing her eyelashes to flutter.

She could have stayed where she was for a hundred years; suddenly all was forgotten and everything felt spot-on. She ran a hand up his chest, his heat emanating through his jumper. She felt his firm body underneath, and his hand, which rested on her lower back, became heavier, drawing her closer. Claudia's fingertips reached his neck. She felt him take her candle from her other hand and bury it, along with his own candle, in his coat pocket. And then he touched her face.

This was no longer a game, no longer something to run away from or giggle about. This was happening now. She rose onto tiptoes, Nick holding her up and tilting her head with his hand. She pulled on his neck so they met halfway.

Soft and warm, gentle and tugging, Claudia was so mesmerised by the sensations of Nick's lips that she barely recognised the two of them were immersed in their first kiss until they were midway through. He tasted of the sweet chestnuts, he bumped his nose against hers, and she could feel that he was smiling through his kisses.

Thank God he hadn't kissed her at the Christmas party. The alcohol would have drowned these sparks. She never wanted to kiss him without the utter clarity she was feeling now.

He breathed her in and she sank deeper into him. He was like a massive cake that she didn't have to share with anyone; she wanted to press her whole face into him and say to hell with the world. His hand moved up from her back and he was clasping the sides of her face. There was barely room for a whisker to fit between them but still she pressed closer, her body craving to be as near to him as humanly possible.

Damn these clothes . . .

Naughty. She dragged her lips off him and they regarded each other with giddy smiles. 'I'm having some very unsuitable-for-church thoughts,' she whispered.

'Me too,' he grinned, his thumb tracing her spine in a way that made her tremble and want to clamber up onto him.

She dived in for one more smooch; she couldn't keep away. Claudia had never wanted someone so badly. Usually sex was something that was fun-ish after a glass or two of wine, or just something to be endured. She'd never felt that movie-style fire. Until now.

They broke away again, panting heavily.

'We shouldn't be doing this here, we'll go straight to hell.'

'Do you want to leave?' Nick asked, the question loaded with meaning.

Conflict churned inside Claudia. She badly wanted to follow her instinct and go with him ... but she needed more time. This shouldn't happen off the back of a situation involving Seth; she was a completely different person with Nick and didn't want it to have anything to do with her last relationship. Her sex drive, or lack of, had burned her in the past and she wanted it to be right. She wanted to be utterly prepared. But her body was begging her not to take too much time. 'Can we have another date tomorrow night?'

'Of course. Where do you want to go?'

'Let's not go anywhere.' She tried to slow her breathing. Tomorrow, she could wait until tomorrow. 'Come over to mine.'

Date Nine

Claudia's flat, West Kensington

'Sorry,' said Claudia to the old lady who rammed into the back of her.

'No time to stand around in the doorway, my girl, I've got shortbread to buy.' With a steely look she stamped into the department store.

Christmas shopping on Oxford Street was one of the best and worst things about Christmas in the capital. The shops bulged with stock – racks of gloves, novelty slippers, gadgets, gizmos, stocking fillers and those special somethings. At every turn, beauty counters offered spritzes of special-edition cinnamon-scented perfumes and food halls filled hungry shoppers' tummies with sample mince pies and flowing prosecco. Elaborate window displays – Santa's grottoes, Christmas mornings, enchanted forests – rivalled the Tate for artistic masterpieces. Shoppers were rosy-cheeked, twinkly-eyed and flinging money at the cashiers like Santa after a little too much Christmas spirit.

But it didn't take long for them to transform into

desperate last-minute buyers fighting over the last jelly bean-pooping reindeer toy. Claudia had one very important present to buy, and even though this was her third department store she still had no idea where to start. To the piped music of 'It's the Most Wonderful Time of the Year' and the reindeer bell-like cha-ching of a hundred cash registers, she stuck out her elbows and marched through Selfridges. What the helling hell was she going to get Nick – her now sort-of boyfriend – for Christmas?

'Excuse me,' she said to a sales assistant, accidently jabbing her in the face with a roll of pretty, overpriced wrapping paper. 'Any chance you could tell me which level man stuff is on?'

'Man stuff?'

'Like, gifts or something. Not Gillette shower gel sets, something a bit more special.'

'Why not try men's accessories, first floor?'

Off Claudia went, joining a queue to go up the escalator, on which she stood with her face pressed against someone's Build-A-Bear box, and emerged on a floor she immediately felt underdressed for. The men's department. All greys and tweeds and more greys and model-types trying on suit jackets in front of mirrors when really they should be reclining with a Scotch and the *Financial Times*.

She fingered the arm of a plaid Vivienne Westwood suit. *What to buy, what to buy* ... But yet again her thoughts drifted to Date Nine. *The* Date. Nick had given her five awesome dates this month, and tonight she'd had an idea for a date he would love. They were to meet late afternoon near the Tower of London for a Dickensian Christmas group walking tour. Then it was back to hers for a home-cooked meal. And then . . .

Anyway, must get on. Claudia strode in a direction that hopefully led to accessories and after a loop and a half of the level she found them. Well, she found some leathery things intermingled with some electronic stuff, which was a start.

'What do you want to buy?' asked a striking waif in a sharply tailored grey dress. She had a thick Dutch accent and icy-blonde hair. Claudia resisted the urge to ask her for a photo.

'Do you work here?' asked Claudia.

'Yes,' said the waif, pointing at a Selfridges badge that said MONIQUE, and Claudia felt like a nitwit.

'I'm looking for a present for my new boyfriend; I'm not sure what to buy him.'

'You should buy him the new iPad. It is new and boys like new.'

'Oooh no, I can't quite afford to spend that much.'

'How about this Aspinal iPad case?' Monique plucked a mock-croc wallet from a nearby shelf and handed it to Claudia.

'Well, I don't think he has an iPad. The boy doesn't even have an iPhone.'

'But it is very beautiful.'

'It is, it's a lovely grey and I like this magnet bit.'

'You will get a second date if you buy him this.'

'We're actually on our sixth date.'

'But you don't like him very much?'

'I like him loads!'

'But you don't want him to have nice things?'

'Of course I do.'

'You should buy this case then.'

It was a nice case, and Claudia didn't want to anger the ice maiden. Maybe she could pop an 'IOU an iPad' inside?

No, that was ridiculous. The case was £250, so she put it back on the shelf. 'Gloves are a nice present; can you show me where they are please?'

'You don't get a classic yellow Selfridges bag if you buy something as small as gloves,' said Monique.

In that case, maybe the case *was* worth it.

'Actually, that's not true,' Monique sighed. 'I just wanted you to buy the case. Follow me; I'll take you to gloves.'

Monique reluctantly handed Claudia a complimentary mini candy cane and left her scouring the racks for any gloves under sixty-five pounds, though she wasn't convinced gloves were a good enough way of saying 'Thanks for being here all along, please be around for a long, long time more.'

The more time marched on the harder it was becoming to concentrate on the task at hand, and the more glued the candy cane became to one of the fluffier gloves, so she edged back to the escalator and hastily left Selfridges. Continuing up Oxford Street, the Christmas lights weaved across the road from one flagship store to the next like vast, frost-covered spiders' webs under the sun.

What was she going to buy Nick? What was girl-friendy and fun but not too 'long-term relationship'?

Hello, Ann Summers.

Goodbye, Ann Summers. Claudia walked straight past and in through the door of Holland & Barrett. She loitered by the hazelnuts. Come on, she was a grown-up, and *sexy things* were perfectly normal and grown up. She exited Holland & Barrett and walked straight back past Ann Summers again, into Dorothy Perkins on the other side.

Stop being ridiculous, nobody's watching and nobody cares. She took a deep breath and launched back on to the street, head held high.

Claudia waltzed in to Ann Summers with faux-pur-pose and headed straight for the first rack of undies she saw. She studied the bridal lingerie with authority while her eyes darted left and right.

'Can I help you with anything today?' asked a girl about ten years younger than Claudia, all oozing confi-dence and burlesque hair.

'Um, I'm just looking for something a bit fun for when I'm with my, um, boyfriend.'

'Sure, were you after toys, or costumes or underwear?'

'Just some undies, I think, maybe something a bit festive?'

'No probs. Special occasion?'

'Just, you know, *sex*.' Claudia shrugged and rolled her eyes.

'First time?' The sales assistant smiled.

'No, I've had sex loads of times, hundreds— Oh you mean with him. Yes, first time.'

'Have you visited Ann Summers before?'

'Pfff, all the time.' *Never*. Claudia had been disinterested in sex for so long she'd never even considered visiting the shop before. The girl led Claudia over to a wonderful array of red and white tasselled, pom-pommy outfits that would make Mrs Claus blush and hide behind her apron. 'This is our Christmas collection, it's all super fun and sexy – it'll be such a treat for him. Trust me, this is his Christmas present covered if you show up wearing one of these.'

'If only I could get enough paper to wrap myself up,' Claudia tittered, examining her hand through a mesh bra. It might as well have been made of cling film.

'Actually, we do have long red satin wraps that you tie around yourself like a present bow, if you want me to get you one?'

'No, that's okay, thank you.' Actually bestowing herself like she was a luxurious present seemed a little narcissistic for the first time Nick would see her naked.

Nick had to see her naked!

'If you need anything, just come and grab me, okay?' the girl said with a grin and wandered off to realign some handcuffs.

Claudia picked up a red tie-front bra with dangly pom-poms. Would Nick like this? She wasn't sure if this kind of thing could even count as a present. Would he say, 'You look great, now where's my iPad case?'

She ran through the unveiling in her head; what might happen, what he'd say, what she'd say. 'Nick, I want to wish YOU a Merry Christmas.' 'Nick, unwrap me, baby.' 'Nick, I want to hang my stockings . . . under your . . .' She cringed. She was going to sound like such a twat. Maybe they should just kiss – over clothes – because kissing him was spectacular enough.

'Would you like to try that one on?'

Claudia blinked. She must have spent the last five minutes staring at the bra like a right pervert.

'No, thank you, I think I'll just take this, and the matching knick-knacks.'

Claudia left the shop, shoving the carrier into her handbag lest anybody see she was a lady who bought rude underwear. It felt nice, though, to *want* to be sexy and exciting. The butterflies awoke with a dance routine to rival a Gap Christmas advert and a beam formed on her cheeks.

Four hours to Nick.

235

Back at home, Claudia spent a long time examining herself in the mirror in her new undies with the heating on full whack. She'd shaved her legs and her bikini line, spritzed *there* with perfume, experienced extreme stinging as a result and quickly re-showered. She dried her hair, leaving it soft and loose. Just how she knew Nick liked it.

She dressed carefully, tucking the fluffy pom-poms inside her clothing. Every couple of minutes she glanced at the clock.

Her stomach was somersaulting faster and faster the closer it got to date time. 'Come on, Claudia, man up,' she muttered. She was a grown woman, and she'd done it many a time. Sort of. Just . . . not with anyone but Seth in a very long time.

What if something had changed? Was sex like fashion? Oh God, she never followed fashion. What if her way was considered really retro?

Did people even shave their bikini lines any more? What if she'd made a huge mistake?

In a panic, Claudia raced to her laptop and frantically zipped around the *Cosmopolitan* website, speed-reading more sex tips than you could fit into a chapter of *Fifty Shades*, and by the end felt so overwhelmed all she thought she'd be able to handle would be a cuddle and a rom-com.

This was going to be fine. It was Nick. He wasn't going to laugh at her or dislike her; he'd wanted her for years. Everything would be *fine*.

Thirty minutes to go.

She finished off the prep on a batch of home-made mince pies in record time and was even able to clear some of the more embarrassing things out of the way of her flat, replacing them with some spicy winter candles.

She passed the little spinning ice-skater she'd bought at Winter Wonderland. 'Not so alone now, are we, Mini Claudia?' she said.

Claudia switched on the Christmas tree lights, giving the room a warm, calming glow. She touched the little tree decoration of Mickey Mouse with a snowboard and smiled at the memory of her and Seth's Orlando holiday two years ago. Then she pulled her hand back. What was that? A memory of Seth with no feelings of resentment or hurt? That was interesting.

The little model swung happily on the branch, raining pine needles onto the carpet. Good job she was spending Christmas at her dad's house, because this tree wasn't going to last much longer. It was her fault really, for buying it way back at the start of December.

Actually, it was Nick's fault. He'd dragged her along as soon as the first advent calendar door opened, and she'd ended up bringing home a four-footer herself, much to Seth's eye-rolls.

Right. Enough day-dreaming about the man, time to go and meet him. Let Date Nine commence.

Claudia waited outside Tower Hill station, a Styrofoam cup of tea in each hand, trying to use the insides of her arms to shuffle her bra back into place – the lack of underwiring was causing it to creep up her boobs.

She couldn't wait to see Nick again. It was very uncool, but she just wanted to bury her cold nose against his cheek and steal a thousand more smooches.

'Hello, you.' Nick bounded over and gave her a ginormous kiss on the mouth. She melted like a snowman by a fireplace. There it was. She considered lobbing the teas over her shoulder and scrambling up into his arms, but instead she burbled something incoherent and handed him a cup.

'Cheers, big ears. This is exciting, what are you going to do with me today?'

What a loaded question. 'You know you love Charles Dickens?'

'More than anyone.'

'And you know you love Christmas?'

'More than anyone.'

'Good. We're going on a Christmas-themed Dickens guided walk. It takes us around where he worked, around locations that were featured in or inspiration for his Christmas books – especially *A Christmas Carol* – gaslit streets ... It sounded quite cool.' She watched him expectantly, praying he didn't think it was the most naff date in history.

'That sounds bloody brilliant!' He pulled her into

him and her heart popped like a thousand Christmas crackers. 'And then it's back to yours?'

'Yep.' She peeped over his shoulder at the snow-covered defences of the Tower of London and was lost in thought about whether Anne Boleyn could ever have imagined, the first time she slept with Henry VIII, that it would have ended with her beheading right there in the Tower, when a small woman in full Dickensian regalia tapped Claudia on the arm.

'Off we go then.'

Nick took Claudia's gloved hand and they joined a small group of people. It was a good job she hadn't spent close to a hundred quid on designer gloves for him, because his own knitted grey ones, scattered with snowflakes, were just lovely. She quite wanted to slide inside them.

'It is cold, bleak, biting weather,' said the woman to the group. 'You may wish to spend this walk wheezing up and down, beating your hands upon your breasts and stamping your feet upon the pavement stones to warm them.'

The group was silent, except for Nick who bent down to Claudia's ear and whispered 'Breasts.' She smothered a laugh.

'I am, of course, paraphrasing from the most Christmassy of tales, A Christmas Carol. Without the author of this story, Charles Dickens, Christmas as we know it might barely exist ...'

Nick was enraptured by the storytelling, his eyes

lighting up with every building they passed that had some significance to his favourite book. Claudia watched him. She couldn't take her eyes off his mouth, and often he caught her peeping. In those moments he would duck down and give her a light, body-tingling kiss. She was utterly distracted.

They were in the middle of an anecdote about goose versus turkey in Victorian London when Claudia felt a cool breeze flutter across her chest. *No.* This was why the majority of bras were held together with an entourage of hook-and-eyes and not just one floaty ribbon. At the front.

The ribbon had tired of its duties and untied itself; her boobs were celebrating their escape by jumping about in their own Christmas parade as she walked over the cobblestones. This was far from ideal. Claudia tried to unassumingly retie the ribbon, but one of the group looked over at precisely the wrong moment.

Claudia turned it into an exaggerated itch.

'Have you been bitten?' Nick asked.

'Yes, maybe, maybe not. Just a tickle.'

'I've been bitten by something too,' a man in woollen hat piped up, and started scratching his own chest.

The guide stopped and turned round. 'Is everyone okay?'

'Something's biting us,' said the man.

'No, it's nothing,' Claudia insisted, crossing her arms over her chest as the whole group turned to look.

'I'm a nurse,' said a woman, stepping out of the crowd. 'Do you want me to take a look?'

'No thanks, it's gone now.' Claudia pasted on a smile and dropped her arms. *Please don't let a pom-pom be hanging out of the bottom of my coat.* 'You were saying?'

The walk stretched into its second hour and Claudia and her unrestrained chest could tell that even Nick was turning his mind to tonight, becoming increasingly fiery with his snatched kisses. As the group rounded the corner of the Royal Exchange, featured in the opening lines of *A Christmas Carol*, and Claudia was pondering if it was too early in the relationship to drag Nick inside and demand a certain ring from Tiffany, Nick pulled her back and pressed her against the cold stone, kissing her hard.

Was it home time yet?

Claudia raced up the stairs, her heart and some other places thumping with anticipation. Nick followed close behind, his fingertips trailing along the edge of her hips.

At the top she couldn't bear to be an inch away from his chest any longer, and she spun around and squashed into him, pressing her lips against his. They stumbled down the corridor, a blur of tongues, giggles and heavy breathing.

Claudia felt Nick's hands edge under her coat and she was hit with sudden panic. The bra. It was still untied, the pom-poms dangling. To Nick they'd feel like weird nubbins on her stomach. She squiggled her torso away from his touch and unlocked her door.

'What's that smell?' Nick sniffed the air. 'It's like … barbecued raisins.'

'My mince pies!' Ooooooooops. Claudia dropped her arms from Nick's neck and her right leg from where it had snuck up around his waist and ran to the kitchen. She yanked open the oven and pulled out a tray of blackened pastries.

'How long have they been in there for?' asked Nick, peering over her shoulder with disgust.

'Since just before our date.'

'Why did you leave them in the oven?'

'I was slow-roasting them.'

'You were slow-roasting mince pies? That's not a real thing.'

'I thought it would make the insides really rich, and the pastry really crumbly.'

Nick prodded one with a fork. It fell apart like ashes. 'You got the crumbly part right.'

'I really wanted these to be nice.'

'I'll try one.'

'No, you'll get, like, lead poisoning or something.'

'Shut your face.' He chewed and swallowed, rubbed his teeth and reached for a cocktail stick to pick at his gums. Then gulped down a pint of water. 'Delicious. What's for dinner, Nigella?'

'Dinner is pizza, bought from Sainsbury's.'

'Nice, can't go wrong.'

'With a festive twist.'

'Oh no.'

'It'll be lovely.'

'What's the twist? You're not putting a Chocolate Orange on the top, are you?'

'Of course not. I was going to put these on it.' She reached into the fridge and pulled out a pack of Bernard Matthews's turkey slices.

Nick laughed. 'It sounds amazing; you are slowly turning into the love of my life.'

They both froze.

'I didn't say that,' said Nick, scrunching his eyes closed. 'You didn't hear that. Let's talk about pizza. Put the pizza in the oven.'

With her back to Nick, Claudia sorted out her custom pizza topping. She smiled to herself. Nobody was thinking about love yet, but she couldn't stop thinking about tonight.

Less than an hour later, Claudia and Nick were polishing off the last of the Christmas pizza. This meant Things were Going to Happen. Which meant Claudia needed a minute to fix her underwear and give herself a pep talk.

'Back in a mo,' she said, hopping off the chair. Nick

caught her as she went past and pulled her down for a gentle kiss. She knew in that kiss she didn't need to be nervous, not really.

Claudia disappeared into her bedroom and removed her clothes. She retied the bra at the front and looked at herself. Her body wasn't perfect; it was a little podgy in places and her skin was as pale as the snow outside. Her boobs would never make it into *Playboy* and her cellulite couldn't be airbrushed out. But in her warm flat, with her fun new underwear and a boy she trusted more than any other boy in the world, she'd never felt sexier.

However. Walking out there in *only* the underwear still seemed a little scary. She couldn't put her jeans and jumper back over the top; it would be a bit of an anti-climax for Nick. Plus nobody looked good hopping out of skinny jeans. She pulled a large pinstriped shirt out of her wardrobe. In movies, girls always looked cute padding about in men's shirts and little else.

It looked ridiculous. Massive and unflattering. And Nick would probably think it was Seth's, which would be a huge buzzkill.

Her dressing gown? Not sexy.

Time was ticking away, and she was – if she could believe it – actually excited about showing off the underwear.

She had a brainwave and delved into a drawer, pulling out a soft, fine-knit man's jumper in charcoal grey. It had a small tear right in the middle, a peephole which showed a glimpse of her stomach. It was Nick's. He'd left it here a couple of summers ago and then had told her to chuck it because of the rip. It was so comfy she'd kept it to slouch about the house in.

Claudia stepped out into the living room.

Nick smiled. His eyes ran over his jumper, her bare legs and up to her face. 'You look lovely.'

'Happy Christmas.' She watched him as he stepped closer.

'Are you shaking?' he asked.

'A little bit.' Okay, she just needed some time. 'Can I get you a drink?'

Nick nodded and she moved to the kitchen, aware of his eyes on her legs. Did he think they looked big? No, she didn't think he did.

'What are we having?' asked Nick, putting his arms around her from behind as she unscrewed the Baileys and a bottle of red wine. He kissed her neck.

'It's a cocktail I've invented,' she stuttered. *Calm down*. 'It's called a Santa's Hat. You put some red wine in a glass, and then top it with Baileys, and the Baileys floats ... Oh.' The Baileys didn't float. It dribbled into the wine, curdling, and looking like a lump of bloodied brain matter.

'Is that supposed to happen?' Nick picked up his glass and took a sip, trickling it straight back out into the glass. 'It's delicious.'

'Bleurgh,' said Claudia. 'How can two such yummy things be such enemies when they come together?'

'Let's hope that doesn't happen to us.' Nick guffawed immediately. 'What a terrible line! Sorry about that.'

'How about just a wine or Baileys, straight up?'

'Baileys for me, please.'

Claudia poured two tumblers of the creamy liqueur while Nick fiddled with her stereo and the mellow sounds of the Michael Bublé Christmas album floated out.

They smiled at one another.

'Cheers,' said Claudia quietly.

'Cheers.'

'This might surprise you,' said Nick, putting down his glass and folding his arms. 'But, tough and manly as I am, I'm a bit nervous about you seeing me in the buff. Not that I don't have the body of Ryan Gosling under here, it's just I don't want you to faint in a rush of oestrogen or anything.'

'I'm nervous, too, though you may mistake me for Mila Kunis in a moment,' Claudia replied. She felt shy, but more than anything she wanted to take the plunge.

It was time.

In time with the brass instrumental of 'Santa Baby', Claudia peeled off Nick's jumper, revealing her Mrs Claus ensemble. Nick let out a low whistle and looked at her tenderly.

'You ...' he whispered. '*Underweary* you. Oh my God.'

Claudia struck a pose, shaking the pom-poms.

'You look magnificent.' He smiled, his eyes briefly meeting hers, then dropping in awe.

Surely not *magnificent*? Suddenly she felt a bit of a lemon standing there. She hopped up on to the kitchen counter and crossed her legs, her hands on her knees. 'You like my lingerie?' She batted her eyelashes.

'I love it,' said Nick, stepping closer. He pulled off his jumper, the shirt underneath rising and giving her a glimpse of a stomach that sent her hormones into a teenage-girl frenzy.

But he couldn't put his hands on her yet! She would collapse into giggles, she just knew it; her skin was already tingling with goose bumps and anticipation. Claudia shimmied down from the counter, surreptitiously removing the wedgie she'd given herself, and danced towards the sofa where she threw another coquettish pose, leaning backwards, one leg kicking up in the air.

'Sexy underwear,' she sang, immediately cementing her unsexiness. *Come on, Claudia, don't mess this up*.

Nick's fingers visibly shook as he undid the buttons on his shirt. He gyrated his hips to the music, the movements getting bigger and bigger until he looked at her, bashful. 'This is just not hot, is it?'

'Why are you nervous? You have *nothing* to be nervous about.'

'Not true. What if I take off my pants and my penis is released and it hits you in the face?'

'Is it really that big?'

'Yes. If I were in *Game of Thrones* I totally wouldn't need a sword. And, um, you do make me very horny.' He cringed the moment the words were out of his mouth.

Christ, this was awkward. 'I want you *so* much.'

'You want me, you, just – why don't you take me.' He ripped off his shirt.

'Why don't you take me?' Claudia kicked her leg over the sofa and strode across the cushions like a giraffe who'd escaped the zoo.

'Right then.'

Claudia leant against the Christmas tree and pulled another pin-up pose. Unfortunately, she kicked the wrong leg out behind her and leant her full weight on her bad ankle, which buckled at precisely the wrong moment.

She stumbled, grabbing the branches of the tree, clinging on to baubles, tugging at the tinsel, until seconds later she tumbled to the ground. Nick reached her just as she wrenched the plug for the Christmas tree lights out of the socket and with a *pff* they were plunged into darkness.

'Are you okay?' he asked, serious, kind, *hers*. Her breathing quieted and suddenly she didn't feel the need for theatrics or lines. She just needed him. She stared up at his dimly lit chest, illuminated only by the Christmas lights of the street outside shining through the window.

Claudia leant up on her elbows and kissed his chest. It tasted salty, of nervous sweat, and smelt like Baileys and man deodorant and all the delicious things that can get a girl going.

Nick stroked her hair back from her face and trailed his fingers, which were no longer shaking, down her neck to her collarbone. She prayed her boob hadn't fallen out in the fall.

She ran both hands around his sides and onto his back, using all the core muscles she didn't think she had to hold her body up off the ground and close to his. His skin was silk. 'You're lovely,' she murmured.

He wrapped defined arms around her torso, taking her weight and pulling her close, putting his face tantalisingly close to hers. He paused and they breathed each other in and out.

'You're covered in prickles,' he whispered. 'And I'm not calling myself a prickle.' Gently, he helped her up and brushed the pine needles from her back, causing a meteor shower to burst across her skin in his wake.

Claudia winced at the needles spiking into her feet and Nick, being so unbearably fanciable in every way – even more unbearable because he'd kept it secret all these years – scooped her up in his arms and carried her across her flat to her bedroom. It took seconds, but felt like hours.

Nick laid her down on the bed like she weighed nothing. Her mind was a blur as he crouched by her feet and pulled out the needles. It was only when butterfly kisses started creeping up her ankles, up her shins, that she snapped back to reality.

'Wait, no, no, no,' she cried.

'What?'

'You have to start at the top. I don't want the first time you see my *thing* to be in extreme close-up.'

'Damn.' Nick grinned and pulled himself up, sliding his body over hers.

They broke apart an inch. 'It unties at the front,' Claudia whispered. Nick held her gaze as his hand moved to the front of her bra, pulling at the pom-pom achingly slowly.

Claudia had never, hand on heart, shriek it from the rafters, wanted to have sex this badly *ever* before.

A feather-light trickle of cold breeze whispered past her breast as it was exposed, before it was covered again by Nick's big hands, his strong fingers. He kissed her lips, her neck, her chest and then back up to her face.

'You're better than I ever imagined.'

'Did you imagine often?' Her fingers crept into the back of his jeans.

'Every day.' He pulled one of her hands up and pinned it over her head, lacing his fingers in hers, and crushing their skin tightly together. She could feel his hardness against her through his jeans and a deep instinct caused her to press her lower body back against him.

'Take them off,' Claudia begged.

'Yours or mine?' he grinned.

'Both.'

And so he did. And he was delicious. And she felt delicious. Their bodies slotted together like a padlock. That night they sweated, they laughed, they were serious, they had make-the-most-noise competitions and they learnt every inch of each other that they'd never got to learn before.

Basically, by the end, they were pretty gross.

For the first time in her life, Claudia woke up having actually accomplished that long-sought-after hairstyle, bed-head. She woke up late, after a relatively sleepless night, and the sun was streaming through the curtains. She sat up and looked in the mirror. Her reflection was flushed, confident, happy. She could hear Nick puttering about in the kitchen and she smiled at the pine needles still resting at the end of the bed.

'Merry Christmas, me,' she whispered to herself.

Claudia stretched. Yep, she was ready for some hair of the dog. Also known as another dose of Nick. She cocooned herself in the duvet and padded to the door of the bedroom. She smelt bacon. That man was amazing.

Claudia opened the door, her eyes drifting around the

flat which was scattered with decorations, glasses, cushions, and Nick's jumper.

And that's when her eyes fell on the kitchen, and the man who stood in her kitchen, and she realised who was nowhere to be seen.

'What the hell are you doing here?' she asked Seth.

Date Ten

Hummingbird Bakery, South Kensington

'Where's Nick?' Claudia asked Seth, as if he might have chucked him out the window.

'Why would I know? Was he here? Did he stay the night?'

'Yes, he just . . .' She didn't want to tell him. 'How long have you been here?'

'About ten minutes. You don't mind that I let myself in, do you? I had a few things to pick up, and thought I'd treat you to brekkie. Bacon sarnie?'

'Of course I mind, you idiot,' she mumbled, checking her phone. Where did Nick go? He wasn't working today. Surely he wouldn't have left without saying good-bye.

She had a text from him. '*Mate*,' it started. Mate? Since when had he addressed her as 'mate', even before they were together?

Mate, I waited so long for her and it was so bad – I had to keep my eyes closed through

most of it! I got out as fast as I could. We
definitely need a night out with the ladies in the
new year.

When Christmas is over, the fun is past and the world greys, ready for a wet and wintry January, great lumps of snow dropping from rooftops. Claudia felt her heart falling in the same way.

The text wasn't meant for her. But it was sure as hell about her. She felt sick.

With her hand over her mouth she read it again and again. This had to be a joke. She looked out of the window at the snowflakes floating by. At the quiet, pedestrian-free street. But if it was a joke, where was he? Where was the 'just kidding' text?

Her eyes welled with tears. Where was Nick?

'Claud, do you want a bacon sarnie?' Seth broke into her thoughts. She shook her head. The only thing she wanted was to not have read that message – for him not to have even sent it, to still be here, bound in this duvet with her, his warm skin on hers, smiling, laughing and making her feel like everything was perfect.

He had to keep his eyes closed? Who was he saying this to?

'Are you okay, sweetheart?' asked Seth, materialising in front of her. She was statue-still, as hard and cold as granite, even when he wrapped her in his arms.

'Get off,' she choked.

'Shh, I know you well enough to know when you're upset. I know I'm a total dick and it breaks my heart that I've made you this sad over the past few weeks.'

'This isn't about you.'

'Maybe not, but even if my apology can make a little bit of you feel better, it's worth it, isn't it?'

Our night was not 'so bad'. It was really good; she wasn't crazy.

'Claud, I *am* sorry, you have no idea how sorry.'

Claudia took an enormous, snotty snuffle against Seth's hoodie and buried her head further into the duvet. She felt him kiss her forehead and she looked up, startled.

'What are you on about? Why are you here with me? Where's your girlfriend?'

'What girlfriend?'

'Stop "what girlfriend"-ing me. The girl from the pub, the girl I saw you with at St Paul's.'

'You were at St Paul's? Why didn't you come and say hi?'

'Why do you think, bell-end?'

'Ha – I love it when your fishwife mouth comes out.'

'You don't love anything about me.'

'That's not true.' Seth caught her eye. 'There's a heck of a lot I still love about you. Your face,' – he ran his fingers over it – 'your body.'

It was so bad …

'Your dancing.'

I got out as fast as I could …

'Your heart. I've missed everything about you, and I don't want to miss anything else. Have you missed me?'

She didn't miss Seth, not any more. But she missed the numbness. Adventure wasn't all it was cracked up to be, and in that moment she would give anything to be back living her flatlining life, because then she wouldn't hurt. And for that reason she nodded.

Claudia sank towards Seth in defeat. He nudged her face up with his nose and smiled that smile for her again. He drew closer.

Seth kissed her and she responded like she was kissing Nick goodbye. Pain collided with confusion, heartache, familiarity and emptiness. Nick couldn't wait to go for a night out with his mate and find a new lady. The chapter was closed as suddenly as it started.

But she didn't want to kiss Seth; it didn't feel like it once had.

The door slammed and she jumped, pulling away from Seth and spinning around. Nick had come back?

No one. 'Shh, it was the wind. Sorry, I left it open to air the flat from the bacon smoke.' Seth tried to pull her back in to him. What a silly girl to jump at the chance of seeing the man who couldn't wait to get away from her.

She shrugged out of Seth's arms and wrapped the duvet tighter around her. She didn't want him to see her naked again; she still had Nick on her skin. She sank onto the sofa, curling her legs under her so she looked like an igloo. 'Did you bring those?' she asked, spying some Starbucks cups.

'Yep.' Seth handed her one.

She sniffed: gingerbread. She never gave Seth credit for paying attention in the same way she had for Nick. He surprised her sometimes.

'If we got back together—' Seth began.

'We're not getting back together. You have a girl-friend. Or at least some chick who thinks she's your girlfriend.'

'She's not … I was *trying* to be her boyfriend. I realised what a penis I'd been to you and was trying to mend my ways. I thought I could build something with her, treat her well, take her on dates, and then in a way I'd have you back, or at least someone like you.'

'She's nothing like me.'

'Exactly. It didn't work. I was really bored on that date.'

'That's because you get bored on dates. You did the same with me, which is why we never went anywhere.'

'No, it was her. It was because she wasn't you.' Seth reached out to stroke Claudia's foot, like she loved, but she moved it away. Nick had touched that foot. 'Claud, we had five years together, don't chuck it away. I can't bear the thought of not being with you.'

'This was your choice.' Her head swam. Nick domi-nated her thoughts, but Seth's words were pickaxing their way through.

'It was a stupid choice. Come on, sweetheart, it's an

easy decision. We already have this whole life together, this home, plans for the future. We could go on the California road trip we've been on about for ages. Let's do it this summer. This Easter.'

'That's not what I want any more.'

Seth moved closer, searching her with his eyes. They'd sat on this very sofa together many times, ignoring who was beside them to focus on the worlds of the characters on the TV.

'Can I have one more chance?'

'No.'

'Please? I could come to the wedding?'

'No.' Nick would be at the wedding.

'Will you think about it? I'd like to show you I'm there for you and your friends. I want to wish Emma and Ellie a happy ever after.'

'My friends hate you, you wouldn't be welcome.'

'They hate me?'

'They have to, they're my friends,' Claudia shrugged.

'Do you hate me?'

'I did. In waves. Now I'm just . . . over you.'

Seth stood up, giving her another one of his famous smiles. 'You can't be over me in two weeks; I'm not giving up yet. Just think about it. If you decide you want us to head down to Surrey together tomorrow, I'm all yours.'

He plonked one bacon sandwich down in front of her

with a wink and walked out of their flat munching the other.

Claudia's home was very quiet.

She stood up, very much alone, with the snow still drifting silently past her window. She didn't know where to start. Did she throw away the discarded mince pies? Did she wash out the glasses with the Baileys and wine mixture? Did she pick up the Christmas tree decorations? Or did she go straight in, knife to the heart, and strip the sheets off her bed?

She bent down and ran her hand over the pine needles that lay like confetti over her floor. The weight of Nick's betrayal was something she couldn't even begin to get her head around at the moment.

As she looked around her, at everything that defined her, she finally understood. She thought she'd built her life around Seth, but she hadn't. She'd built her life around Nick.

His latest text message was cold.

Let's just pretend last night never happened.

She stared at the screen for some time. She'd expected some kind of a 'this was a mistake' conversation, since he'd made his feelings pretty clear, albeit accidently, but there was no sugar coating on this. Did he think he was doing her a favour by not beating about the bush?

> Good idea, she typed back sadly. I was glad you'd left this morning.

She reminded herself that it wouldn't hurt him – though would maybe dent his pride – but she was only acquiescing to his feelings.

Her phone tinkled. She sparked with hope that it could be an explanation, something a bit more personal.

> If you need a booty call again, you've always got plenty of other men on the go. Don't call me.

Ouch. Her soul hurt. Conclusive proof from two ends of the spectrum that no good can come of sex, whether she was having it lots or arguing about having none of it.

She typed back,

> As if I would. You didn't exactly rock my world.

The wedding was going to be horrible. What if Nick met one of these new ladies there? It would be beyond awkward if he was snogging some bridesmaid up against the photo booth while she stood on her own, watching. Because she'd totally watch; she wouldn't be able to help herself.

What a stupid girl to think she was lucky enough to recover from one failed relationship by immediately having a brighter, better one. She'd given everything over to hope and it had left her cold and discarded in the real world.

Perhaps giving Seth another chance wasn't a bad idea, because maybe Nick would see them together and regret how he'd treated her. Was it worth a try? What would she really be gaining here? Nick didn't like her – he'd made it pretty clear that she was a mistake – and did she want to get back with someone that heartless?

Maybe not, but she wanted to spite him, to make him feel as replaceable as he'd made her feel.

She dialled Seth's number. 'This is such a bad idea,' she muttered as it rang.

'Claud!'

'Come to the wedding,' Claudia said with little emotion.

'Seriously?' Seth sounded like he couldn't believe his luck.

'Yes. Last chance, don't be a dick. We leave tomorrow. And we're not back together.'

Claudia was furious. With herself for kissing Seth and inviting him to the wedding. With Nick for playing her like a fool. And with all the Sellotape in the world for curling up like a fortune-telling fish every time she tried to stick it to the wrapping paper.

How *dare* he laugh about her bedroom skills behind

her back? Nick, always so funny, always had to make a joke.

How *dare* he – the other he – cook bacon in her kitchen when she was all naked and vulnerable and then trick her into smooching his stupid face?

Boys were crap, like crappy Sellotape.

'That'll have to do I'm afraid, Dad,' Claudia said to the simple square picture frame that more closely resembled a deflated football by the time she'd finished her awful wrapping. 'DAMNATION!' She yelled at the photo of the two of them she'd forgotten to put in the frame.

She got up and snorted angrily. Right. There were three more days to go on her chocolate advent calendar, but she scoffed the lot. In your face, Christmas.

She paced about her flat like an angry bull.

She wasn't grateful to Nick. Yes, he'd shown her a wonderful couple of weeks and said some lovely things, but whether it was to satisfy his own curiosity or because he thought he was such a hunk and he was doing a favour by offering his services, she didn't know, and she wasn't grateful. She didn't need saving. He should have just left her alone. Should she text him again?

Yes, she should.

> The minute I split up with Seth you swooped in.
> From now on, leave me alone. You've always
> been too overbearing.

She stared at her phone, waiting for a reply.

Still waiting ...

She didn't mean he should leave her alone *yet*. Only after he'd texted back, to apologise or something.

Was her text too cruel? He hadn't technically swooped in, no more than she'd let him. But then she remembered *I got out as fast as I could* and her stomach flipped.

Claudia went and got herself a cup of tea, then checked her phone again. She switched it off and on. She took the battery out and put it back in. She painstakingly covered it with a tower of every single sofa cushion, waited exactly sixty seconds, then slowly removed them one at a time.

Still nothing.

Claudia needed some time alone. It had been a busy month, full of activities, people, well-wishers, to-do lists and, for better or worse, dates. And it would continue to be busy; tomorrow Penny wanted to meet for a cupcake and a coffee, then Claudia was driving home for the Christmas holidays with Seth in tow, then the following day was Christmas Eve: wedding day.

But this afternoon Claudia had to herself. And with her head swimming with tarnished memories of amazing sex, and the looming feeling that she'd somehow made an awful mistake, or two, she had to get out and walk off some of her nervous energy.

She dressed in all of her favourite winter garments at once: her woolly polka-dot tights, an overly expensive black knitted dress she'd bought at a Hobbs sale because it was as soft and fuzzy as a cat and made her feel like Kate Middleton, her Christmas-tree earrings, and her big Paddington Bear duffel coat.

The sky was bruised, like her heart, and even in the early afternoon it was already twilight. The lamp-posts created pools of amber on the still-thick snow and the wet tarmac of the Mall. Claudia walked to the front of Buckingham Palace and looked through the towering black and gold iron gates, the metal ice-cold and wet through her gloves.

'You don't have these problems, do you, ma'am?' she whispered up at the imposing off-white building, with its famous balcony, her teeth chattering. 'You could send a man to the Tower if he crossed you.'

'Isn't it beautiful?' breathed a woman with a strong American accent and a camera the size of Claudia's head. 'Do you live here?'

'Here? Um, no, this is the Queen's house.'

'I mean in London, honey.'

'In that case, yes, I live here, but I sure wish I lived *here*.' She pointed a glove through the railings.

'You're lucky to live in this city at Christmas, there's so much tradition and culture. Why, I feel like I'm in a Dickens novel most of the time.'

'I know that feeling. Are you having a good trip?'

'I just love it. We arrived two days ago and are here until after New Year's. Do you have any must-dos, as a local?'

Claudia thought about it. Last Christmas she would have been stumped after 'I hear ice skating is fun', but this year she'd done much more. 'Have you been up the Shard? It's spectacular to see London in all this snow.' She smiled. That was a good date. Thank you, Billy.

The American woman nodded. 'We were thinking of doing that sometime next week – hopefully the snow will hold until then. We went to that Winter Wonderland in Hyde Park, but I didn't like that much – a bit too fun fair for me.'

'I didn't like it much either, I had a horrible date there and I threw up. Not my best Christmas experience.' Claudia chuckled. *Ah, Eddie, it seems like a lifetime ago that you were bleeding on my face.* 'A traditional British pub might be right up your street. There's a lovely one on the South Bank called the King's Inn, it's all log fires and good roast dinners.'

'Perfect, thank you! Any other tips?'

'Well, if you can find any carol concerts at St Paul's Cathedral, it's just ... magical,' said Claudia sadly.

'Talking of magical, we're going to the Royal Opera House tonight to see *The Nutcracker*. Have you been?' The woman's cheeks were glacé-cherry red with excitement, a merry flash of colour among the grey and off-white scenery. 'I just love the ballet.'

Have I been? 'Yes, my friend is a ballet dancer, actually. Look out for her; she's the short girl in the red and white dress in the opening scene. And my other, um, friend built the sets. He works backstage.' *And he's buff and sexy and I love him – in some way – and he thinks I'm crap in bed.*

'We were lucky to get tickets; it's the last performance before Christmas.'

'Well, I think you're going to love it. Completely love it.' Claudia took a deep breath of cool air. 'So what do you think the Queen's put on her Christmas list?'

'I expect she wants the same kinda thing as you or me,' said the woman. 'And what I want is a Michael Kors watch. What about you? What do you want for Christmas?'

What did Claudia want for Christmas? Mariah Carey hummed in her head. 'I heard that Prince Harry once gave the Queen a bath hat that said "Ain't Life a Bitch". Maybe one of those.'

The woman whooped a jolly laugh. 'Did you know that the Queen watches the Queen's Speech on her own on Christmas Day because she can't bear being on TV in front of her family? I guess we all get a little stage fright sometimes.'

'I didn't know that.'

'Now then. I might not have a Michael Kors watch yet, but this old one tells me I have to go. I'm getting my nails done with my daughter, a snowflake design, before tonight.' She snapped a final photo of the Palace. 'Now, whether it's a bitchin' bath hat or something special, I hope you get what you want. Merry Christmas, honey.'

'Merry Christmas,' smiled Claudia. She quelled the overwhelming desire to ask the woman if she could come and get her nails done, too.

Claudia missed her mum.

Truth be told, Claudia missed everyone right now.

Claudia walked through the door of the Hummingbird Bakery the next morning, pausing under the exuberant heater to peel the scarf off her sweaty neck. She scowled at the pink walls. She scowled at the other customers, and she scowled at the friendly-looking server with the MERRY CHRISTMAS, I'M MANPREET name tag. She then scowled in turn at the cupcakes, the brownies and the whoopie pies.

'Hello, grumpy,' Penny said, coming up behind her and also removing her coat and scarf. Claudia tried hard not to scowl at her, too.

'Season's greetings,' she said, laced with sarcasm.

Penny raised an eyebrow at Manpreet behind the counter. 'Can I have a red velvet cupcake please, and a hot chocolate.'

'Sure.'

Penny turned to Claudia. 'What do you want?'

Claudia peered at her. Penny wasn't sounding very friendly. To be fair, Claudia wasn't being very friendly to her, but she had a good reason to be down in the dumps. She turned to Manpreet.

'Please can I have a pumpkin whoopie pie, a tiramisu cupcake and an extremely dark coffee with loads and loads of cream.'

'Coming right up.'

'Shall we sit?' Penny asked Claudia stiffly.

Claudia slouched behind Penny as she led them to a window table. 'So guess what?'

'What?'

'You're my tenth date of December,' Claudia said.

'Mmm, aren't you getting around?' said Penny. What did that mean?

'Not ten different people.'

'Some just keep coming back though, don't they?'

Manpreet brought the loaded tray to the table. 'Enjoy. Let me know if you need a sick bag,' she grinned at Claudia.

'So, what's going on?' Penny asked.

'What's going on with what?'

'What's going on with you and Nick?'

'Beats me. We had a date the night before last. *The* date. And this morning he'd left.'

'Why did he leave?'

'I don't know, Penny, do you want me to list my faults? He had sex with my terribly offensive vagina. He

270

literally had sex with me and ran away from my bits, straight out of there, didn't want to see them in the cold light of day. And frankly,' Claudia pointed down, 'she's really hurt. She'd been to the salon and everything.'

'Are you back with Seth?'

'No.' She squirmed. 'What?'

'Are you?'

Penny knew something. 'I'm not back with him but he's coming with me to the wedding.' So there.

'Claudia, this is a really bad idea.'

'Why is it bad? He was my boyfriend for five years.'

'He was your boyfriend for five years and then he dumped you! And was with someone else, and you were miserable.'

'And then I was with someone else, and now I'm still miserable.' Of course she knew it was an awful idea, but it was too late now and she wasn't in the mood for someone else to point out her mistakes. She felt she'd had enough of that from one, horrible text message. 'Has Nick said something to you?'

'I called him yesterday. He's under the impression you were stringing him along while you worked things out with Seth.'

'I'm not working things out with Seth, but at least Seth stuck around for five years. At least it took him five years to figure out how not-sexy I am. Nick had one ride on the rollercoaster and was like, "Yawn, when's the next bus home?"'

'I don't get it. I don't get you. You didn't give Nick a chance to stick around for another go.' Penny glared at Claudia, who mashed her fork into her whoopie pie and refused to look up. 'Nick's heartbroken. I don't know exactly what happened, but it's a pretty horrible way to treat a friend.'

'What are you talking about?'

'It seems to me that you led Nick on, like he was a rebound, and the minute he left you were back in Seth's arms.'

'I am not back in Seth's arms at all.'

'He saw you kissing!'

'What? Nick saw? When?'

'At your flat, after he went out to get you a bloody gingerbread latte.'

'Oh . . .' He'd just gone to Starbucks? Those drinks were from him? She could see why that would look bad. Really bad. But he started it. And bloody Seth! Yet another lie. She actually was the idiot he took her for. 'The only reason we were kissing was because Nick sent such a mean text that wasn't meant for me, basically crapping all over our night together.'

'Did you ask him about it?'

'No.'

'You didn't even ask him about it?' Penny shook her head in disbelief. 'So it was probably a misunderstanding.'

'There is no way it was a misunderstanding. You don't

know anything about anything. It detailed how rubbish it was, how he couldn't wait to get out, and basically how I was just a conquest.' Claudia's voice wobbled, she was ashamed saying it aloud. 'He just wanted to see if he could bed his best friend. He'll probably see if he can do you next.'

'Yeah, Nick is such an arsehole, that totally sounds like him. Can I read the text?' Claudia handed over her phone and Penny read it, nodding. 'I get that this sounds bad, but "I kept my eyes closed the whole time" – you're hardly a minger, Claud, I just don't believe this can be about your night together. And I'm surprised you can; you know Nick better than this.'

'It wouldn't be the first time this month I was surprised by the behaviour of someone I trusted,' Claudia sulked. Why wasn't Penny more shocked? It seemed so easy for her to believe there was a mix-up.

'But *what* behaviour? One minute you're both besotted, the next minute you're throwing it out the window, snogging Seth and moaning about a text that mentions you how many times? Oh, that's right, none.'

Was Penny right? Was it Claudia who had buggered it all up?

'If you think Seth's a better option that Nick, who is *awesome*, you're insane,' Penny continued. 'You're a glutton for punishment. And you're not the girl I thought you were.'

They took a moment to simmer down.

'What is this about?' Penny asked slowly. 'Do you want to find out what's going on with Nick? Or do you want an easy way out so you can get back with Seth?'

'I don't know.'

'I wish you could just make your mind up for once. I don't mean this in a nasty way, but you can't make your mind up ever, about anything. You run for the easy option rather than fighting for what you supposedly want. You didn't even bother asking Nick what this text meant, you were just like, "Ah well, Seth's being nice now so he'll do."'

Claudia sat in silence. It was true. Sometimes she felt so far from the strong, assertive, Beyoncé-type woman she longed to be. She remembered with a deep pang that she still hadn't given an answer about the Royal Ballet job. How many years had she been passively job-hunting now? Was she going to mess this opportunity up as well because she was so afraid of change? She talked the talk about taking risks, but when was she going to grow up and make some decisions?

'I think you should talk to Nick, ASAP.'

'I think you should just—'

'Just what?'

'Stay out of it,' Claudia mumbled. Her head hurt and she felt sick thinking she might have made the stupidest, most monumental mistake. But she could come back from it ... couldn't she? If she explained it to him? But every time she remembered that message she felt a rush of pain all over again. What other explanation was there? Surely it was better not to kid herself: it had obviously been about her.

Penny's face was pink. 'You're right. Far be it from me, the outsider, the gooseberry, to invade on the private little world of Claudia and Nick.'

'I didn't mean it like that. You're still my best friend.'

'Am I?' It hung in the air like a threat. 'It was so easy for you to dismiss him, to imagine the worst. What if I make a mistake, or there's a misunderstanding? Am I out, too?'

'Of course not.'

'I can't believe that at the moment.'

But now is when I need you the most. Stop making it harder.

The Michael Bublé Christmas album started in the background – a sad reminder of Claudia and Nick's night at her flat. Claudia glared at Manpreet and then turned back to Penny. 'Did you ask for this to be put on?'

'Yes, that's exactly what's at the top of my priority list right now. Not trying to make my two best friends see sense before everything falls apart, but to make sure that the Michael Bublé album is playing whenever you're in the room, because everything is about you.'

'I feel like you don't get it, Penny, like you want answers from me that I don't have right now.'

'Fine, I'll keep out of it. I'll keep out of your way while you swan about in your own world, kissing the best friend, kissing the ex, whatever. You're absolutely right – it's not my problem.'

'You should be pleased: Nick's all yours now. You can waltz off into the sunset together.' Claudia immediately regretted saying it.

'Yeah, I'm desperate for your sloppy seconds. Thank you, Claudia, for stepping aside and bestowing him on me.'

'I'm just saying. Maybe you should go for it – you liked him first.'

'And we both know how bitter you get about me having things you don't.'

There was silence. That was true, but Claudia was not about to admit it.

'I am *not* jealous of you.'

'I should go.'

'Yes, please, I've had enough bashing for today.'

'I'm so tired of listening to you feel sorry for yourself.' Penny rolled her eyes, standing up.

'Sorry for being such an inconvenience to your life.' Claudia's heart stung. Was this really what Penny thought of her? She brushed a hunk of cupcake across the table in front of her, which soared directly onto Penny's dress in a big blob of buttercream icing. She raised an eyebrow at Penny. 'Whoops.'

Penny looked at the mess as it plopped from her dress onto the floor. Slowly she leant over the table and picked up the discarded half of Claudia's whoopie pie.

'No,' said Claudia, pushing her chair back into the middle of the bakery. Penny prowled after her. 'Stop it, leave me alone.'

'Um, ladies, you're scaring the other customers,' Manpreet said, trying to position herself between the two.

And right there, in the middle of the charming South Kensington branch of the Hummingbird Bakery, Claudia sat on a chair while a sticky, squashy whoopie pie was mashed onto her face.

'I'm going to kill you until you're dead, Penny,' Claudia yelped.

'That's not necessary,' Manpreet said, napkins in her hand. 'I think it would be good if you'd both just leave and continue this snowball fight outside, with actual snow, further down the street.'

'I'm going to kill you till *you're* dead,' Penny fumed, tugging on her coat. 'You got icing on my favourite jumper dress.'

'Now you'll just have to choose one of your ten thousand other slutty dresses.'

'*Slutty?* Well good luck finding another dress to wear to the wedding, because you're not borrowing mine.'

'LIKE I CARE. IT LOOKED SHIT ON ME ANYWAY.' Hang on . . .

The girls stormed from the bakery and stood staring at each other on the snowy street, nostrils flaring. 'Well, see you tomorrow,' Penny said, and spun around, stalking off down the street.

'See you tomorrow,' said Claudia, stalking off in the other direction. Which was kind of annoying as she actually needed to go the same way as Penny.

What had Claudia learnt today?

That she was probably no longer welcome in the Hummingbird Bakery.

That Penny didn't seem to like her very much at all. And that the two of them were frighteningly capable of being total cows to each other.

That she'd potentially made the most monumental mess of everything, and Nick wasn't the heartless shit she'd been so quick to assume he was. The thought made her whole body ache. Why was she such a screw-up?

Essentially, she'd lost them both through words and actions she couldn't take back.

'I'm a Billy no-mates,' she said to a headless snowman she passed, as if he didn't have enough problems of his own.

And she now had a trafficky couple of hours' drive with Seth, who she really shouldn't have invited. What was her dad going to say when she turned up with him at their family home?

And tomorrow, at the wedding, they'd all be together in one room.

Date Eleven

The Wedding, Frostwood

Claudia cranked up the car stereo so Chris Rea sang 'Driving Home for Christmas' at full volume, but still Seth remained sleeping. He was the worst road trip partner ever.

She wound down the windows and let in a rush of freezing air. Seth stirred. 'Are we nearly there yet?'

'Shut up.'

'All right.'

Maybe he was better silent; she found everything he said at the moment grated against her already scratchy emotions.

'Can you pass me a Quality Street?' she muttered before he could drift back into snoozeville. 'Are there any strawberry creams left?' Out of the corner of her eye she saw him shuffle one up his sleeve.

'No, 'fraid not. How about one of those green triangles? There's loads of them.'

'GIVE ME THE GODDAMN STRAWBERRY CREAM. YOU'VE EATEN EVERY OTHER ONE OF THE STRAWBERRY CREAMS.'

'Fine, take it. Time of the month, is it?'

She narrowed her eyes at the road ahead.

'Can we put the window back up? It's chuffing cold,' Seth asked.

Without another word Claudia whirred the window upwards, cocooning them once again. She drove through the pretty outskirts of Surrey, the red-brick houses getting bigger the further they were from the capital. Icing-sugar snow decorated the gardens and rooftops, and Christmas trees twinkled through windows. By now, schools and offices were breaking up and the pavements were filled with children padded to the eyeballs in coats, onesies, scarves, hats and mittens, and adults struggling under the weight of excessive food shopping bags.

Resting on the back seat of the car was a huge, sticky panettone (not made; bought from Harrods Food Hall) wrapped in wide red and gold ribbon. A peace offering to her dad and his sweet tooth, to take away the bitter taste of her bringing Seth home.

The second Claudia pulled her car into the neat driveway of her family home, the living room curtain twitched. Moments later the front door swung wide open and out bounded a Bernese Mountain Dog wearing a tinsel necklace and a dopey smile, his paws throwing snow up into the air behind him.

Claudia stepped out of the car and crouched down, embracing the dog and squashing her face into his warm brown fur. 'Flippers, you big silly thing. You, me, sleeping in front of the fireplace and ignoring the world over Christmas, how does that sound?'

Flippers plonked a heavy paw on her lap and beamed.

Seth came around the side of the car. 'All right, Flippers?'

Flippers snorted indignantly and turned away from Seth, sticking his nose through the open car door and sniffing at the panettone.

Claudia looked up at her childhood house. Her dad had done a good job with the outdoor lights this year. Even the big oak tree had what appeared to be the fluffy fairy lights from her teenage bedroom draped on it.

'Welcome home, love.' He appeared at the door and smiled at his daughter. If there was ever a moment in the past twenty-four hours that she regretted re-inviting Seth to the wedding, and therefore having him spend Christmas with them, it was now.

'Dad . . .' She smiled back sadly and waved her arm towards Seth, who was half buried in the boot of the car, pulling out their luggage.

Joe stepped over and pulled her into a hug.

'I'm sorry he's here,' she whispered to him.

'Are you?' he whispered back. 'Do you want him to leave?'

'No, but I think I made a mistake. Are you really angry?'

'Of course not, Claudy, but the minute you decide you want him gone I'd be happy to be the one to tell him.' He pulled away and squeezed his daughter's hand. 'Seth.'

Seth heaved a bag of wine and whisky onto the snowy driveway. 'Hello, Joe, merry Christmas.' He stepped over and cautiously held out his hand.

Joe shook it with a smile that faintly resembled a sneer. 'Hello. I'm surprised to see you back here.'

Seth slung an arm around Claudia's shoulders. The air solidified to ice. 'Yep,' he said. 'We decided to give things another go.'

'No, we didn't,' said Claudia, slipping out from his arm to bend back down to stroke Flippers, who was now holding one of the panettone ribbons in his mouth. 'Especially after that Quality Street lie. And don't think the other lie about who really brought the Starbucks over yesterday morning went unnoticed.'

She stood and looked him square in the eye. Seth shuffled under her gaze. He turned to Joe and laughed heartily. 'In-jokes, eh? Shall I pop our stuff straight in our room?'

'You're in the spare room,' said Claudia and Joe at the same time.

After an achingly awkward dinner, Claudia had retired to her bedroom to try on every dress/skirt/blouse combo she owned. Following the cupcake war that morning, and subsequent dress-retraction from Penny, Claudia had raced back to her flat and packed a whole extra suitcase of anything remotely weddingy.

She pulled out the sequined dress-cum-top that Nick had given her on their date to the Christmas party. 'What do I want to achieve here, Flippers?' she asked the dog, who was lying across her bed, gazing adoringly at her *Friends* poster.

Despite what Penny had said, she still couldn't get the words of Nick's text out of her mind. What could it have been about other than her? She wanted him to hurt as much as she did. She wanted to parade in with Seth, looking a million dollars, without a care in the world for Nick and his *I had to keep my eyes closed*.

But also . . . she desperately wanted him back. For it to all have been a misunderstanding. For it to be all right.

There was no backing out or sending Seth home now. She was just going to have to see how it played out at the wedding.

'Thanks, Flippers, as usual you've been a big help.' She flapped his big ears and he rewarded her with a big panettone-scented yawn.

The following morning Claudia woke up as early as she had at Christmas time when she was little. Only this Christmas Eve it wasn't excitement that had her up and at her window in the deep darkness of half-past four, but a tightening knot of apprehension in her stomach at the day ahead. On the window ledge was a dense layer of snow, and she could see a blizzard swirling in front of the orange glow of the street lamps.

What if it's too snowy and the wedding's called off? she thought with hope. No, she wouldn't go that far. She wanted to be there for Emma and Ellie's big day more than anything; she'd just rather not have to face her demons. Her demons being her two best friends.

As the sky lightened the clouds wandered off, taking the blizzard with them, and before she knew it the sun was waking and the gritting lorries were grinding past the house.

She supposed she should play nice with Seth and try to have a good day, so when they passed in the corridor, him fresh from the shower, warm steam rising from his skin in the cool air of the house, wearing nothing but a towel around his waist, she said begrudgingly, 'Morning.'

'Morning, chick,' he grinned.

'I'm just popping to the shops if you want to come?' *Please don't come.*

Seth snorted. 'Trailing round the shops and going to a wedding all in one day? No thanks. Thought I'd have

286

an early morning festive tipple and start the Christmas TV watching, since we have to be out for most of today.'

Good, that was him occupied then.

'Dad?' she called, jogging down the stairs.

'Good morning, angel. Happy Christmas Eve,' he said, coming out of the kitchen holding a box of corn-flakes.

'And to you. I'm just going for a quick shop, do you want to come?'

Joe looked at his cereal box.

'You don't have to . . .'

'Would you mind me coming? Would I be any help?'

'I'd love you to come!'

'Still not bought all your presents, missy?'

'Presents done, but no idea what I'm going to wear to the wedding in three hours' time. So I feel it's time to get out the emergency credit card.'

'Why not, eh? You deserve a treat. You know, I'm looking forward to this; it's been years since I've been shopping with my little girl. Maybe we could use *my* emergency credit card instead.'

Sometimes, dads were the best things in the world.

Claudia and Joe walked along the barely visible pave-ment.

'What kind of dress are you looking for?'

Claudia shrugged. 'Whatever, really. Who cares?

There's no time to go to more than a couple of shops anyway.'

'Why did you invite him down again, love? You don't seem happy about it at all.'

'It was a knee-jerk reaction to something that had made me sad. I really don't want to get back with him, Dad. But it's Christmas Eve. I can't just send him home now; it's me who's been fickle.'

'Of course you can. I'll drive him back into London if it'll make you feel better.'

'Thanks, Dad, but his family are so far north he wouldn't have time to get up there and even Seth shouldn't spend Christmas alone on the floor of his mate's empty flat.'

Joe humphed.

'Evryonehtsme,' she said quietly.

'What's that, love?'

Claudia glanced up at her dad. 'Everyone hates me.'

'Not true. I don't go dress shopping with people I hate.'

'Penny hates me ... and Nick.'

'Do you want to tell me what happened?'

'No.' They trudged on for a couple of minutes. 'Penny and I had an argument and she squashed a cake in my face, and I kind of deserved it.'

'It's not like Penny to waste cake; it must have been a hell of a barney.'

'I thought Nick had done something really horrible to me – and he still may have – but Penny said I might be wrong, and by that time I'd already done something horrible back to him.'

'So you're still not sure if Nick was horrid to you or not?'

'Not as sure as I was.'

Joe nodded, digesting. 'So where does Penny and her cake fit into this?'

'She was standing up for Nick.'

'Not for you?'

'*Exactly*, and that's what was making me angry. But she thinks I just misread the whole situation and was being a bit silly.'

'Do you think you were being silly?'

Claudia did feel quite silly. She'd let Seth's bad behaviour make her assume the worst, when Nick's whole appeal was that he was not the same person as Seth. Why oh why hadn't she asked Nick straight out what that message meant? She might still have ended up hurt and heartbroken, but at least she'd *know*. 'It's possible,' she mumbled.

'Will you try to talk to Nick today? As soon as possible? Sort this whole thing out.'

'I don't think it's going to be that easy. I don't think he'll want to hear my side.'

Joe chuckled. 'Nick's hardly the sulky type. You two have been close as cucumbers for a million years; of course he'll listen to you. As will Penny. Just don't have that talk anywhere near the wedding cake.'

Claudia kicked at the snow, throwing powder into the air and filling her shoe. The thought of talking to Nick gave her goose bumps. Nervous goose bumps, but also the kind of goose bumps when you suddenly become anxious to do something, knowing there's a tiny sparkle of possibility that it might fix everything. 'Okay.'

'You'll talk to them?'

'As soon as I can. Sorry we're going to be out for most of today. Do you have any plans?'

'I think I'll prep some veggies for tomorrow, and Christine was going to come over and watch a Christmas movie.'

'Christine? Like a date?'

'No, not like a date,' Joe spluttered. 'I'm too bloomin' old for dates. But she's nice company, quite a talker as you know, and her little boy's also spending Christmas Eve at the Wedding of the Year.'

'What are you going to watch?'

'She's bringing over *Elf*. I've never seen it.'

'It's good, you'll like it – it's set in New York.'

'Ah, I love New York. Maybe you and I should take a trip there again some time next year.'

Claudia nodded, smiling at her dad. 'That would be nice.'

They stepped into one of Claudia's favourite boutiques in Frostwood, and there it was: *the dress*.

Knee-length, forest green, sprinkled with tiny clear and silvery beads. Claudia tried it on and it fitted like a glove, the colour matching her eyes and the style instantly lifting her spirits. She felt elegant and ready to rise above anything. Even a day with two sort-of-exes and a best friend who hated her.

She stepped out of the changing room and Joe beamed. 'Look at you. You look beautiful, my love.'

'You think?'

'Like a Hollywood star. Perfect for a date. You could make any boy at the wedding weak at the knees.' He winked.

What was he getting at? By the time Claudia had changed Joe was already holding an empty bag and the receipt.

'There you go, love, pop it in here.'

'Dad! You didn't have to pay for it, really.'

'I wanted to. It's Christmas. So hush.'

She gave him a huge squeeze. 'You're just brilliant. I kind of wish I could stay home today and hang out with you and Christine.'

'No, you don't, you'll have a great time. And if it's eventful, it'll make for some funny stories around the Christmas dinner table in the future.'

There were just two topics of conversation among the guests in the ceremony room of the country hotel where

291

Ellie and Emma were to be married. One was how lucky the happy couple were to be having such a picture-perfect winter wedding, now the sky had cleared to a bright blue and the snow was deep and Tippex white. The other was how blooming annoying pashminas were, and how at the next winter wedding everyone would opt for a cardigan.

The room had large windows that looked out over the glistening grounds. Bunches of fir cones, thistles and holly leaves decorated the ends of the rows of seats and a string quartet played Christmas classics softly in the background.

Claudia waited nervously, her heart jumping every time someone new entered the room, as edgy as the brides-to-be. Beside her was her eleventh date of Christmas, Seth, taking selfies while she wished he was someone else. Neither Nick nor Penny had arrived yet. How early in the day could she get Nick on his own and ask him exactly what that text was about? Her conflicted feelings couldn't stop squabbling until she knew where she stood with that. And once she knew the answer she either had some serious grovelling, or serious heart-mending, to do.

The door opened and Claudia turned in her seat.

Billy? What was he doing here?

He caught her eye and threw her a huge wave across the room. Behind him, holding his other hand, walked Penny, who looked directly at Claudia with a look of defiance, and then her jaw dropped.

Claudia was so bowled over by Billy being there with

Penny that it took a moment to notice why Penny was staring at her dress.

It was because she was wearing the exact same one.

Oh, for crying out loud.

Penny composed herself and pushed Billy into a row of seats near the back. Billy kissed her on the cheek and took her hand with such affection it nearly made Claudia smile tenderly at her best friend. What a good match. But then she remembered that she and Penny currently disliked each other and were wearing the same outfit. She turned back to Seth.

'Penny's here.'

'Is she?' he said, uploading one of his photos of himself to Facebook.

'She's wearing my dress.'

'Tell her to give it back.'

'No, not *my* dress, the same dress as me.'

'I'm not surprised; you two are always borrowing each other's clothes. You have the same taste, so buying the same thing was bound to happen some time. What's the problem?'

Claudia stole another glance at Penny, just as Nick walked in. She caught his eye. Last time she'd looked directly into his eyes they'd been inches from hers, in her bed.

He looked sad as his eyes shifted to Seth. Claudia's heart ripped. That didn't look like the face of someone who'd dodged a bullet. *Penny was right*. She didn't know for sure, but something in his look made her question how she could have ever jumped to the conclusions she did. Had she completely misinterpreted that text? And if so, was it possible she could apologise enough? She was about to mouth 'We need to talk' when the string quartet switched to the bridal chorus.

Nick ducked into an empty seat and avoided looking at her again.

Then in walked the bridesmaids.

Seth sniggered. '*Now* I see the problem!' he whispered in her ear.

Four bridesmaids, all wearing that same green dress.

Now not only did Claudia and Penny look like everyone's wedding nightmare, they also now looked like two spare bridesmaids who weren't special enough to be part of the wedding party.

Claudia caught Penny's eye and despite everything they shared a tiny moment of amusement, which fluttered her heart like breeze over a feather.

The brides stepped into the room together, dragging their eyes from each other to beam at their guests. Both dressed in off-white gowns that perfectly matched their different, but complementing, personalities.

The wedding was beautiful, funny and filled with anecdotes about the two brides that had Billy roaring with such loud laughter that Claudia had to smile.

'Right, you lot,' said the registrar to the guests. 'These lovely ladies need to do the important signing-stuff part now. While that happens, the quartet are going to accompany you while you have a little sing-song.'

Muttering rippled through the room.

'You'll notice there are twelve rows,' she continued. 'And at the end of your row is a number. The numbers are all mixed up – it's not one at the front, twelve at the back – and your number is the line of the song that your row will sing.'

'What's she on about?' Seth said.

'The song will be "The Twelve Days of Christmas". Lyrics are in your order of service. Row one, you kick us off.'

The string quartet started playing and row one, who were halfway back, grudgingly stood up and mumbled, 'On the first day of Christmas my true love gave to me a partridge in a pear tree . . .'

Claudia remembered with a flash her first date of Christmas. Way back at the Opera House. When she lost the man who was sitting next to her again now.

'Row two!' called the registrar.

Row two stood as row one sat. 'On the second day of Christmas my true love gave to me two turtle doves—'

'And a partridge in a pear tree!' sang row one, getting the gist and hopping back up in unison.

Her second date of Christmas – Starbucks. With the man at the back whom she'd since lost.

Row three contained Penny and Billy. Billy looked like he was having the time of his life, while Penny was just desperately trying to squeak out the correct notes. Claudia smothered a laugh at the exact moment Penny looked over. Her eyes narrowed, mistaking Claudia's humour for cattiness.

Row four were mostly the elderly guests, who took a speedy vote to remain seated for their line. Row five really went for it with their line – the best one – and Billy couldn't help himself so belted it out too.

Her fifth date of Christmas ... Nick again. That perfect afternoon on the South Bank. The BFI, the pub, and then Penny saying she liked him.

Row six was Claudia and Seth. As Claudia started to sing she was aware of Penny doing an exaggerated snigger from behind her. She sang louder, and with as much X-factor as she could muster. 'Six geese-a-laying ... '

Her sixth date of Christmas: the Shard with Billy. She glanced over her shoulder at him warmly.

The rows bobbed up and down, up and down, Emma and Ellie in fits of giggles trying to focus on signing the register, and Seth getting increasingly huffy next to her. Claudia dragged him up by his jacket, her nails digging into his skin through the fabric. 'Try harder,' she seethed between lines.

Nick was stuck on row twelve, so only got to sing one line, and then it was all over. Sounded about right.

Would she even get a twelfth date of Christmas?

Mulled wine and cream fuzzy blankets were handed to guests as they went out for photos on the lawn. Groups of school friends and work colleagues huddled together, wrapped up warmly, while the photographer crunched about in wellies capturing the moments.

Seth was staring wide-eyed at the other guests.

'What are you gawping at?' asked Claudia.

'Nothing, there are just so many ladies here.'

'It's a lesbian wedding; Emma and Ellie have a lot of lesbian friends.'

'I'm going to go to lesbian weddings more often.'

Was he deliberately trying to irk her?

'Can we get school friends of Ellie's, please?' called the photographer. Claudia's heart started to race and she left Seth staring at a couple sharing a romantic kiss by the fountain. She couldn't bring herself to make eye contact. Since Penny and Nick stood together to the right of the newly-weds, Claudia deliberately positioned herself on the other side, with a couple of men she hadn't seen since sixth form.

The photographer snapped a picture and checked her camera. 'No, that looks a bit crap. You in the bridesmaid's dress,' she said, pointing at Claudia. 'Could you move to the other side of the handsome chap.' She motioned to Nick.

Claudia froze, feet in the snow. 'Now?' she asked.

'It's not going to work if you wait until the next

wedding.' Claudia skulked over and stood stiffly, an arm's length away from Nick.

'Can you move in closer?' asked the photographer. 'Put your hand on his arm. Or on his chest. And handsome man, if you're interested, I'm not a lesbian.'

'Neither am I,' called Nick, his mind elsewhere. Claudia saw him blushing, unable to look at her as she edged closer and pasted on a smile. But he didn't look embarrassed. He looked hurt. She felt her armpits sweating against Nick's suit jacket and was very angry at her nether regions for lighting up like an electric hob just because she was near him.

'Try not to keep your eyes closed the whole time,' she murmured to him, testing his reaction. It wasn't what she'd been expecting.

He glanced down at her, surprised, looking directly into her eyes in a way that chilled her. He'd never looked at her so coldly before. 'That's the first thing you say to me? No apology?'

'Shut up you two,' hissed Penny.

Nick and Claudia went back to grinning at the camera. 'I got your text,' Claudia said quietly.

'And I got yours. Don't worry, message received.'

'I mean your first text. About me. About us.' She held her breath.

'What are you talking about?' He faced her again, clearly confused.

Just then an Australian accent rang out across the

grounds. 'Once a cheater, always a cheater!' Claudia, Nick and Penny turned to see Billy and Seth having a glare-off.

'Shit,' muttered Claudia.

'Thanks, all,' said the photographer. 'Okay, the uni friends now please.'

The three of them walked as briskly as you can over snow in smart shoes. 'Your new man seems to have a good head on his shoulders,' Nick told Penny pointedly.

'Billy,' cried Claudia, reaching them first.

'Hey, Claud,' said Billy with a big grin, leaning over and kissing her on the cheek. 'Good to see ya. Love your home town, it's so quintessential.'

'You know this guy?' spat Seth.

Claudia ignored him. 'I didn't know you were coming today,' she continued to Billy.

'Penny invited me. I was going to be spending Christmas with a couple of the guys from work – bit sad – but this lovely thing took me under her wing and is letting me spend Christmas with her. Isn't she ace?' He wrapped an arm around Penny, whose icy exterior melted a little as she relaxed against him. It was sweet.

'She's ... something,' Claudia agreed.

'How you doing, Billy, isn't it? I'm Nick,' Nick said, reaching out to shake his hand.

'All right, mate. Good to finally meet you. You're looking sharp.'

'You too. I'm quite jealous of your hair.'

Seth huffed. 'Well this is all very cosy, isn't it? Shall I leave you all to catch up?'

'Yes,' chorused Billy, Penny and Nick.

Seth turned to Claudia, who was hesitating. 'No,' she said reluctantly. She saw Nick roll his eyes just before he turned and walked away.

'Come on, Billy,' said Penny. 'I'm feeling a bit of a chill here. Mind if we go inside?'

'Sure, sweets. See you in a bit, Claud.' The two of them left Claudia and Seth standing awkwardly far from each other.

The meal and speeches were a casual affair, thankfully, with a buffet and a lounge filled with free-for-all comfy armchairs and sofas near fireplaces. Claudia had been dreading a seating plan forcing them all together, but she ended up eating a large plate of profiteroles on her own in a corner, the hotel cat sleeping on her feet.

It had been a while since she'd seen Seth. She was aware of him staggering back and forth to the bar from time to time, but she'd kept her distance, hoping to run into Nick alone.

Well, that wasn't going to happen if she sat in the corner like a crazy cat lady all night. She put the remainder of the profiteroles aside and plonked the grumpy mog in her place on the chair. She had to find Nick. Though it gave her an overwhelming urge to run away with a whole bottle of brandy, she had to face this and talk to him.

Claudia smoothed down her dress and started across the room.

Emma appeared, enveloping her in a hug. 'Thanks for coming today, hon, I love that you went all out with the colour scheme.'

Claudia laughed and took a step back to admire Emma's dress. 'Hey, I could have worn a wedding dress; *that* would have been awkward. You look gorgeous. Are you having an amazing day?'

'Yes, it's brilliant, my wife is such a drunk!'

'Your *wife*,' Claudia squealed. *Is that Nick in the corner?*

'I know. Claudia you have to get married really soon because then *you* can be the drunk wife we all laugh at. It's making amazing photos for the new house.'

Seth sidled up, draping a heavy arm over Claudia's shoulders and staring at her with drowsy eyes. Why couldn't he just go away? It was her fault he was here, though. Everything was her fault.

Ellie danced over, her eyes twinkling with tipsiness. 'I've taken off all my underwear! I feel so much more comfortable.' She saw Seth. 'Urgh, what are you doing here?'

'Ladies, you look *beautiful*,' Penny said to the newly-weds, appearing behind Claudia's shoulder. She hissed into her ear, 'We need to talk about something.'

'I'm going to get another drink,' sulked Seth, mooching off to the bar.

Penny turned towards the corridor. Claudia considered being stubborn, but she didn't want to mess up anything else by not listening to what needed to be said. She followed Penny out of the room.

'Nice dress,' Claudia deadpanned when they were alone.

'You too.'

'What happened to the LBD?'

'I was worried it was too slutty.'

Claudia felt a twist of guilt. 'It wasn't. Sorry about that.'

'That's okay. Listen, I've got something to tell you.'

'Did Billy make you pregnant?'

Penny chuckled. 'No. You don't mind me bringing him, do you?'

'It was a surprise, but I'm actually really happy. He's the nicest guy I've met in a long time.'

'You don't ... like him like *that*, do you?'

'No, absolutely not. So what do you want to tell me?'

Penny shuffled on the spot and tugged at her dress. 'I'm scared that what I tell you will make you think I'm being a bitch, but I'm not, I'm just trying to be a good friend.'

'What's going on? Is it about Nick?'

'No, it's about Seth.'

'Oh.'

'Claud, one of the bridesmaids just told me that Seth asked for her number. He was being smarmy and all

302

over her, and then said they should hook up while he's down here.'

Claudia's mouth dried and she became very aware of the sound of her breathing. 'Did she give it to him?' she asked, as if that were important.

'No, she'd seen him here with you and told him where to go. Plus she's a lesbian.'

'He's really drunk,' Claudia said.

'I know. Maybe it was just that—'

'No, I'm not excusing him. Who wants someone who can never get drunk because he'll cheat on me?' Her eyes filled with tears. It was Christmas Eve, why did she have to have tears on Christmas Eve?

Penny pulled her into a hug, their matching dress-beads clacking together. 'I don't know what's going on between you two – if you're getting back together or if you're just trying to figure some things out – but I just think you're brilliant and he's such a massive arsehole and I hate him.'

Claudia mopped her eyes on Penny's shoulder. 'I don't even know why I'm upset: I don't want to be with him any more.'

'It's understandable; he hasn't treated you very well,' she said tactfully.

'Ah yes, that's why.'

'Can I make a couple of suggestions?'

Penny took Claudia's big, snotty sniff as a 'yes' and went on.

'Firstly, I'm going to go and find Seth and send him home to your dad in a taxi. No one wants him here, and he's not going to ruin your evening.'

Claudia snorted another 'yes'.

'Then will you go and find Nick? You have to find out once and for all whether that text meant what you're obsessing over it meaning. I was going to ask him but Billy told me not to stick my nose in.'

'What if it did mean what I think it did?'

'Then Nick's a knob and we'll send him home to your dad as well.'

'What if he *says* it was something else, but he's just being a big fat liar?'

'Do you remember what happened to my birthday cake at my twenty-first?'

'Nick ate it.'

'Yes, Nick ate it. And do you remember how he tried to lie his way out of it, and the story got more and more elaborate and he broke out in hives and ended up having to lie down?'

'Nick's not very good at lying.'

'Exactly.'

Claudia sighed and gripped her friend harder. 'Penny, why are you being nice to me when I was such a cow to you yesterday?'

'Because I was just as much of a cow to you. I didn't even want to hear your side of the story.'

'My side was pretty weak. But I said horrible things

304

and called your clothes slutty, and they aren't – they're lovely, I really am just jealous.'

'What I did was much worse,' Penny cried, squeezing Claudia back. 'I squashed a whoopie pie on your face, which was mean and childish. And not being able to make decisions isn't a bad thing, it shows what an interesting, varied life you have. I wish I was you. I'm the one who's been doing the same thing day in, day out since I was a teenager. At least you've tried other stuff, at least you still have a world of opportunity in front of you. What options do I have? I want a baby, but then what if I'm too old or too out of shape to go back into ballet again? I'm scared, Claudia. As much as I want a baby I don't want it to be the end of me, and that's why I put *that* monumental decision off. So I feel really crap for berating you about not making your mind up. Sometimes it's just too *hard*.'

Now Claudia was bawling all over again, but thoughts of Seth had floated far away. 'Don't you dare feel crap, *I* feel crap. I need your help and opinions. I never meant for you to feel like a gooseberry, I was just feeling bitter and grumpy and it was easier to put my hands over my ears than hear what a cock-up I am.'

A bartender walked over and handed them each a hot toddy. 'Here you go, ladies, it's our crying bridesmaids' special. Chin up.'

'We're not—' Penny started.

'Shh.' Claudia clinked glasses with her and they both

gulped the fiery liquor. 'Okay, I need to find Nick.' Her hands were shaking as she put down the glass. Penny, her most brilliant friend in the whole world, went off to deal with her very-much-ex-boyfriend. Would her other best friend be as forgiving?

'Nick.'

She found him by the vast Christmas tree, absent-mindedly fiddling with a glass decoration in the shape of a sledge. He turned, the Christmas spirit draining from his eyes, and glanced behind her for Seth.

'Can we talk for a moment?' she asked.

'You don't need to, I've got the message. Can we just leave it?'

'No.' As soon as he said it she knew without a doubt she didn't want to 'just leave it'.

'Guys, come and dance,' ushered one of the brides-maids.

'We'll be there soon,' Claudia lied and turned back to Nick.

'Nick and Claudia, you bloody gorgeous pair,' shrieked a passing school friend.

They smiled politely and when he'd gone Claudia took Nick's hand, an act that still felt natural, even in the current state of their relationship, and pulled him into the gap behind the Christmas tree.

And there they were. Alone, and so close that they

breathed together. Surely they could just forget everything and go back to this. His face looked down at hers with sadness and a seriousness that made her feel very grown up, and scared for what was to follow.

'Why are you here with me? Where's your boyfriend?'

'I need to know what that text message meant.'

'What text message?'

She couldn't say the words aloud, even though they were imprinted on her memory, so handed him her phone.

He read it and Claudia studied him carefully, holding her breath. 'Oh. I wondered why Greg hadn't replied.' No embarrassment, no guilt. Then the penny dropped. 'You thought this was about you.'

He pulled her into him with such force that she crushed her face against his suit. *It wasn't about me*. She didn't need to hear any more. She gripped her arms around his back but he gently unhooked them and stood back.

'It's not about you, I swear. I'd never say anything like that about you, or our date – you meant too much to me.'

Meant? He couldn't be saying it was too late? Her hands were shaking. She tried to put them back around him, but he resisted, pulling her off.

'This text is about work. Not you. How could you ever think I'd write this about you?'

'I – the words, and the timing—'

'Greg needed me to interview a possible new set

designer for the team because she was running late and he had to go. She finally showed up and her portfolio was awful, like a rubbish GCSE art project. It was a huge waste of time so I cut it short and got out. Then I came and met you. The next morning was the first time I even thought about work and remembered I had to let Greg know how it went.'

'What about the "night out with the ladies" bit?'

'*That's* about you. Greg suggested we join him and his wife for a post-Christmas blues meal in January.'

Claudia almost fell into her second Christmas tree; she was so bowled over by a wave of relief and mortification. 'I'm the world's most humongous idiot.' She smiled at him, but he didn't smile back. A chill ran through her. *Please smile at me.*

'I can see why you took that the wrong way, it was bad timing and bad luck that I sent it to you, I guess my brain was all Claudia at that moment, and maybe I should actually think about getting a slightly more modern mobile, but do you really think so little of me?'

'No I don't – it was a mistake. I was heartbroken.'

'But Claud, I've worshipped you for so many years; if you ever did anything wrong I'd always be adamant you had a reason, that you were right. But where's your faith in me?' She tried to reach to him but he flinched. 'You were so quick to think I was a horrible person, to throw it all away and run back to him.'

'I'm not with Seth, that was just a kiss, a bad reaction.'

'It's not just a kiss when it's with him. He's been a huge part of your life.'

'Not as huge as you.'

'He's more to you than you want to admit, and I can't compete with that any more.'

Don't do this. 'I need you, Nick.'

He shook his head, withdrawing from her further. 'You don't need me. You need to be on your own for a while; I can't be your crutch.'

'Don't tell me I need to be on my own. Don't put words in my mouth.'

'You're both my best friend and the person I'm in love with.' He touched her face, painfully. 'How is this ever going to work? I can't be those things and see you keep going back to him.'

'Listen to me: I'm not going back to him. I don't want to be with him at all, I love you,' she said fiercely. She clung to his suit but his arms hung at his sides.

'I think you only love me as a friend.'

'I did, once. But Nick, Seth is just … nothing now. Don't let his stupid face ruin us.'

'Every time I turn around he's back there with you.'

'*No.* That morning I thought you'd left and I felt used, and I missed you like I'd lost a limb, and he was just *there.*'

'What happens next time he's just "there"?'

'There won't be a next time!' She was tired, fading to ashes. *Come on, Claudia, it's not over yet.* She pushed her hair back from her face and looked at him. Looked at her best friend, the one who'd always been there, the one she'd fallen for hard as soon as she'd realised. 'What can I do to make you forgive me? Tell me how to make it better.'

'I don't think it can be. We should have just stayed friends.'

'Bollocks we should have. That's not what either of us want.' No way. They had to be together. 'Let's try, Nick, don't give up – is this just a way to avoid my cooking?'

He smiled faintly. 'Yep. Your cooking sucks. Christmas pizza, for Pete's sake.'

'But I'm good at other things. I can ice skate. We can go ice skating again.'

'I got arrested.'

'Well, it's good to have new experiences, isn't it? We can have all these new experiences together.'

'Claudia, I don't think we can be friends now. It's too hard seeing you with him, or with other men.'

'But I don't even want to be friends with you, I want to be *with* you, so there won't be any other men.' Claudia tried to take his hand but he pulled it away. She found it and gripped it, hard. 'I want you to annoy me with your huge build-ups to everything, I want you to flirt with me, I want you to throw snow at me because you know exactly when I need you to break the ice—'

'Good one.'

'What? Oh, ha. And I want to spend Christmas with

you because you make it more magical than it's ever been. You *are* Christmas.'

Nick looked over her face one last time. 'It's been a great month in a lot of ways, but I don't think that can change anything.'

'It's been the best month I've ever had because of you, because of your crazy dates and your lovely, distracting arms and your . . . please don't go.'

'I need to be away from you for a while. I just need your face to fade away a little.'

He tore his eyes from her and edged slowly out from their hideaway, leaving her alone behind the Christmas tree.

Claudia collapsed to the floor. It really was over. The damage was done. Nick was a big part of her life and without him she'd never be herself again.

The strong scent of pine needles made her nauseous. Shaking, she stood up and wiped her eyes. It was time to go home.

Suddenly the branches were pushed back, the peal of tiny decorative bells rippling through her sorrow. Nick stood in front of her for no more than two seconds before he pulled her into a kiss that took her breath away. He crushed her against the wall and she kissed him back, afraid to let go and take a breath. What did this mean? Was it a goodbye kiss? Had he changed his mind? As he pulled back she linked her hands behind his neck, keeping close, if only for a moment longer.

'Why am I being such a stubborn twat?' he asked, searching her eyes, his lips millimetres from hers.

Claudia held her breath.

'Are you really done with him?'

She nodded. 'I was done with him when you bought me my first gingerbread latte this Christmas. It just took me a while to figure some stuff out. But I'm getting better at decisions and new adventures and stuff.'

Eventually he smiled softly. 'Well, I am quite a rip-roaring adventure. What do you say, bestie, shall we just say to hell with everyone else and shack up together?'

Claudia answered by launching herself into him and covering his lovely warm face in kisses.

Date Twelve

*Christmas Day at Claudia's
dad's house, Frostwood*

'You're getting lipstick all over me!' Nick laughed, stumbling out from behind the Christmas tree, his arms still wrapped around Claudia.

'Good, I'm marking my territory.'

'Ahem.' Emma cleared her throat and Claudia and Nick broke apart to see the entire wedding party gathered around the bride and bride. Some stared with surprise at two of their schoolmates hooking up, others with contempt at the slapper who was snogging a different man from the one she arrived with. They shuffled apart, but Claudia kept a strong grip on Nick's sleeve, just in case.

'It's not that we don't approve of your lifestyle, we just don't want it pushed in our faces,' Ellie slurred with a big, drunken wink.

'Listen, everyone,' Emma continued. 'Since we've been having a gay old time in here, quite the blizzard's been building outside. The front desk have told us no more taxis are coming in or out, the last one left a few minutes ago, and they can't get a gritter here until tomorrow. Ellie and I will be dancing our way into Christmas Day anyway, and if you can't make it home they've offered us a handful of their rooms for free.' She took a pause. 'I'm really sorry.'

Reactions were split – some whooped at the continued party and free hotel room, while others huddled in worried chatter about how they were going to get home for Christmas.

Claudia turned to Nick. 'We have to go home.'

'I don't think we can – no taxis. We can get a room here though; I'll pay if the free ones are taken.'

'No, we have to go home. I can't condemn poor Dad to spending Christmas morning alone with Seth.' She shuddered at the thought of Joe and Seth miserably pulling a cracker, Joe willing the toy to fly out and hit Seth in the eye. 'I don't know how we're going to do it, but I have to get back tonight, blizzard or no blizzard.'

Nick peered through the window. 'Okay. It doesn't look like it's snowing that heavily right now, it's just dumped about three feet already.'

'I'm going to walk it.'

'Yes, you're perfectly dressed for trudging through snow in the pitch black. Those heels have crampons, don't they?'

'I'll be fine, I'm very good with cold. Sometimes I have cold showers just for the hell of it.'

'Wow, my very own Bear Grylls. It's not that far – I'll carry you.'

'You can't carry me all the way back to the house.' Though the thought was rather yummy. Would he carry her over his shoulder? *Calm down, Claudia.*

'I carry heavier things than you backwards and forwards across the stage every night.'

'We'll take it in turns.'

'No offence, I'm all for women's rights and equality but there's no way you could carry me for more than about five seconds.'

'I could try. Jump on my back.'

'Shut your stupid face.' He took her hand and led her to Emma and Ellie, where they said their goodbyes and thank yous, then stepped out into the freezing night air. Fat snowflakes blustered around them while Nick wrapped Claudia in both her coat and his.

'You wear yours,' she demanded through chattering teeth.

'I'm already going to be wearing you, I'll be fine.' He crouched down, his back to her. 'Hop on.'

Claudia climbed on to his back, shook the powdery snow from her heels and nestled her cheek against the back of his head. He set off, slow and steady, taking enormous, BFG-style footsteps through the deep snow.

'I reckon we'll be there in about three quarters of an hour,' Nick called back. 'Once we get up to the road there'll be the streetlamps and *oof*—' he shouldered a tree that appeared in front of them. He stumbled briefly, chuckling, with Claudia clinging on.

'Are you sure I'm not breaking your back?' Claudia murmured into his ear after a while.

'Yes. I just can't ... stand ...' He started to tip forwards.

'Stop it!' Claudia screeched as the snow loomed close to her face.

Nick stood upright again and they continued. It was hard work, the dense snow and black night causing every step to take planning and effort. But not once did Nick complain or ask for a break. And although it was very selfish, nuzzled into the back of him was exactly where Claudia wanted to be.

Finally they reached a quiet residential street where silhouettes moved about behind curtains, stacking presents under iridescent Christmas trees. Small faces kept appearing at upstairs windows, looking up at the sky and then running back to bed. One house was holding a party, and the faint sound of Slade seeped through the windows, through which Claudia could see sparkly-dressed friends clinking champagne glasses, and one couple standing in the doorway looking at the snow. They raised their glasses at Nick and Claudia across the street. Claudia waved back.

'You can put me down now, the snow's much clearer here,' she said reluctantly; she would have been quite happy to stay in this position all through the holidays.

'We're nearly there now. And it's going to win major brownie points from your dad if I turn up with you on my back.'

'You don't need brownie points from him. He's been hinting about you and me getting together for yonks.'

'*Yes!* One-nil to Nick.'

In no time at all they were turning onto Claudia's driveway. Nick carried her all the way through her front door and into the living room.

He only dropped her to the ground when they came face to face with Seth.

'What has been going on here?' Claudia asked a guilty-looking Joe and Christine, who were standing in the corner giggling. Joe was holding Seth's phone.

Seth was propped upright on the sofa, snoring his head off and clutching a bottle of port. In his hair were copious pastel-coloured butterfly clips hijacked from Claudia's bedroom. His face was decorated with thick, clumsy make-up. He was draped in necklaces and clip-on earrings.

Joe stepped forward and handed Claudia Seth's phone, which was logged on to Facebook. 'I hope you don't mind, love. Penny called us and warned he was coming home, and what he'd been up to at the wedding. Well, he's not going to treat my daughter like that under my own roof. So . . . we did this.'

Claudia scrolled back through Seth's timeline. Joe and Christine had been busy. Photo after photo of Seth looking a far cry from the immaculate poses he only allowed online. Status updates of embarrassing 'confessions'. Inappropriate comments on other people's photos.

'What's this?' she asked, noticing several statuses that were chunks of text.

Joe put an arm around his daughter. 'I'm sorry, sweetheart, we looked at his messages and there were rather a lot to girls, saying things a chap with a girlfriend shouldn't be saying to others. Especially not when that girlfriend is my daughter.'

'They're horrible.'

'I know, not quite the smooth-talker he thinks he is. Then I thought: these girls are someone else's daughters – they probably have no idea what he was up to either. So I decided they, and everyone else, should know. Are you upset?'

She wasn't. In fact, she was really quite impressed with her dad. 'Actually, I feel like I dodged a bullet.'

'His number of friends is decreasing by the minute,' Christine told her with pride.

Suddenly Nick burst into such loud laughter over her shoulder that Seth stirred and nearly woke up. 'Joe, this one's *amazing*.' He pointed at the screen. Seth's profile photo had been changed to what looked uncannily like a picture of him with his willy poking out of his flies. His incredibly *tiny* willy. It already had forty-seven 'shares' and over a hundred 'likes'.

'That's his little finger – I did that!' Joe grinned. 'My *pièce de résistance*.'

'Seth's going to be really angry,' Claudia warned with a smile.

'Well, I'm really angry with him,' said Joe.

'Me too,' said Nick and Christine at the same time.

'Me too,' Claudia agreed.

'Come on then, Mum,' said Nick, turning around. 'Your turn for a piggyback – let's get you home for Christmas.'

'Don't leave yet.' Claudia held on to his hand. 'Dad, it's still blizzardy out. Nick and Christine could stay here, couldn't they?'

'Absolutely. Don't think you're leaving me to deal with this on my own on Christmas morning,' he said to Christine. 'You'll spend Christmas with us. I think we'd quite like a bit more of a full house, wouldn't we?'

Claudia nodded and turned back to Nick. 'Spend Christmas with me?'

'Another date? *Fine*. But you can't be lazy and sleep in tomorrow, okay? It's the most important day of the year.'

❄

'Merry Christmas.'

Claudia opened her eyes to find her eyelashes

pressed into Nick's bare chest and a light dribble coming from her mouth. She'd been gripping him in her sleep, afraid of him not being there again in the morning.

'Merry Christmas,' she answered. 'What time is it?'

'Christmas time,' he grinned. 'It's coming up to nine. You slept in way longer than I can on Christmas morning.'

'Sorry, but you're very comfortable. I think I'll go back to sleep.' She snuggled back down and he wriggled away from her.

'No you will not.' He rolled out of bed and padded across her room, throwing open the curtains like a delicious, naked illusionist.

Claudia sat up in bed and watched him. She'd already received her best Christmas present of all.

He scuttled back under the warmth of the duvet. 'Does spending Christmas Day together count as a date?'

'I think so. Which makes this my twelfth date of Christmas.'

'Twelve dates?' He whistled. 'What a goer. "The Twelve Dates of Christmas". Ha! See what I did there?'

There was a knock on the door.

'Merry Christmas, you two,' Joe called. 'Claud, your mum's on the phone.'

A childlike rush of happiness burst through Claudia and with a quick smooch on Nick's lips she jumped from her bed and pulled on some pyjamas. 'Do you want to meet me downstairs when you're dressed?'

Nick sniggered. 'I'm naked in your dad's house on Christmas Day. Don't tell Jesus.'

Claudia took the phone from her dad and curled up in a window seat. Flippers was leaping in and out of the snow on the lawn below, making a fine mess.

'Mum?'

'Merry Christmas, sweetheart! I didn't wake you, did I?' Her mother's voice was crystal clear and more familiar than it had ever been, despite being over ten thousand miles away.

'No, I'd just woken up. What time is it over there?'

'Just gone ten – it's the end of the big day for us.'

'Did you have a good Christmas?'

'It was lovely – hot and sunny, same old. I do miss England at Christmas, it's not the same here. I miss you.'

'I miss you, too.'

'Your dad tells me you have a new man.'

Claudia had always felt a bit funny talking to her mum about boys. Perhaps it was because her mum had always tried to be her girlfriend more than her mother, a fact that left her feeling more annoyed than happy. Even now the feeling remained a little, and she didn't want to go into too many details. 'It's just Nick, do you remember him?'

'The one who stared at you all the time? Of course.'

'No he didn't.' Claudia smiled. 'But yes, him.'

'Seth all gone?'

Claudia glanced at the spare-room door. 'As good as.'

'Do you want to tell me what happened?'

'We were just in a bit of a rut ... It doesn't matter.'

'I get that, you wanted a new adventure.'

'No,' Claudia said quickly. 'I mean yes, but it's just a one-time thing.'

'Sweetheart,' her mum said softly. 'I know you don't want to end up like me.'

'It's not that I don't want to be like you, it's just ...' Claudia tried to form her words. 'No matter how much adventure you had, it never seemed to be enough. You never seemed satisfied. What if I get everything I'm looking for and then start feeling in a rut again?'

'That's a risk you're going to have to take. You can't not take risks just because they might not suit you in the long run. If they're worth taking then they're worth taking. You think I regret for one second taking the risk of marrying your dad and having you? Just because an adventure comes to an end, or changes into something else, doesn't mean it wasn't worth doing.'

Claudia mulled this over. 'I'm scared.'

'But Claudia, you're not me. Wanting a new adventure doesn't mean you're *always* going to be wanting complete lifestyle changes. You've never been like me in that respect. You're able to find magic and adventure within a solid life, sharing it with other people. I know you've felt stuck but that's just because that situation was wrong for you, not because you can't ever enjoy a situation.'

'Thanks, Mum.'

'Here's an adventure for you. How about you and Nick visit me in New Zealand next year?'

Something stirred inside Claudia. Her mum had invited her over many times, and although she'd been once she usually declined, always feeling resentment at having to go crawling across the world after her mum. But her bitterness was shifting. Her mum was just a person and she'd tried, in her own way. Maybe it was time.

'You want to meet the new boyfriend?' Claudia asked with a smile.

'I want to meet the new you. But yes, I also want to properly meet the boyfriend. What do you reckon?'

'I reckon that sounds perfect.'

Her mum squealed down the phone. 'Hon, that is the best Christmas present – I can't wait. Now you go and enjoy your day, eat lots of Christmas pudding for me, and I'll phone you again in a couple of days and we can discuss dates.'

Claudia rang off, her mind turning to Christmas presents. Before she joined the extended family downstairs there was something she wanted to go and find.

'No, honestly, it's a real thing – it was even on *National Lampoon's Christmas Vacation*.'

'But I need that for the parsnips.'

'Let's all just have one go and then we'll bring it back in.' Claudia entered the kitchen to find Nick, wearing her dad's jumper and stonewash jeans, holding a baking tray and a bottle of spray oil. Christine was wearing an apron, hands on hips, and Joe was pulling on his hat and gloves.

'Happy Christmas, all. Nick, are you doing what I think you're doing?'

'Yes! Mum, Claudia'll tell you – it's so much fun.'

Claudia hugged Christine and her dad, wishing them a merry Christmas. 'It really does work; a baking tray makes an excellent sledge. We tried it a couple of years back on Hampstead Heath. Dad, are you coming?'

'Too right. Though I'll go last because I might bend the tray.'

'There'll be no bending the tray; I'll have unevenly roasted parsnips,' said Christine.

'Come on, Mum, come and have a go. This can wait.'

'Why are you doing this anyway, Christine?' asked Claudia. 'You're the guest.'

'I want to, it's a thank you for letting us stay over, and because I don't have any pressies with me to give out.'

'Fine, then as part of the thank you we command you to slide down a hill on a baking tray.' Claudia pulled on her coat over her pyjamas.

'Aren't you getting dressed first?' Joe asked.

Claudia popped a Chocolate Orange segment in her mouth and headed for the door. 'Nope, it's Christmas Day. Can't be bothered.'

It wasn't until she stepped outside that Claudia remembered Seth.

'I just remembered Seth,' she said to no one in particular. 'We don't want him here today, do we?' There was a rousing chorus of 'no's and a growl from Flippers, whose lower body was buried in snow. 'Right, could one of you call a taxi and I'll go get him up and send him on his way.'

'Tell him he's an absolute idiot for letting you go, but I'm very glad he did,' said Christine, flushing pink.

'Tell him if he ever steps foot in my house again I'll make sure he has *no* friends left, on and off Facebook,' Joe added.

Then Nick said, 'And tell him he's got crap hair and I've always thought he's a dick. Sorry, Mum.'

'Oooh, he's such a dick with a teeny tiny dick!' Christine clenched her fists.

'Christine!' laughed Claudia. 'I'll tell him all those things. Back in a mo; save a ride for me.'

Claudia went up the stairs two at a time. She thought back over the last few weeks, at how much had changed. How nervous she had been approaching Seth for a confrontation that night of their date. Even when they first arrived in Frostwood she was afraid of sending Seth home to a Christmas on his own, before he threw it in her face with his behaviour at the wedding. Now she felt nothing but eagerness: he was nothing more than a bug on the windscreen that she was looking forward to washing off.

She threw open the spare-room door and Seth shot up in bed, fully clothed, and immediately gripped his head.

'Bloody hell, did you pickaxe my head last night? It feels awful.'

'Nope,' she said, opening the curtains and picking up his duffel bag. She unzipped it and started chucking his clothes in. 'Didn't give you so much as a passing thought last night, to be honest.'

'What are you doing, hon?'

'Just helping you pack.'

'Why?' It never took Seth long to bore of a conversation, and he was already reaching for his phone. He frowned at the screen. 'I've been popular overnight – got about a million Facebook notifications.'

'You're leaving.'

Seth yawned and scratched his balls, still scrolling through his phone. 'Why? Isn't it Christmas Day? Did I sleep right through it? Hmm. People have said some very un-Christmassy things to me on here. Not much Christmas spirit . . .'

'It is Christmas Day. Merry Christmas. Get out.'

Finally he put down his phone. 'What have I done now?'

'I know about the bridesmaid, I know about the other girls on Facebook—' She held up her hands as he started to protest. 'Listen to me. I'm not asking for explanations, or excuses, or apologies; believe me when I say I'm not asking for anything from you any more. It's finally okay that you don't care, because I don't care either.'

'But I want to be your boyfriend,' Seth sulked, rubbing his head.

'Boo-hoo.' She zipped up the bag and pulled back the covers. 'Bye then.'

She went back down the stairs with Seth close behind, blabbering something that was pretty much white noise. As they exited the house a large snowball zoomed past her and landed with a wallop in Seth's face. Claudia studied three guilty faces, and then spotted Christine brushing the snow from her gloves.

'*Bloody hell*,' Seth fumed. He wiped his eyes and glared at the four of them. 'Oh, of course you're here,' he snarled at Nick.

'I was always here,' he laughed. 'Just waiting for you to cock it up.'

The taxi rolled up outside the house and Seth stamped over to it. He climbed in and miserably got his phone out. As the taxi pulled away Claudia saw realisation dawn and the expression on his face transform to mortification, and then rage as he looked back at them out of the window. Joe gave him a thumbs-up.

Christine got so into baking tray-sledding that after getting into a heated race with a child from across the road she had to be coaxed back inside with the promise of a glass of port and first pickings of the chocolates hidden on the Christmas tree.

Once back in the house Joe put on his triple CD of Christmas music and Christine went back to cooking what was sure to be a stonking Christmas lunch.

Claudia excused herself and went to warm her legs by the crackling log fire that Joe had been up early lighting. She dialled Penny, who answered the phone laughing her head off.

'Claud!' she cried, between giggles. 'Happy Chrimbo!'

'And to you. Are you having a good day?'

'The best – Billy is hilarious, everyone loves him.' Claudia beamed inside. Penny hadn't sounded this happy, this content, for a long time. She asked, 'How about you?'

'Really good. Seth's gone. Nick's still here. Let's have a Boxing Day coffee? No cake, though.'

'Ha! That would be perfect – we have so much to catch up on; I won't have seen you for a whole twenty-four hours.'

Back in the kitchen, Nick was crouched in front of the oven gazing at the turkey when Claudia reappeared beside him. 'I have a Christmas present for you.'

'I have one for you, too, but it's at home,' he apologised.

'That's okay. Mine's small, it's nothing really. I just thought it would be nice to give it to you finally.' She pulled him out of the kitchen and back up to her bedroom. She handed him an envelope containing a hastily written Christmas card. Inside the card was a folded piece of faded, lilac paper.

'What's this?'

'It's a letter I wrote to you when I was eighteen, on the day of the leavers' ball. I never got to give it to you but I kept it here. Sorry about all the hearts instead of dots on the "i"s.'

"Hi Nick."

'Don't read it out loud,' she cringed, but looked over his shoulder.

Hi Nick,

Wassuuuuuuup? I can't believe tonight's our LAST NIGHT OF SCHOOL STUFF!! You're going to college soon to be a mega-famous set designer. Don't forget me!!!!!!! We'll have a brilliant time tonight. I hope they play Rollin' by Limp Bizkit because you look really cool dancing to that. Hey, you always look cool!!!!!!

'This is true, I do always look cool,' said Nick.

'I'm so sorry about all the exclamation marks,' laughed Claudia.

I'm just writing you this letter — this is so embarrassing!!! — to say that I'm going to miss you and there's something I've wanted to do for a while. Hopefully by the time you read this we'll have had a kiss and then maybe the memory of me will stay on your lips while you're away.

'I never knew you were such a cheestring,' Nick said tenderly.

I think I fancy you, and I hope you fancy me!!!!! Maybe when we're thirty we'll have a big mansion and loads of babies and we'll tell them about tonight as being when we first got together.

'You would have run a mile if I'd given you this at the time, I'm sorry I was such a stalker.'

Righty-roo, time to get ready. Do you like me in glitter eyeshadow? I hope so. I won't be wearing lip gloss tonight. Hopefully I'll just be wearing you (on my lips).
    Loadsa lurve, Claudia!!!!!!!
    Xoxoxoxoxoxoxoxoxoxoxoxoxo

'So.' Claudia took the letter from Nick and set it aside. 'Some things have changed since then. I don't want loads of babies – at least not yet – and I know I look awesome in glitter eyeshadow; I don't need you to validate that any more. But I am still a bit of a cheestring, so I want this to show you that you have nothing to ever feel insecure about, because, really, it's always been you. Exclamation mark, exclamation mark, exclamation mark.'

Nick pulled her into him. 'Oh, Claud, I just don't know if I can be with someone that says "wassuuup".'

'It was 2001. It was cool back then. *I* was cool back then.'

'Thank God you're not cool now, eh?' He gave her a kiss. 'Thanks for saving this. I was such a chicken for not kissing you that night. But it's nice to know you wanted to, and it wasn't just Malibu and hormones. Now, since we're up here, how about a bonk before the big meal?'

'We can't do that – our parents are downstairs.'

'Fine. But I'm going to eat a lot so don't expect anything from me this afternoon.'

Thankfully Joe's big appetite meant he always bought far too much food at Christmas, so there was plenty to feed the four of them. Christine's Christmas feast was as good as Nick had been raving about: buttery turkey; big, dark roast potatoes; mounds of seasoned vegetables; the biggest platter of pigs in blankets, which made Nick's eyes fall out of his head; crunchy chestnut stuffing and endless sherry-spiked gravy.

'Do you know what the best thing about getting together with you is?' Claudia asked Nick, whose plate resembled Mount Fuji.

'Is it my hat?' His too-small gold party hat sat tall on his head.

'That's the second best. I do want that hat. The best thing is that we've known each other for years, which means we've eaten in front of each other countless times, which means I don't have to eat delicately or be paranoid about gravy dripping down my chin like I would with a real new boyfriend.'

Nick guffawed. 'I love it when a girl doesn't feel she has to make an effort around me.'

When the meal was over Claudia carried the plates back to the kitchen, Christine right behind her with the gravy boat.

'I've always thought you two should be together.' Christine winked and scuttled out of the kitchen. Claudia picked up the Christmas pudding and was heading back to the dining room when Joe passed with the leftover roast potatoes.

'I've always thought you two should be together,' he whispered.

As Nick served up the rich Christmas pudding

Claudia looked around the table at this funny, snowed-in, makeshift family spending their first Christmas together. If only she'd known that all it took was twelve simple dates to change her life. She'd tried so many subtle things, not wanting to rock the boat too hard, and all she'd really needed to do was be herself. With Nick, she could be herself. With the decision she'd made about her future, she could be herself.

Nick was lying on the sofa holding his stomach like he was about to give birth, his eyes drooping.

'Before Nick falls asleep, I just have something I want to tell you.' Nick opened an eye, Joe put down the *Radio Times* and Christine folded up the Monopoly instruction sheet ('I'm not having Nick making up rules again this year'). Flippers plodded over and sat in front of Claudia, blocking her from everyone's view. She pulled him in towards her.

'I've decided to try something new.' She looked at Nick. 'I'm going to take the Royal Ballet job.'

That woke him up. 'You are? That's brilliant news!'

'It's just for a year, right?'

'Yeah.'

'Here's the plan. I've decided I want to get back into dancing. I'm not kidding myself, I'm not as skilled as I used to be, though I'm still good. But I'll need some time to train up. I'm going to use this year as a new adventure, and it'll allow me to have the time to get some qualifications and get something lined up so that by the end of the year I'll be ready to teach dancing.'

'You want to teach?' asked Joe with a smile. 'I think you'll be absolutely brilliant at that, love.'

Claudia blushed. 'I've been thinking about it and I think it would be kind of perfect for me. But I couldn't just waltz into a dance studio and do it now; I do need some training, to get up to speed.' She turned back to Nick. 'I figured, why not have an extra little life adventure in the lead-up. Make a name for myself at the Royal Ballet.'

Nick combat-rolled off the sofa and shuffled over to her, wrapping her and Flippers in a big duvet-like hug. 'I'm going to annoy the hell out of you next year. I'll always be there, gagging for a snog, making you put photos of me in your book. I can't wait.'

'I can't wait either,' Claudia laughed.

Joe handed out some tiny glasses. 'We don't have any champagne, but let's toast with some sherry.'

They'd just clinked when Nick yelled, 'Stop!' He looked at his watch. 'The Queen's Speech. Places, everyone.'

Obediently they all settled around the TV, sherry in hand.

'Do you reckon the Royals are doing this right now? Gathering together, quaffing the sherry, rubbing their full stomachs, to watch their gran on TV?' asked Joe.

'Maybe she gives them a live version,' said Nick.

'Actually, she watches from a different room,' Claudia said. 'She can't stand seeing herself on TV.'

'Oooh, neither can I.' Christine shook her head, as if she'd experienced similar television coverage to the Queen of England.

Nick looked at Claudia. 'How do you know that?'

'I just heard it somewhere.'

When the speech was over Joe reached under the tree and passed a neatly wrapped parcel to Claudia. 'It's just a little something, love. So you can start building up your own little adventures.'

She unwrapped the parcel and inside were four Rough Guides. One for the UK, one for Europe, one for New York and one for New Zealand.

'The New Zealand one's from your mum.'

This was so thoughtful. 'How did you know to get such a perfect gift?'

'I know everything.'

'You really do. Nick, there are so many more dates we can go on now.' She turned back to her dad. 'The New York one—'

'I'm going to take you on that holiday next year, but you can plan the itinerary. Deal?'

'How about we go next December? We could all go: Christmas in New York is supposed to be amazing – we could see the Rockettes, go up the Empire State Building, go shopping in Bloomingdales, see ice hockey in Madison Square Garden—'

Joe yawned. 'That sounds perfect. You plan whatever you like love. Merry Christmas.'

❄

Christmas Day stretched to an end. Outside the candlelit houses of Frostwood the sky painted itself bleak again and the snow returned, dusting over the footprints and sled-tracks, preparing a clean palette for Boxing Day fun.

On the sofa, Claudia relaxed back against the warmth of Nick, who wouldn't take his arms from around her. He sprinkled the top of her head with kisses as he lazily watched *Miracle on 34th Street* and she flicked through her guide books. Joe was snoozing quietly, his Santa hat falling over his eyes, while Christine snored loudly from the opposite armchair. Flippers lay upside down in front of the fireplace, his belly toasting happily.

Claudia rolled over to face Nick. 'You know last night, when we were behind the Christmas tree?'

'Mmm-hmm,' he smiled sleepily.

'You said something. Do you remember?'

'I said a lot of bollocks, sorry about that.'

'But there was one other thing. You said you loved me.'

'That I did.'

'Was that bollocks? I mean, we haven't been together long – I don't blame you if you haven't fallen in love.'

'I haven't fallen in love,' he yawned. 'I've loved you for years.'

Claudia stretched up and pressed her face against Nick's, giving him a happy kiss.

He dragged over the tin of Quality Street. 'Here, I saved you all the strawberry creams.'

'You did? You can have one.'

'Nah, that's okay, they're your favourites. Can I have some of the toffee pennies?

She knew she shouldn't base an entire relationship upon Christmas chocolates, but it was one heck of a way to start.

Merry Christmas!

Acknowledgements

I think we all know that Charles Dickens wrote the best Christmas story of all with *A Christmas Carol*, so with a big thanks to him for starting the trend, may I take up just a smidge more of your time to thank a few others for their help with my little festive offering?

Manpreet (AKA Mampers), what can I say? Thanks for taking a chance on me and believing I could write something that wasn't *too* Beyoncé fan-fiction. You deserve way more than a box of Wispas for putting up with my questions every five minutes. Let's go the Hummingbird Bakery again soon (but not have a food fight). And everyone else at Little, Brown – Hannah G, Marina, Zoe, Liz, and the copyedit team, Frances and Clara, Sarah, Hannah W, Jo, AndE, and all the others who put their time and effort into helping my silly old book – thank you, and Chocolate Oranges all round!

Agent Hannah, thanks for loving *Twelve Dates* and

then loving me, because I know I'm totally your fave.

My husband Phil, who shunned manlier books to painstakingly read every word of *Twelve Dates* several times over. I would have been a procrastinating mess without you, and I promise we'll get our own Flippers really soon.

Emma – who in real life is not a lesbian, nor is she marrying my g-stringed matey Ellie – you're the best reader/writer I know, thanks so much for all your input.

Yes, Dad – you were indeed right when you 'always said I would do it'. Thank you for always keeping the faith in me. PS Claudia's dad bought her a dress. Just saying.

Mum – you're my best pal and brilliant in every way. Thanks for listening to me blabber on for hours, not just with this book, but all the time. PS Let's make Dad buy us something.

There are so many family and friends who've been amazing and supportive – Paul, Laura, Beth, Mary, David, Jude, Robin, Eleanor, Peter, Katie, Ross and everyone at the day job. And Liam and Kath – thanks heaps for the brilliant, shiny website (at www.lisadick-enson.com). You guys are ace. Aren't they ace?

And finally, thanks to Wham!, Mariah, The Ronettes, Bublé, Bing, Ella, East 17 and all the singers of my favourite Christmas songs who kept me in the festive spirit as I wrote this all summer long.

Twelve Tips to Dating in London

1. *Be open to new people.* London is a big bubble bursting with people who are just bursting with life. Sure, it has its fair share of weirdos, but there are a lot of diamonds in that rough, and everyone looks good under Christmas fairy lights anyway – haha.

2. *Do something festive.* Find yourself some ice skating, a carol service, or a Christmas market. Walk around Winter Wonderland or share a bag of sweet-smelling roasted nuts from a street vendor. All good excuses to huddle close and brush your begloved hands against each other.

3. *Be different.* Dinner dates are lovely and romantic and full of twinkle and light, but why not try something new and meet for a breakfast date instead? From creperies in Brixton, to Jamie Oliver's Recipease in

Notting Hill, to the Cereal Killer Café on Brick Lane, there are plenty of reasons to start a crisp wintery morning with something other than a lie-in.

4. *Get your cheap on!* One of the big, beautiful qualities of London is how it lobs free things at you from all angles. So don't panic and think dating equals an empty wallet, it just equals a chance to do some things you wouldn't normally do. Visit the V&A together, curl up at a Christmassy outdoors music event, rock up to a light switch-on, the possibilities are (nearly) endless.

5. *Take them to places they've never been before* ... NOT IN A RUDE WAY! Maybe a bit in a rude way ... But what I mean is, take your date to a place neither of you have visited – that way it's new and interesting for both of you, and there's no pressure or embarrassment if anything goes wrong.

6. *Pick somewhere near a Tube line* ... My most romantic of tips. But seriously, London Tube closures and delays can cause panic when you're due to meet someone, made worse if there's a massive walk the other end. Also, you can then eke out your date at the other end, without the worry of missing the last train.

7. *So many Christmas movies, so little time.* Sometimes in December, we all just want to flop down and watch a Christmas movie (this is me like, every day). Combine this wonderful laziness with a special date and visit the BFI (British Film Institute) on London's South Bank and catch a Christmas classic together on the big screen.

8. *Choose a location with a view.* Dates – especially first dates – can be hard and awkward and basically *the worst* (have fun!) so damage-control this by picking a location with a lot to say about its beauty or its history. London can help you so much here! E.g. 'Did you know outside this pub was where Jack the Ripper actually killed one of his victims?!' You're welcome.

9. *Have a big night out.* Christmas is a great time to go to the theatre, and whether you prefer enticing plays, festive pantos or classic musicals London has them all. Pick something you'd both be into and start the holiday season with a bang. And some expensive wine gums.

10. *Plan ahead, just a little.* London is one of the top destinations in the world at Christmas (in my opinion) thanks to its history filled with kings and queens and Charles Dickens, and its architecture of

castles and palaces and pubs and parks. It's no wonder the tourists pour in, and so they should, but if there's a date you're desperate to have, book it in advance to avoid sadness and ruining the relationship for ever ;)

11. *Do a festive-drink crawl.* I refuse to believe that a fantastic Christmas date can't be found in Starbucks. You can be in an out within half an hour if it's bad, or you can sample every festive drink on the menu while the rain pitter-patters against the windows if it's good. And if it's *really* good, then you can step it up a notch and take your partner elsewhere for some mulled wine or hot toddies.

12. *Ignore the dress codes.* Yes, Londoners are stylish. But they're also quirky, or cosy, or grungy, or pretty. There are so many people in London, and in winter especially it can be chuffing cold, so I don't think you *at all* need to follow a certain type of outfit etiquette when dating. There's plenty of 'types' for everyone, so be comfy, be warm, and be you.

Twelve Mini Breaks of Christmas

You've had your twelve dates, you little lovebirds, now are you ready to up the commitment to twelve cosy Christmas mini breaks?

For the Mr & Mrs Darcys . . . Bath

Baby, it's cold outside, but when you're neck-deep in a warm thermal pool with views over the beautiful city of Bath, and an equally as hot hottie by your side, frankly, let it snow, let it snow, let it snow. With gingerbread-coloured architecture, Christmas markets and lots to explore, Bath is a great little love nest.

For the falling in lovers . . . Devon

Snowy hills, weather-beaten tors, and ponies as far as the eye can see, Dartmoor National Park is a great place for some fireplace R&R with your other half. Two Bridges Hotel in particular offers amazing food and beautiful, historic rooms, and not a huge amount to do but relaaaax into each other.

For the traditionalists ... Various Christmas markets, Germany
It's an obvious one, but something everyone who loves Christmas should experience at some point. Walking around snow-covered streets, Prince or Princess Charming on your arm, and munching on waffles drenched in melted chocolate is pretty much what Christmas is all about. Sort of. Mmmm chocolate.

For the big kids ... Disneyland Paris
You can't say holding hands and screaming your heads off as you zoom up and down on a haunted hotel-themed roller-coaster isn't an interesting way to spend a date. Unleash the laughing and let your hair down at a place that literally sings *Joyeux Noël* at you both from the minute you arrive.

For the wannabe-nakeds ... Dubai
If frostbite and fireplaces ain't your thang over Christmas, and you're desperate to see a little more of your partner's skin (you dirty girty) then hot hot hot winter sun is a doable seven hours' flight from London. So stick your bikini and your roast turkey in your bag and get ready for luxury and luuuurve.

For the Claudia & Nicks ... London

Perhaps you don't live in London, or perhaps you do but the two of you never do the touristy stuff. Experience the magic of this amazing city and soak in the history, the skylines, and all the mulled wine and gingerbread lattes you can manage. And wear a Christmas jumper while doing so, please.

For the drunk in loves ... Edinburgh

Smooching over hot whiskies with a stunning castle backdrop is a pretty fiery way to spend some time away with someone special. If you can, time your mini break to Edinburgh so you're there over Hogmanay (New Year's Eve), for extra fun and magic.

For the adventurers ... Iceland

Step your dating game up by treating that hunk or hunkess of yours to a whirlwind trip to see the Northern Lights. Three-night breaks with flights start around £300 per person in December, and *man*, will they owe you a good Christmas present after that experience!

For the surf dudes with attitudes ... Cornwall

Steely grey seas and waves as big as love-story emotions, the Cornish coast has a drama to it in the winter that begs for couples to eat fish and chips under thick blankets. For a bit of calm, Christmas magic, head to pretty

Mousehole, famous for its festive light display, and potentially never return home.

For the love machines ... Lake District
Take a break from work and cities and brick walls and rent a beautiful log cabin in the Lake District. You can bag one with an open fire and your very own hot tub, and who the heck cares if it rains! Winter is coming, bring it on.

For the pre-Christmas pamperers ... All over the world
Perhaps you both need a break from work, festive drinking, or just to relax your minds and bodies before all that family craziness over the holidays. Book yourselves into a spa weekend somewhere beautiful, and red wine and couples-massage yourselves up to your hearts' content.

For love like in the movies ... New York City
There's a good reason New York is the heartbeat of so many romantic tales – its charm, magic and wowability, especially at Christmas, make the streets and skyscrapers sparkle like Tiffany diamonds. Book lovers should cosy up at The Library Hotel, where a certain author happened to get engaged ...

Did you enjoy
The Twelve Dates of Christmas?

Turn the page for an extract from
Lisa Dickenson's hilarious
You Had Me at Merlot ...

'I've done it!' I paced around in my little flat in my heels, slowing my breathing. 'Six years after it came out, I've finally just perfected the "Single Ladies" dance routine.'

'Congratulations,' said Laurie down the phone. 'Does that mean you haven't left home yet?'

'I'm not getting a boyfriend now – all this hard work's not going to waste,' I warned her.

'Fine, you don't have to get a boyfriend today, but you do have to get on the Tube and get down to Wimbledon.'

'Are you there already?'

'Not far. Now take off that leotard—'

How did she know?

'—and get your smelly self into the shower.'

I put down the phone and peeled off my sweaty leotard and heels, chuffed to bits with my achievement. I hummed and danced all the way into my lovely waterfall shower in my lovely turquoise bathroom, surrounded by only beautiful-smelling girl stuff, feeling as happy as ever to be living alone. And after I stepped out, I pulled on a dress and flung open the curtains as if I hadn't been doing anything weird.

'Hello out there,' I said to the brightly dressed people of Notting Hill. 'How's the furnace this morning?'

The Tube train shuddered to a stop, allowing another heave of bodies to clamber aboard, while two more rivulets of sweat pole-danced their way down the backs of my legs. It was pretty sexy. London hadn't been this hot since the great fire in 1666 (possibly), and the residents were dropping like flies and grumbling all the way round the Circle line.

I like London in the heat – the more *scorchio* the better. I like it when tourists flock in and their preconceived idea of an England gushing with rain is carried away on a warm breeze; cloudy, bruised skies windscreen-wiped to reveal bright, royal blue.

And there's nothing a Brit loves more than sitting out in the midday sun at the first sign of summer, which was why I was joining hundreds of people on the annual pilgrimage to Wimbledon for the start of the tennis. My friend Laurie is an event photographer, which means she gets coveted seats at amazing stuff, and as I'm the only stable other half in her life I'm often along for the ride.

I lifted the hem of my maxidress off the floor, cooling

my ankles. I'd seen Paris Hilton wearing a similar maxi at Coachella this year, and thought it would be perfect for Wimbledon, but looking at my fellow passengers in their Jack Wills and Ralph Lauren I felt a bit silly in the tie-dye ensemble.

The doors finally dragged open at Southfields, throwing up its contents upon the platform, and I followed the crowd on the fifteen-minute walk to the famed tennis courts.

As I entered the All England Lawn Tennis and Croquet Club Laurie flew at me, an excited bundle of cameras, bags, merchandise and messy black hair. 'Elle! I just saw Venus Williams coming out of the toilet!' she shouted as a greeting.

'Are you sure? I feel like she'd have her own toilet, like in a dressing room.'

Laurie considered this. 'Well, I took a photo, so we can check later on. If not, I have a photo of a stunning girl coming out of a toilet.'

'What did you buy?' Laurie's house was chock-a-block with memorabilia from everything she goes to – she's the only one I know who will buy up everything on the overpriced merchandise stalls at a concert, or will actually purchase the robes, flannels and soap dishes from a hotel gift shop rather than just stealing them from her room.

'Everything. I got us T-shirts, pencils and sweat-bands,' she said, slipping a fluffy white one on my wrist.

We made a pit stop at a strawberries stand and the bar before hauling all of Laurie's equipment over to Centre Court and positioning ourselves on the green plastic seats, blobs of cream threatening to fall off our strawberries and land with a splat upon the head of the spectator in front, and plastic beer cups splashing foam on my flip-flopped feet. It was only when I noticed the empty seat next to us that I realised someone was missing.

'Hang on, where's Tim?'

'I can't believe I forgot to tell you!' Laurie cried. 'We split up.'

'I can't believe you forget to tell me as well!'

'Well ... he was kind of forgettable. You just proved that yourself.'

We took a moment to mourn the loss of Tim, who was indeed forgettable, so much so that I regularly forgot his name when we were out and kept calling him *m'dear*.

'What happened?'

'I just couldn't see myself still with him in a couple of years, let alone growing old. He was very nice and everything, a lovely guy really, and I wish I'd felt more towards him, but it was all just a bit "meh". So I broke up with him.'

At that point the crowd shushed as the players, glistening men in crisp white shorts, took their places on opposite ends of the court. We chomped on our juicy strawberries and watched the sweating gents on either side of the net, their balls thunking back and forth, so to speak, accompanied by primal grunting, which turned my thoughts back to relationships.

'Are you sad?' I whispered.

'No. Just disappointed that it didn't work out, again.'

'The ladies aren't going to be happy about this set-back,' I reprimanded her. 'The ladies' are our group of girlfriends, brought together through university, a mis-matched group of opposites who all attracted. All of them, except for Laurie and me, grew up and are now in one or more of the marriage, mortgage and baby clubs. And they are positively, plague-infestedly itching for us to join.

'Tell me about it. When Tim and I met Jasmine for drinks a few weeks back she actually started suggesting ideas for our honeymoon. I just ...' Laurie trailed off and sighed heavily into her strawberries and cream. 'I just don't want to keep dating and never feeling like I'm actually getting close to anyone.'

'I know,' I soothed. I didn't know. The thought of getting close to someone, having them move into my home, having to make joint decisions on what TV to watch and what to have for dinner, knowing that if I want to work late I should let my 'other half' know just all seemed like a lot of effort.

'I don't want to feel like I'm putting on a show,' Laurie said a while later.

'No.'

'I don't want to feel like I'm always the bridesmaid.'

'But you've never been a bridesmaid. It's actually really fun. You feel super-important.'

'I just want to feel . . .'

'What?'

'Love.'

'—*LOVE!*' boomed the umpire down on the court.

'Leave me alone!' Laurie cried back, then hid behind her camera as about twenty people turned to shush us.

We settled back to watch the game, neon-yellow balls whizzing across the blue sky and getting thwacked back where they came from with a grunt. I was itching to give my attention back to Laurie, worried she was sat there suffering in silence, and eventually there was a break in play and the stands broke into excited chatter.

'I'm over internet dating, you know,' said Laurie, turning to me, her tongue wedged into the bottom of her bowl, licking the cream.

'Really? You're taking a break from men, joining me as a happily single lady?'

'Hell no, I'm just going to do things the old-fashioned way, and meet someone face to face.'

'Well that sounds sensible. Are you going to join a new gym or something?'

'No, no, we're not going to do that . . .' Laurie smirked at me with her *I've had an idea* face. 'I've had an idea. And it's a really, really good idea that I really, really want you to join me on. I think we deserve a holiday.'

'Ooo yes! I love holidays. It's been too long. Where shall we go? Cancún? Greece? Thailand again?' I raised my eyebrows at her.

'Well actually I've already chosen the holiday, but I think you'll love it.'

'Oh.'

'Hold this.' Laurie handed me her empty, saliva-covered strawberry dish and reached down between her legs to her handbag. After some unladylike struggling she picked up her beer and gulped the remainder, handing me the empty cup as well. She then yanked out a thin, glossy brochure and placed it on her lap, laying her hands over it. On the cover, between her fingers, I saw a large, glistening glass of wine with a sun-drenched background of a vineyard. Interesting – I do like wine and sunshine.

The crowd cheered and Laurie lifted her hands to clap, as if she knew what was going on, and my eyes caught the title of the brochure.

'"*You Had Me at Merlot*" *Holidays*,' I read. 'What kind of a holiday is this?'

'It's a vineyard holiday, in Italy.'

'That sounds nice. A little red, a little white, a little siesta in the sun.'

'A little smoochy smoochy with some *full-bodied* men?'

'What?'

'Nothing, I mean, except it's, like, a group trip.'

'Like a tour?'

'No, more like a get-to-know-you holiday, where you do activities with other people ...'

I watched one of the players pour a bottle of water over himself at the side of the court, much to the swooning of one of the women in the Royal Box. 'So you *have* to mingle with the other guests?'

'It's kind of an essential.'

'But what kind of a— Is this a *singles'* holiday?' I hissed.

'Yes, but I really want to go, and I really want you to come with me.'

'No way.'

'Please, Elle. It'll be so much fun.'

'I really don't want to do this.'

'Why not?'

'Because ... *You Had Me at Merlot*? It just sounds incredibly cringey.' I took the brochure from her. 'It's going to be all greasy Casanovas and titillating drinking games.' But, flipping through the pages, I saw pictures of sunrises over medieval villages, rolling vine-covered hills, delicious Italian platters and no bondage-masked men or booze buses in sight.

'You're always saying how much you *loooove* being single, so why wouldn't you love a singles' holiday?'

'Because the whole point of a singles' holiday is to meet potential partners!'

'I guess—'

'Or is it just to have a romp in the sunshine?'

'No, the first one. Well, maybe a bit of the second. But this isn't an eighteen-to-thirty holiday, Elle, it's a really classy affair. Just like you.' She prodded my sweaty arm and gave me a look that told me she already knew I'd agree.

'I can't leave work.'

'Yes you can. You haven't taken any holiday yet this year.'

'Can't we go to Cancún?'

'Next year, I promise.'

I sighed. 'What would I have to do on this holiday? Is there anything to occupy me while you're off sampling the ... selection?'

'There's loads to do.' She opened the brochure at a page that showed a smiling middle-aged couple leaning against a row of Vespas, the immense terracotta frontage of Bella Notte vineyard rising behind them. 'You can pick grapes, you can go for walks, you can borrow a Vespa and explore the area. Or you can just taste-test all the wines and fall asleep in the sunshine.'

My friend is annoying. It's like she has a built-in algorithm that targets my weak points and knows exactly what to hard-sell them with. And the thought of sleep and sun and endless wine had me considering her proposal. In a way, you could say she had me at 'Merlot'. Dear God, what was I getting myself into?

*

It was late the following week and the office was having an early-closing day due to fumigation following a fruit-fly invasion (thanks to some over-zealous juice dieters in Accounts). I was meeting the ladies – Jasmine, Helen, Emma and Laurie – for drinks by the water in Greenwich, and the ice was already melting in the first round by the time our final femme, Marie, arrived with squidgy little baby Daisy.

'It is so hot; my nipples will not stop lactating.'

I put down my White Russian.

'They lactate when you're hot? Is that even a thing? What about the women who live in countries like Tunisia?' asked Laurie, holding her beer bottle to her hot forehead.

'I think my body's just trying to find any possible way to cool me down. I actually had to stand in the paddling pool at midday yesterday because they were just flowing like Timotei waterfalls.' She stared at my cocktail. 'I want your alcohol.'

'By all means.' I slid the milky drink across the table.

'No!' Jasmine smacked my hand with a *you don't know ANYTHING about being a new mum* glare. 'You're doing so well; not long now.'

'I just want some wine, just four big glasses of wine.' Marie grappled around for her orange juice, unable to see the table thanks to her ginormous breasts. 'Gah – these things are ridiculous!'

'I think your boobs look amazing,' said Laurie jealously.

'You'll have them soon; Tim is going to baby you up in no time.'

I grabbed the White Russian back again. Here we go. 'No, Tim and I split up.'

There was a chorus of 'Oh-no's and all four heads tilted to the right. 'Why?' demanded Jasmine, personally offended. 'He was The One.'

'No he wasn't,' I said. 'She wasn't that into him.'

'But I thought you were going to get married.'

'We really hadn't been together very long.'

'He would have made a great dad, though,' Emma sighed, and the others nodded in sorrow.

'It's okay, because Elle and I have a new plan.' Laurie shuffled in her handbag and pulled out the brochure. 'We're going on a singles' holiday.'

Squeals of delight.

'A *posh* singles' holiday,' I clarified. 'To a vineyard in Tuscany, to do wine tasting and suchlike.'

'The company's called *You Had Me at Merlot*!' said Laurie with pride. The ladies sniggered.

'Can I have a little less cheese with that wine?' asked Jasmine, and Marie guffawed so hard she started spouting again and had to hand Daisy over to Emma.

'The vineyard itself is called Bella Notte.' I was aware I was bristling, which was ridiculous, as I'd had exactly the same thoughts. But hearing them bash my first holiday in for ever smarted.

'That's pretty,' said Marie. 'I envisage you both

gazing at the stars, mambo Italiano-ing with signors, utterly happy-drunk on wine. Are you gonna snog someone?' Her eyes glazed over as she transported herself into our heady, single world.

'I am.' Laurie put her hand up.

'Really? With tongues?' Helen breathed.

'Who doesn't use tongues? Isn't that standard? Do people kiss differently these days?' asked Jasmine, turning to us for answers.

'I'm not kissing anyone,' I said.

'*You have to.*' Helen slammed her wine on the table. 'I mean, wouldn't it be rude not to on a singles' holiday? What else will you have to do?'

'I don't think it's a tally-sheet, notches-on-the-bedpost type of singles' holiday. I think it's probably going to be older single people, not your eighteen-to-thirty crowd. We might be the youngest there.'

'Older men can be very hot,' said Helen, she of the younger husband. 'Think of George Clooney.'

'Hold on,' said Emma. 'George Clooney lives in Italy, and he's often single, and he's older – maybe he'll be there.'

'He's so going to be there!' cried Helen. 'You're going to marry George Clooney!'

'Nope, George is married now. But even if he wasn't, although I'd be willing to have a summer fling if he wanted one, I don't think either Laurie or I are going to be getting hitched off the back of one holiday.'

'There's something about holidays though – being in a new place and not having to do dishes—'

'And drinking carafe after carafe of wine,' added Marie.

'—it just puts you in the mood for romance. Brian proposed to me after five too many Bahama Mamas in Barbados.'

'Ellie proposed to me at the bottom of Snowdon,' said Emma.

'At the bottom?'

'We couldn't be bothered to climb it, when it came down to it. But we were still on holiday. My friend Claudia's taking Nick to New Zealand next week; they're bound to come back engaged.'

'But these are all established relationships. I have no plans to walk down the aisle any time soon.' Jasmine and Marie exchanged raised eyebrows, which irked me even more. I know myself better than they know me, and why did they think I could only be happy if I was like them? I wasn't single because no one loved me, nor because I surely must give out too many desperate vibes, nor because I won't find a man unless I stop looking, and no (Dad), not because I'm a lesbian. It's because I like my life, I like being able to come home to my own flat and be by myself and learn dance routines, and I've *chosen to be single*. And I was getting pretty fed up with having to justify myself to everyone. Of course, that little speech didn't come out as planned, and instead I grumbled like a sullen teenager: 'I'm not swapping my life for anyone else's idea of my Mr Perfect. So there.'

'I'm just glad I don't have to go on singles' holidays any more,' sighed Jasmine.

'It's not that we have to, we want to.' Laurie grinned, opening the brochure to a page with a large photograph of a girl riding on the back of a Vespa, sunglasses reflecting the Italian sunshine. 'How could you not want to go here?'

'Exactly,' I said. 'Sometimes it's nice to go on holidays without kids and couples all over the place.'

'Talking about kids' holidays,' said Jasmine, 'does anyone know where I can buy good, organic travel nappies? As you might have seen on Facebook, Max used his potty for the first time last night, and it was just the most adorable thing ever, but we're going . . .'

I'm a horrible friend, but I faded out. I looked beyond the ladies to the baroque white architecture of the Old Royal Naval College and wondered if I'd ever fancy going back to university. Or joining the navy. Then I thought about the YouTube clip of the cat dressed as a shark, rolling around someone's house on a Roomba. *That* is the most adorable thing ever, surely? I just don't think a child weeing into a bowl compares.

The week before my holiday, work seemed even busier than usual, if that were possible. There were a million loose ends I wanted to tie up, and a million more 'little things' people wanted me to do for them before I left. I hated saying I couldn't do something, so I always said yes. But tears tickled the backs of my eyes sometimes. Not coping wasn't an option.

I'm one of three marketing managers at a PR agency in the City, and I'd been at work since seven fifteen that Thursday morning. By two thirty I needed to stretch my legs, having only gone as far as the loos and the coffee machine since I arrived. I decided to go and wander about by Donna.

Donna is our managing director, and kind of my idol, though I've never said more than a 'Hello' and a 'Yes, I *love* working here' and an 'Actually, it's Elle' to her. But she's a woman – the only woman – near the top of the company, and one day I want to be up there near her, so I need to make myself known.

I smoothed my hair, grabbed a ringbinder (no idea what was inside) and headed downstairs to her floor with a plan to pass her office.

Here's how I was hoping it would go:

I stride past Donna's office, confident and professional, and she looks up.

'Elle?'

'Oh hi,' I say, going in. 'How's your daughter?'

'She's great, thanks for asking. I've been meaning to run something by you. You're in this for the long haul, right?'

'Absolutely, I'm not going anywhere.'

'That's fantastic. You have such an admirable work ethic. I've noticed the extra hours you put in, the passion you show for the company, your drive to achieve results. Oh, and everyone absolutely loves you. There's a position opening up that you'd be perfect for. It's very high up and important, and you'd have your own office and a company credit card and a six-figure salary, and people will add you to their LinkedIn accounts.'

'Donna, how nice of you to think of me! I'd love to!'

Here's what actually happened:

I walked past her office five times; eventually Donna got up and closed the door. I had a mild panic attack that she'd think I was useless if I had enough time on my hands to be wandering about all day, and decided to put in an extra couple of hours before home-time this evening.

Ah well, I'll try the same routine tomorrow.

The rest of the day flew by in the usual blur of conference calls, marketing plans, PowerPoints and problems until my stomach let out a large growl and I glanced at the clock in the corner of my screen, which read 19:25. I looked up and there was no one else on my floor. No one at all.

Turning my chair, I used my feet to drag it and myself to the window, where I leant my forehead against the glass and gazed down at the street below. Colleagues and suited strangers spilled out of the bars and restaurants, enjoying the warm evening air that I couldn't feel now the sun had dropped below the building opposite, and the lack of life made the air-con seem all the colder.

Why did I try so much, when those people seemed to be actually having all the fun?

I decided I'd leave early for a change, and treat myself to dinner out, somewhere in the last of the sun. I rolled my chair back to my desk and went to shut down my computer when an email came through from Donna. I replied instantly, unashamedly hoping for brownie points, and then sat back and waited.

I waited fifteen minutes, just in case a message pinged back, commending me on still being at my desk, but nothing. And then the cleaner switched out the light and I was forgotten, invisible.

For a moment I just sat there, staring at the pod after pod of empty desks, which looked eerily dead in only the shaded light from outside the tinted windows. I *was* important to this company, wasn't I? I was needed, an asset. I was one of their best workers. Maybe they didn't always notice when I was here, but I was sure they'd notice next week when I wasn't here. Wouldn't they?

Fine, I'd bloody go home then. I'd be back in less than twelve hours anyway.

The following day I was indeed back at work, my last day before my holiday, and I was slouched in the board-room with fifteen other people, waiting for a meeting to begin.

I wondered how soon this meeting could be finished with, so I could get back to the never-ending to-do list upstairs.

Then I wondered if Dan from Accounts knew how much he looked like Anneka Rice.

Damn it, my new work shirt was gaping open at the boobs again.

As the clock ticked around to ten past the time the meeting was supposed to start, I let out a ginormous sigh with an accidental audible 'Uuurrrggghhhhhh.'

'Bet you can't wait to get out of here and start your holiday,' murmured Kath, one of my executives, who was sitting next to me, polishing off her third tepid coffee.

'There's just something so annoying about us all waiting for one person when we're all busy. Who are we even waiting for?'

'Chill out, think of all the gelato you'll be eating this time next week.'

My team knew I was going to Italy, but no more than that. I really didn't need them on my case about my single status too. Or, worse, asking me when I got back if I'd met anyone 'nice'. 'Will you be okay while I'm gone? Are you happy with everything that needs to be done on the Lush Hair account?' I asked Kath.

'Of course, just go and have fun and stop being such a worry-arse.'

The door opened and in strode Donna, and immediately I pulled myself up, tugged my shirt closed and nearly toppled off my chair trying to look like the most professional person in the room. There was something about Donna which always made me feel I should be on my best behaviour.

'Morning, all, let's begin,' she said, no nonsense. The meeting started and I tried my hardest to look interested, confident, to ask insightful questions, which I only fudged once when I said, 'And did you want the full title, Prime Minister Boris Johnson?'

'No, Ellen,' said Donna, 'let's go with *Mayor* Boris Johnson.'

'That's what I meant – ha ha ha, silly me – oh, and it's Elle, just so …' My voice was swallowed up by Dan starting his Excel presentation.

Kath leaned over to me. 'Don't worry, I get them mixed up all the time. Just remember this: *Mayor Mayor blondie hair.*'

I'd decided to take a quick weekend trip down to the Devon seaside to visit my parents and eat a cream tea before my Tuesday-morning flight to Italy. Although the holiday was only for ten days, last year I got into trouble for not taking all of my holiday allowance, so I took two full weeks this time. I was already on edge, thinking they'd realise they got on fine without me, didn't need me at all and I'd be fired before I could say *arrivederci*.

So, late at night on the Friday, when I finally left the

office, I leapt on the train to Exeter where my mum picked me up and drove me home, putting me to snoozeville in my teenage bedroom, complete with purple walls, a blow-up chair and a big faded poster of Craig McLachlan that I won't let her take down.

I woke up to seagulls thumping on the roof, squawking loudly about the appalling lack of chips at six in the morning, and our cat, Breakaway, standing all four heavy paws on my stomach as if to say '*You see how much my feet sink into you? LOSE WEIGHT.*'

Mum was already up, because whereas I can't start my day without a handful of crisps and checking my work emails before I've taken off my PJs, she can't start the day without a walk along the seafront. I had a cheeky dip into a tube of Pringles and scuttled off to join her.

The sea was calm, but a cool breeze was hanging out with the clouds that had scattered themselves over the pink skies.

'Cold, isn't it?' I yawned, curling my arm around Mum's.

'These clouds'll blow away by lunchtime, I'm sure. It never rains down here, in the Fiji of England. I expect it'll be lovely and warm in Italy, won't it?'

'I hope so. My aim is to leave Laurie to it and just lie back in the sunshine with some vino, and eat every scrap of Italiano food that passes by.'

'It sounds blissful. I love Italy; I could eat antipasti for every meal of the day.'

'Then you should! Yolo, Mum.'

'Yellow?'

'Yolo. It means "you only live once".'

'So if I was at a funeral I'd say, *"Well ... yolo"*?'

'Probably not – it's more of live-for-the-moment saying. Not a ha-ha-you're-dead saying. It's what us hashtag-cool-kids say.'

'Are you drunk now?'

'No, hashtagging is . . . never mind. Yes, antipasto is *delizioso.*'

'Did you know my first holiday with a boy was to Italy?'

'Urgh, a boy that wasn't Dad?'

Mum threw her head back and laughed. Is there anything better in the world than someone laughing? Seeing that spontaneous burst of joy take over their face, and knowing that it's the most wonderfully infectious disease in the world? 'I'm afraid so! He took me there with the intention of proposing to me at the Trevi Fountain, but just as he was about to do it I looked down at my strawberry gelato and realised I loved that more than I loved him, and that was the end of that.'

'Blimey, Mum, you heart-breaker.'

'We'd only been together a couple of months. I think his mummy was just wanting him to find a bride.'

'You've never been to Tuscany, have you? With or without potential dads from the past?'

'No, but it looks absolutely beautiful. One day I'd

like to go for a month or two, and just paint pictures and—'

'Eat antipasti?'

'Eat antipasti.'

'I wish you could come on this holiday with me.'

'I'm not sure a singles' holiday's quite up my street. Plus it would be a bit mean to your dad.'

'It's not up my street either.'

We stopped to lean over the railing and watch the rolling waves, the wind blowing our hair about. Half-asleep dog walkers and early-risers with metal detectors were the only others out at this time.

Mum put her arm around me and I shuffled closer. 'Just don't be closed off, sweetheart. There's more to life than work.'

'Antipasti?'

'You know what I mean. It won't do you any harm to experience some of the other lovely things in life. Hashtag yolo.'

Read more by
Lisa Dickenson!

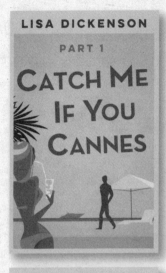
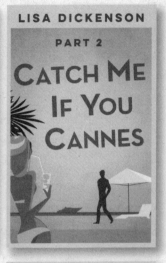
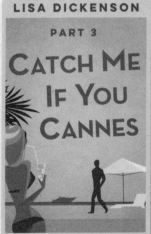
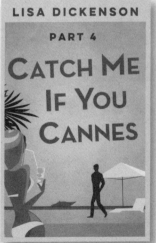

Available as a four-part
ebook serial now.

Join the fun online with
Lisa
Dickenson